ACROSS THE BORDER

Cash offered his hand, but Jack didn't take it. He loathed what Cash had become, a quivering doper with bloodshot, yellowed eyes, so unlike the Cash Bailey who was star quarterback of Benrey High.

"You know why I'm here," Jack said. "Two people dead on Main Street. One of 'em just a kid. Almost killed a mother and her baby."

"Don't like it one bit myself, Jack. Nasty piece of business. I need enforcement by local authority, so that nothing like this will happen again. I need you, Jack. We could work together." Cash paced. "Hell, Jack, nothing would make me happier than to see you with a little grubstake of your own. Maybe a hundred thou a year, off the top?"

Jack snorted derisively. "I catch you in Benrey, Cash, you're dead. Hear? You cross that border, your ass is mine."

Cash's eyes went cold, his voice steely. "Don't push me, *friend*. You're on the wrong side of the river and your badge don't mean shit here."

Jack saw his opportunity. He whipped the Winchester from under his poncho and leveled it. "If I pull this trigger, you'll be bloody ribbons," Jack snarled. "Does that mean shit here?"

EXTREME PREJUDICE

by
RICHARD DOBBINS and EVAN SLAWSON

screenplay by
DERIC WASHBURN and HARRY KLEINER

story by
JOHN MILIUS and FRED REXER

PUBLISHED BY POCKET BOOKS NEW YORK

Another *Original* publication of POCKET BOOKS

POCKET BOOKS, a division of Simon & Schuster, Inc.
1230 Avenue of the Americas, New York, N.Y. 10020

ISBN: 0-671-64016-X

First Pocket Books printing April, 1987

10 9 8 7 6 5 4 3 2 1

POCKET and colophon are registered trademarks
of Simon & Schuster, Inc.

Printed in the U.S.A.

FOR ELSA PETERS MORSE AND FOR MARJORIE

Acknowledgments

Thanks to:

Andrew Vajna, Mario Kassar, and Robert Brenner at Carolco Pictures, Inc. (and midwife credit to Jeanne Joe) for giving us the opportunity to write this. More thanks to all the other fine people at Carolco who provided advice, encouragement, and wherewithal, especially Alice Andrade for her technical help and Lynwood Spinks, who came through for us in the nick of time.

Walter Hill, Deric Washburn, Harry Kleiner, John Milius, and Fred Rexer. This work is only a conduit for theirs.

Mae Woods, who welcomed us onto the set from the very beginning, gave us access to everything, and helped us throughout the process.

Regina Gruss, our first contact with the cast and crew.

Nick Nolte (and his partner Bill Cross), Powers Boothe, Maria Conchita Alonso, Michael Ironside, Clancy Brown, Larry B. Scott, William Forsythe, Dan Tullis, Matt Mulhern, Tiny Lister, Luis Contreras, and J. D. Johnston, for sharing their insights and research into their characters.

The production team on *Extreme Prejudice,* for innumerable kindnesses and pieces of useful information.

David Malvani for his expertise in *español*.

Elizabeth Beier, our editor, for grace under pressure.

Family and friends, who had to put up with us.

Anyone who should have been thanked here, but wasn't —like Freeman Davies.

These people share our accomplishments but not our culpability or our shortcomings.

"This is hard country, brush country, mean country, heartbreak country; harsh sun, bitter dust, pale shadow."

JOHN HOUGHTON ALLEN
Southwest

"Say what you mean, mean what you say, and cover the ground you stand on."

TEXAS RANGER MAXIM

"No man in the wrong can stand up against a man in the right—who keeps on coming."

CAPTAIN MCNELLY, TEXAS RANGER

I

RINCON

1

Jack Benteen—Texas Ranger, the Department of Public Safety's chief district officer for Benrey County —white-knuckled his cruiser through a thick downpour. His headlights barely cut through the deluge as the car hydroplaned through each turn. Hank Pearson, Benrey County sheriff, rode shotgun. Pearson was in his early sixties but still tough and hardy. He peered out into the rain and tightened his seat belt. The police radio sputtered calls that Jack and Hank ignored.

Jack snapped off the headlights and slid to a halt by a small roadside honky-tonk. A neon Budweiser sign flashed in the window. Above the door, an unlit weathered wood sign read RINCON NORTE—North Corner. Jack's eyes moved to a faded yellow pickup truck and a beat-up Volkswagen Beetle among the shabby cars in the muddy parking lot.

Jack pointed out the two vehicles to Hank. "The pickup is T.C. Luke's. The VW must be what come through the border when they cut the fence."

Hank was matter-of-fact. "You called it right. The Luke boys stoppin' to celebrate—before heading home with the dope."

Jack shrugged. "Beats me how the Border Patrol could lose that bucket of bolts. Even in this rain."

"Only hot pursuit they ever win is when they try to get laid. Even then they have to pay full price." Hank chuckled and picked up the radio microphone. "Let's get some backup, then have ourselves a little fun."

"Just tell 'em to hurry the hell up. I don't want to wait. They get wind of us and they're gone."

Hank reached for the microphone to call Dispatch as Jack watched the bar.

Jack cursed softly. Three men were coming out of the Rincon Norte and climbing into the VW. One, Chub Luke—a shaggy, bearded hulk in a cowboy hat and a long slicker—had his arm around a whore who he pushed into the car ahead of him. The VW sputtered to life and drove away.

Without turning on the headlights, Jack spun the cruiser into the parking lot and almost up to the front door. He grabbed the cut-down Winchester clipped onto the ceiling rack overhead and, without turning toward him, told Hank, "I don't want to lose T.C. Tell the goddamn useless Border Patrol that Chub is headed back their way! Then go 'round to the back door and cover me."

Jack jumped out of the car and ran up to the building. He plastered his back against the wall, pulled his sheepskin coat closed with his free hand, and sidled toward the door, rainwater pouring off his Stetson.

Hank spit Jack's message to the Border Patrol into the radio, grabbed his 12-gauge pump riot gun from the dash mount, and slogged through the mud to the back of the building.

Hank remembered how Jack cut his reputation as a no-nonsense hard-ass when eight or nine prisoners in the county jail cooked themselves up some "raisin jack" prison liquor and got crazy drunk. They managed to seize control of the top floor of the jail and to issue a list of demands, the first of which was an ice-cold keg of Lone Star beer. Hank figured what the hell, just wait them out, but Jack grabbed an M-16 and a few over-sized magazines from the gun locker, then went up-stairs and peppered the ceiling with a long furious burst. The would-be rebels were found cowering in the eight-inch crawl space under two lower bunks. Each of them swore off drinking for life. Jack's follow-up assignment—patching the roof—didn't cure his hot-headedness. No bunks in the Rincon Norte, was Hank's thought as he covered the rear door, trying to see through a filthy window.

Inside the smoky bar, a worn-out 45 of José José's "Quien Puedo Ser" crackled on the jukebox, loud enough that the Tex-Mex clientele had to shout to be heard by the bartender. It was a full house; so many people were standing it was hard to see the tables. The lights and music flickered with the strokes of lightning; the din of rain on the honky-tonk's metal roof was frequently drowned out by thunder.

A bolt of lightning knocked the lights out for a few seconds. When they came on again, Jack Benteen blocked the open doorway, water dripping off his coat and hat. He kicked the door shut behind him and walked into the room. The roar of conversation died away. Jack didn't offer a badge, but nobody needed to see one. The customers knew him—and backed off quietly into the shadowy corners of the room.

Jack understood the whispering in Spanish around him, mostly harmless stuff—*what the hell is he doing here, who is he after*. Jack crossed to the bar, keeping his eyes on everything. José José was silenced with a pop as the needle on the jukebox lifted. The bar was quiet now, except for the thunder and the pounding rain on the roof. Jack looked hard at the bartender, figuring out if the bartender would lie even before he'd told him what he wanted.

"T.C. Luke." Jack kept his voice down.

The bartender shrugged. *"No entiendo. No hablo inglés."*

Jack smiled tightly and asked again in Spanish, though he knew the bartender had understood him the first time. *"Busco T.C. Luke. Está aqui?"*

The bartender shook his head, but glanced nervously toward the rear of the bar. Jack moved away from him and headed for a corner table. Three Anglo men were sitting in shadow with their backs to the wall. The one in the middle was T.C. Luke. He was as big and ugly as his brother Chub, and he quietly slipped something —Jack couldn't see the old army-issue Colt .45 semi-automatic—amid the bottles, glasses, and other debris on the table.

Jack focused into the shadows. "Luke?"

T.C. Luke forced a mossy-toothed grin, keeping his hands under the table and his eyes on Jack's Winchester. "Right here, Jack. Hell of a night. But you sure come to the right place to get in out of the rain."

"Say adios to the lady, T.C. You're going with me." Jack sounded apologetic, but he was wary, watching T.C.'s eyes shift around the bar and T.C.'s arm moving under the table.

Luke pushed the hard-looking woman off his lap, dropping the cold gun on the warm spot where she had been sitting.

Jack saw something bulky under Luke's feet —probably the dope. Come on, he thought, bring your hands up, T.C.—with or without a gun. Fishing around in his coat pocket, Jack pulled out a pair of handcuffs and tossed them on the table.

"You'll find they fit. Get into 'em."

Luke's eyes narrowed as he looked from Jack to the cuffs, then back to Jack. He gauged his timing: the Winchester was cradled in Jack's left arm, not really

6

ready for action. T.C. figured he might have a fighting chance. "How much help you got outside, Jack?"

"How much you think I need?" Jack didn't return Luke's grin. He was watching T.C.'s arm, waiting for him to make his move.

"You're pushing me, Jack. You're working me too hard."

"Your choice, T.C." Jack saw Luke shift uncomfortably in his chair, possibly moving clear of the table just a little.

"Ain't right to take me in." Luke frowned. "Goddamn it, Jack, I'm just a poor old dirt farmer. Can't make ends meet chopping cotton."

Jack shook his head. "You're going about it the wrong way."

"It ain't right, Jack."

Some of the other customers started to move in behind Jack. He knew his life depended on keeping his eyes on Luke, but he had to be aware of what was behind him and to his sides as well. Suddenly, Hank pushed through the back door, all business, his 12-gauge leveled, sweeping the crowd.

"Anybody want a piece of this?" Hank nodded at Jack to continue. He had waited outside, looking for the right opening, helping Jack maintain a psychological advantage.

With the advantage of the distraction, Luke rose swiftly, gun in hand and firing. But Jack was ready. The Winchester idled, but his right hand shot out of his coat with blinding speed, his pistol spitting muzzle flashes, hammering Luke backward into a cigarette machine and tearing him open. Luke's .45 flew out of his hand and crashed onto the table as he died.

The man on Luke's right made a break for the door, but Hank clipped him in the temple with the butt of the 12-gauge, knocking him cold.

Panic broke out with the shooting. The Rincon Norte filled with screams. Patrons stampeded for the door, until Hank fired a shotgun blast into the ceiling. The roar of the gun stopped them in their tracks, as rainwater poured through the fresh hole in the roof.

Jack homed in on the rear table. One man was left beside Luke's corpse. Jack put away his pistol and leveled the Winchester. He motioned to the set of handcuffs on the table next to Luke's .45.

"Your choice." Jack cocked a fresh round into the chamber.

The man at the table looked around, terrified. He slowly brought up his hands, wrists first, until Jack could see they were empty. The man snapped the cuffs onto his own wrists and raised his hands over his head.

"Now let's see what you got, *amigo,*" Hank said. "Make yourself useful. Pick up the bag and put it on the table."

Carefully, the man picked up the canvas bag and dropped it on the table.

"Dump it out," Hank ordered.

The man reluctantly upended the bag on the table. Several large plastic bags full of white powder fell out—enough cocaine to keep Houston wired for a week.

Hank tossed Jack his shotgun, then stepped forward and booted the table over. A nickel-plated Model 10 Smith & Wesson with a four-inch barrel and pearl grips lay at the handcuffed man's feet. Hank pocketed the gun and forced his prisoner to his feet.

Hank snorted. "I figured pig shit like you for pearly grips."

The man's eyebrows knitted, puzzled. Then he started to understand. "You . . . wanted me to go for the gun?"

Jack stepped forward and nudged the man under the chin with the muzzle of the Winchester. "Don't want to worry about walkin' manure shooting us in the back someday."

The handcuffed man turned livid. "You sonofabitch murdering bastards . . ." He continued ranting until Jack pushed him hard with the Winchester.

"You want another chance?" Jack's eyes were cold slits. The man shut up. "Then live with it, sucker." Jack grabbed the man by the neck and threw him stumbling toward the door.

Hank called Jack from the doorway. "My boys will be here in five." He cracked a smile. "Damn, Jack, this is like the old days."

Jack smiled back mirthlessly. "I take that as a compliment."

"You would."

As the sirens of their backup units howled into the parking lot Hank slipped cuffs on the man he'd knocked unconscious and Jack pushed his own prisoner outside. Hank stopped in the doorway and tipped his hat to the remaining patrons. *"Buenas noches,"* he said, then turned and walked back outside into the rain.

Jack also moved slowly out into the rain, wishing the downpour would wash T.C.'s blood off his hands.

2

Jack sat in his wood- and glass-paneled corner office at the Benrey Sheriff's Station. He looked at the clock on the wall, watching the second hand sweep toward the fact that he *had* to go home eventually. He held out his gun hand. It was steady as a rock. Shooting T.C. hadn't affected his nerves, even if it was eating into his conscience.

Jack's Colt .45 automatic sat, gleaming and cold, on his desk blotter. He fingered the sculpted bronze grips that showed the profile of an Aztec king above a horse's head inside a horseshoe, bordered with curlicues. The grips were souvenirs of an unauthorized pursuit into Mexico. He had chosen the images: the Aztec represented power and leadership, the horse represented mobility, the horseshoe was for luck.

The man who had handcuffed himself at the Rincon Norte turned out to be Mac Parker, a local small-time con artist. Jack knew the name because once he had taken a young woman's screeched complaint about Parker getting her pregnant and deserting her. Jack had

10

tried to find Parker, but all he came up with was a rumor that Mac had been seen in Mexico. The child was given up for adoption.

Now Parker huddled, glaring mad and still drunk, in his cell. Jack walked right up to the bars and peered into the man's face. He realized it was Parker and smiled. "Get any Father's Day cards this year, Mac?" he jibed.

"Aw, shit, man, cut me a break," Parker complained, looking pained at the memory. "Would you have married her?"

"I wouldn't have balled her," Jack shot back. "Better watch out if you make bail. Your ex-sweetheart's daddy still wants to tattoo your face with a hot branding iron." Jack licked his lips and cracked a wide smile. "Maybe I'll tell him you're here." He headed for the door, flicking the lights out behind him.

Across the street, a faded brown GMC Value-Van with the words WEST-TEX CABLE & SATELLITE SERVICE painted on the side in large yellow and red letters sat dark and quiet. Inside, Sergeant Charles Biddle, U.S. Army Special Forces, watched Benteen cross to his cruiser and fire it up. The image was reproduced on one of the video monitors over Biddle's head. Moments later, a video printer scrolled out a close-up of Jack's face. Biddle, a wiry black man, was surrounded by half-a-million dollars' worth of sophisticated surveillance and communications hardware, which he ran with calm expertise. The truck's contents presented an ironic counterpoint to the slogan ENJOY GREAT ENTERTAINMENT AT INCREDIBLY LOW PRICES which appeared below the West-Tex logo on the outside.

As Jack pulled out of the parking lot he idly wondered if a neighbor's new satellite dish would soon be blocking the view from his office.

* * *

It was nearly sunrise when Jack killed the cruiser's lights and motor to roll noiselessly into his driveway. The Tudor-style house sat on a low rise along the outskirts of Benrey. His grandfather had started the building, but the house still wasn't finished. It probably never would be. Jack joked about it as a work-in-progress. The house was surrounded by a stand of scrub oak and had no lawn to speak of—it just sat baldly in the dry natural landscape as though it still hadn't gotten used to being there.

The lethargy Jack felt as he entered the dark house had less to do with fatigue than with a deeper weariness. If you still had a soul, it hurt to kill another man, in self-defense or not. Jack had spent all night trying to blank out his emotions, without success.

The bedroom door was closed. Jack inched it open to watch Sarita Cisneros—his lover, his consort, his *muchacha*—sleeping peacefully, her long dark hair flowing around her head, her negligee shimmering in the light from the hallway.

Jack quietly entered the room, stripped off his coat and shirt, then moved to the adjoining bathroom to wash his face. The image in the mirror was haggard, tired, looking older than he remembered. He couldn't help thinking he might have brought T.C. in alive instead of feetfirst, if he really tried to.

Jack reached for a towel and knocked the water glass off the sink, breaking it on the pink-tiled floor. Cursing softly, imagining the shards cutting Sarita's bare feet when she woke up, Jack stooped down and carefully gathered the broken glass. When he looked up, Sarita was standing in the doorway, looking at him as she tied her bathrobe around her. She was slim and sexy in an innocent way, with a proud fine-boned face. Her hair fell over her shoulders as she hugged herself to ward off the dawn's chill. Her olive eyes met Jack's and they shared a smile, which dissipated awkwardly. Sarita broke the silence.

"Hola, stranger. Good to see you again." Her voice was soft and soothing. But right now, Jack would rather she were yelling at him, doing anything that would take his mind off what happened at the Rincon Norte.

"Sorry . . . didn't mean to wake you."

Sarita shook her head. No apology was needed. *"Está bien.* The hours we work . . . Sometimes I feel like we need an appointment just to pass each other on the street."

Jack didn't say anything, just kept holding out the broken glass. Sarita handed him the wastebasket and Jack dumped the shards into it.

"You haven't been happy in a long time," Sarita said, searching Jack's face.

Jack remained stoic. There was truth in what she said, but he didn't want to admit it or lay any blame. Sarita was a good woman, the best he'd had. But he still wasn't satisfied. And he knew it was something inside himself that kept them apart, kept Jack from being able to share his feelings with her. He was a man whose job consumed him to the exclusion of anything else in his life. Sarita understood this and for the most part accepted it.

She had met Jack more than half a lifetime ago, when he played on the Benrey High School football team with her older brother, José. She grew up in a *colonia,* a shantytown carved out of fallow ranch land near the border. The owner had divided a far corner of his property into tiny parcels, which he sold for a few thousand dollars each to migrant workers who had no other hope of owning a home. The workers built their own houses, rickety and plain, with no conveniences and not even any utilities.

The Cisneros family paid a neighbor to let them fill

jugs for their cooking and bathing from his garden hose. Their only bathroom was an outhouse. When it rained, the unpaved roads became rivers of mud that Sarita and José had to walk through barefoot on their way to school, to keep from ruining their precious shoes. Their father had died at the age of forty-two during such a flood, felled by a heart attack as he pushed a friend's car out of the mud. Sarita took some comfort from the fact that her father's soul was released as he was helping somebody.

José had married just out of high school, and within a few years earned enough money as a mechanic to leverage the *colonia* shack into a house within the Benrey city limits. He and Sarita split the rent on a nearby apartment for their mother. Even after three years with Jack, Sarita made it a point to spend at least one night there each week.

Jack had been able to keep the aura of forbidden passion that had electrified their first bedroom encounters alive in her longer than Sarita expected. But now Sarita felt this too might be gone forever, that Jack was now so accustomed to her that he didn't appreciate what she brought to their romance. Like most people, Sarita hated feeling taken for granted.

Jack had been ready to collapse into bed, but now his adrenaline was pumping again. He went to the kitchen for a beer, avoiding Sarita's close look as he passed her. She stood there for a moment, hurt, then followed Jack to the kitchen.

"So? What's wrong?" Sarita asked him.

Not now, Jack thought, not now. "It's okay. Go back to bed," he said, slumping into a straight-backed chair.

Sarita could always read Jack. She knew he was hiding something, something bad. She walked behind the chair and put her arms around him. "What happened?"

"A fella tried to shoot me last night." Jack paused. "He was a little slow."

"And you were a little fast." Sarita knew the score. The things Jack did in the line of duty could turn a man's conscience into a tomb of guilt and recrimination. Jack needed somebody to help purge the doubts, the self-criticism, but Sarita couldn't figure out how to do it for him. "Chicano?" she asked, a little coldly.

Jack shook his head. "Anglo. Just another farmer struggling to hold on to his piece of the world by running dope across the border . . . for Cash Bailey. And I had to blow his shit away."

Instead of looking to Sarita for her reaction, her sympathy, Jack went back into his shell, turning away and gulping down the rest of his beer.

Cash Bailey, Sarita thought. She had been with Cash first, before Jack. At first, Cash was wildly attracted to Sarita; he sensed a kind of purity in her. It was as if he felt her innocence could somehow redeem his lack of it. But he ultimately grew tired of her and longed for new women to conquer. When Cash told Sarita adios, Jack picked up the pieces. Now, it seemed, their paths might cross again. Sarita returned to the bedroom and threw herself on the mattress, without any hope of going back to sleep.

3

At ten the next morning, a motor-drive camera whirred and clicked as its shutter opened and closed on fragments of Benrey: the city hall, the police station, power lines and utility poles, the bank. Major Paul Hackett, an intense man with thinning hair and an amoeba-shaped scar on his left cheek, wearing jeans and a flannel shirt, pointed a zoom lens at Main Street and pressed the trigger on his motor-driven Nikon FE.

The midmorning sun broke through the storm clouds and softened the harsh outlines of Main Street's brick storefronts into patches of cool shadow. By some trick of the light or the mind the streets had the look of weathered smuggler's trails cut through dry chaparral, desolate and unwelcoming. Benrey had the used look of a place drifters go to die. But to Jack Benteen, Benrey was home.

Jack Benteen was part of the Texas Rangers before he was born. His father and grandfather were old-school Rangers who lived by their wits and a fast gun; they enforced the law but remained outside of it. Their reputations were what Jack measured himself against.

16

At thirty-five, Jack wore his badge with a sense of history, if not a sense of style, and he exercised his authority with his own willful disregard for the powers that be—both of God and of man.

Like most Rangers, his uniform consisted of whatever he saw fit to show up in. Today it was a plain brown shirt and matching pants. His trademark was a double-hung hand-tooled gunbelt, twin silver buckles slung low, his .45 in a quick-draw mini-holster. A Schrade folding lock-back knife in a pouch that slid into a back pocket kept the gunbelt from falling down.

Hank Pearson had adopted the Texas Ranger maxim, "Say what you mean, mean what you say, and cover the ground you stand on," as his own. In earlier years, he spent a good deal of time drilling the Ranger legends into Jack, gruffly cultivating a shared heritage in law enforcement. Hank sat in the passenger seat of Jack's cruiser flipping down the visor to deflect the low glare as they turned toward the sun and rolled down Main Street. A Sheriff's Department cruiser slowly passed in the other direction, the radio sputtering a "howdy" along with Deputy Ranger Purvis's grinning wave. Purvis was one of the crop of "poets," Hank's word for those who got into law enforcement via a written test.

Hank shook his head. "Purvis always looks about as sharp as week-old whipped cream on a used rubber."

"Guess we don't live up to the old days, huh?" And probably never did, Jack completed the thought to himself.

"Purvis is a runt, too." Hank was matter-of-fact as he recited one of his frequent litanies on the old ways: "In your daddy's day, he wouldn't take 'em under six foot, and your grandpa wouldn't take 'em under six-foot-eight—measured barefoot on broken glass. And only then if they were mean and ugly." Hank took vicarious pride in the Rangers' history. "A man puts on a legend when he puts on that badge." He wrinkled his forehead. "But it don't fit many of them these days —present company excepted, of course."

Jack appreciated the rare praise. Being a Ranger was something a Benteen did when he became a man—or to prove he was a man. When his father died, Jack abandoned the nomadic life he had fallen into, returned to Benrey, and joined the Rangers, out of a newfound sense of duty as well as from an ironic acceptance of "destiny," which he preferred to think of as "tradition." Impressing Hank, or at least being on his good side, was important to Jack. Hank was an important link to Jack's past, to his father and grandfather; Hank's approval was the closest thing he could get to theirs.

"I was just jabberin' on the phone with the head honcho in Austin about an hour ago," Hank began.

Jack, used to his actions being "misinterpreted," was ready for the worst. "I suppose headquarters wants my ass for breakfast, sunny-side up."

Hank shook his head. "Not this time. It's going down as self-defense. No departmental review." Hank paused as the cruiser stopped at one of Benrey's few traffic lights. "Case closed, Jack . . . except for Chub. One bet's for sure. That hunk of trash won't rest until he gets even for you stretching his brother out in a box. It's only a question of when and where he'll try to sock some hot lead between your shoulder blades."

"Won't be the first to try," Jack said. "If I had a nickel for every death threat . . ." He grinned at Hank. "I could make a few phone calls and have enough left over for some coffee."

Hank smiled. "Funny, I never figured a dumb hairy-assed hillbilly like T.C. Luke would get himself killed over a dope deal. I put him and his brother in jail a couple of times for drunk and ornery, but never thought they'd come to this."

"He was just an old farmer gone broke," Jack said. "A good man until Cash got hold of him, told him he could make some quick money. But old T.C. couldn't take the pace."

"You take it too personal, Jack. I'm telling you that."

"It is personal. Three times in the last six months I've used my gun. Every goddamn one was in a drug deal with Cash Bailey behind it."

"We don't know it was Cash's boys last night. Not for a fact."

Jack snorted. "You take my word, it's Cash all right."

"He's got you spooked." Hank caught Jack's arm to get his attention. "Put in for leave, Jack. A long one. Before you get bent out of shape."

"It's Cash who's going to need a vacation by the time I'm through with him." Backing away from this wasn't what Jack had in mind.

Jack pulled the patrol car into a diagonal parking space in front of Smiley's, a workingman's dive with a water-stained ceiling and greasy utensils, in the center of town. He shut off the motor and idly watched in his rearview mirror as a rusted old pickup truck rattled past behind him. But old pickup trucks were common in Benrey—more so as the local economy ground itself into the dust, crushed by falling oil prices and Mexican inflation. The new trucks almost always belonged to the ambitious and the greedy who profited from the fast, illegal border commerce.

Hank sized Jack up and stopped him as he reached for the door handle. "You're a moody sonofabitch today. What's on your mind?"

"I'll tell you," Jack said, reflectively. "I keep lookin' out there at Mexico, across the river, and I can't see shit 'cept Cash Bailey grinning. Daring me to shut him down."

Hank had heard it before. He had known Jack and

Cash since they were kids, had tried to keep them out of trouble when their wild oats were sowed too far afield. Jack was okay, but Cash had been a lost cause.

Hank nudged Jack. "All you have to do is wait. Cash is bound to self-destruct without you even lifting a finger."

Jack drawled, "It's no favor to hang a man slowly." Hank laughed as they walked into the cafe. That was another of Hank's sayings, but Jack first heard the story of the slow hanging as a child when his grandfather tucked him into bed one night. Gramps Benteen grew up in Yuma, Arizona, where in 1898 the sheriff jailed two men who murdered a local rancher and a saloon keeper. When the sheriff was called out of town, a self-appointed vigilante committee broke the murderers out of jail. As Gramps watched, the two men were made to stand on a board laid across the bed of a wagon. Nooses were slung from a tree near the town hall, then slipped around the condemned men's necks. As soon as the wagon started to move, one of the men jumped as high as he could and his neck broke, instantly and loudly. Somebody in the crowd yelled, "He must have been hanged before. He knew just how to do it!" But the other man might have fainted, or the noose was too tight, because he just sank down on the rope and endured an agonizing, gurgling, choking death that lasted nearly half an hour.

Gramps described it down to the last twitch of the unlucky man's feet, touching off weeks of nightmares in young Jack. Even now, when things were bad, Jack sometimes felt like he was living a slow hanging, his rope woven out of endless Texas highways and unwanted family ties. Like his forebears, Jack preferred to cull the worst apples from the barrel, the ones whose removal put a fear of the law into the small-timers and made them want to stay small. And in theory at least, Jack liked justice to be swift and final, frontier-style. But the nightmares were returning as Jack realized that closing Cash Bailey down might force him to kill the man who was once his best friend.

4

Inside the brown West-Tex van parked on Main Street in Benrey, Major Hackett, Sergeant Biddle, and another man, Sergeant Larry McRose, were watching the approach of an old pickup truck through high-powered Steiner binoculars. McRose was big and muscular but his soft beard and light brown hair mellowed his looks a bit. At six-foot-three and wearing cowboy boots with faded denims, he towered over the other two men. None of the men was in uniform. Biddle wore a V-neck sweater over a light pink oxford shirt with chinos and loafers. He looked like Benrey's first black yuppie. McRose would have looked more at home at a rodeo than surrounded by the truck's surveillance gear, while Hackett, for all his intensity, might have been mistaken for the owner/manager of a fast-food franchise.

"Here we go, sir," said Biddle. "One 1958 beat-to-shit, dirty blue pickup with white wheels and no hubcaps. That's them."

"Intell readout?" Hackett asked.

Biddle consulted a clipboard. "B-K-eight-four-zero-eight—Sonora, Mexico, plates."

Hackett checked the truck out with the binocs again. "B-K-eight-four-oh-eight . . . Intell on target."

"Unbelievable," McRose chimed. "We actually got some recon that's worth a good goddamn."

McRose slipped the West-Tex truck into gear and followed the pickup.

The old pickup, its once-blue paint and primer worn away by years of glaring sun and blowing sand until it was finished in only a fine coat of rust, rumbled down Main, stopping in front of the Benrey Bank. Merv, whose thick glasses clashed with his tailored mauve-colored western suit and ostrich boots, jumped out with two heavy suitcases. The truck pulled away as Merv struggled into the bank with the suitcases.

Inside the bank, Merv made himself comfortable on a new sofa and blithely contemplated a Remington-esque mural of a cowboy leading cattle across the Rio Grande, which took up half the wall behind the tellers' cages. Clarence King, the bank's president, hastily finished a phone call, then crossed to Merv with a look of alarm.

"Jesus Christ, *two* suitcases?"

Merv stood up to shake, but his hand just dangled as Clarence fretted. "We're overflowing, Clarence. From now on, it's two per day. You should be happy, business is good."

Clarence, a beefy man, who used his height and bulk to intimidate, wasn't pleased. "You know I can't handle that much." But Clarence knew that complaining to Merv was futile. Cash didn't give a damn about the problems of running a bank or running money through one, and he had Clarence by the proverbial balls. His only choice was to comply.

Merv picked up the suitcases and headed for the back room, Clarence trailing behind him. "Cash says open more banks. Branch out, Clarence. Grow. Think big."

"Real goddamn easy for you to say, you don't have the feds looking in your books." But Clarence dropped the subject, anxious to conclude the transaction.

Clarence and Merv quickly thumbed through the cash in a private counting booth, Clarence's palms clammy and wet as usual. He needed a drink. For all his appetites, he didn't have the temperament for being an outlaw. "Damn it, Merv, what am I gonna do with all this cash?"

"Cut the shit, Clarence. You're going to be a rich man." Merv grinned.

"I'm already a rich man."

Merv stopped smiling. "Don't forget how you got that way." Merv headed for the door. "See you tomorrow. Same time, same station, same show."

As Merv walked out of the building he nearly bumped into someone. Merv looked up, startled by the steel-blue eyes that met his. The eyes had an infinite depth and the calmness of inner vision, but they also had a hard edge that made Merv uneasy. He grunted and hastily stepped around Sergeant Declan Patrick Coker, nearly walking into a tall, potted cactus. Merv had no idea that his picture had just been taken by a camera hidden in Coker's briefcase. Coker was another member of the "West-Tex" team. He, too, wore no uniform. Instead, for now, he wore a sports jacket and slacks. With his briefcase, he could be taken for a traveling salesman or an insurance broker.

Hector, at the wheel of the old blue pickup, stopped in front of a garish yellow building with a huge plastic CHICKEN CHAMP sign over the storefront. His sunglasses, tan suit trimmed with dark piping at the seams, and his neatly trimmed goatee were incongruous with the battered old truck.

Inside the restaurant, Scotty Gould, a teenager wearing the yellow polyester franchise uniform, mopped the floor before the place opened. Hector grabbed a rabbit cage from the back of the pickup and tapped on the glass.

Scotty unlocked the door and let him in.

Hector looked around. "Where's Andy?"

Scotty shrugged. "Be here in ten minutes."

Hector set the cage on the stainless-steel counter, slipping a bit of carrot to the rabbit. "Good, tell Andy that I bring him a nice rabbit."

"Who do I say gave it to him?"

Hector smiled. "Don't worry about that. He's gonna know."

Scotty stared dumbly at the rabbit. "He's already got two hundred rabbits at home."

"Well, now he's got two hundred and one." Hector pushed his way out the door, got in the pickup, and drove back to the bank, where Merv was already waiting for him.

Inside the bank, Coker's briefcase camera captured the positions of the tellers, the bank officers, the vault. Satisfied, Coker left the bank and crossed the street to the West-Tex truck. As Coker got into the truck, Major Hackett was peering into Smiley's window through a rifle scope. Hackett handed the scope to Coker, who trained it on Jack Benteen, the crosshairs intersecting just behind the Ranger's left ear.

Jack's too-hot coffee burned the roof of his mouth as he watched the cook fry his eggs over-easy on the griddle across the counter. Hank noisily slurped a spoonful of milk and cornflakes alongside him. Jack fished an ice cube from his water glass and dunked it in his coffee cup.

"Half the new business in Benrey is a Cash Bailey front. The damn town's a laundromat, Hank. Cash Bailey's Money-Wash. Dope money. Prostitution money. Blood money. The more money he cleans, the dirtier the town gets."

"Doesn't say much for the efficiency of local law enforcement, does it?" Hank said dryly.

Jack was obsessed with Cash, but he was often obsessed, consumed with a burning intensity that wouldn't let him rest until *whatever* problem was resolved. Not jealousy, Jack reflected. This was territorial: Cash could have whatever he wanted—*south* of the border. But this was Jack's turf. Benteen turf. An outpost of law and order. And Cash Bailey didn't belong there anymore.

Hank chewed a mouthful of cereal. "No point letting it stick in your craw. Cash Bailey's where he is and you're where you are and you both go back too far together." Slurp. "You've *still* got a grudge over that woman of yours."

"That was four, five years ago. Ancient history," Jack said dismissively.

"Predates the fucking pharaohs," Hank agreed, with a laugh.

Andy Anderson, the paunchy, bespectacled owner of the Chicken Champ franchise, parked his new Blazer in back and let himself in. He looked absurd wearing a ten-gallon hat as he walked through the kitchen and called out to Scotty, wondering what the hell a cage was doing in the restaurant. Scotty grunted Hector's message and, smiling, Andy flipped open the cage door to stroke the rabbit.

A block away, Hector and Merv watched from the rusted pickup truck as the Chicken Champ erupted in a massive roar of flame and smoke and showering plate glass, blowing over a passing car, tossing it like crumpled paper into a parked sedan. Hector pulled away as Merv whistled his awe.

"Anybody there besides Andy?" asked Merv.

"Teenage fuck who deals dope at the high school," Hector replied, as he steered the pickup toward the border. "Or used to, anyway."

"But no customers."

Hector shook his head. "May have singed a few passersby."

"I think we should have handled Andy a little more quietly," Merv reflected.

Hector turned down a side street to avoid two approaching police cars. "Cash told me he didn't just want to punish Mr. Chicken. He's more interested in sending a message to anybody else who might try to chisel him."

"The trouble with that," Merv went on, "is he's also sending a message to the law."

"You got that right, *amigo*. The message is 'don't fuck with us!' "

Merv disagreed, believing that the best way to keep the sheriff and Captain Benteen off their backs was not to antagonize them. But he knew his perspective was a lot different than Hector's. Hector had grown up in a Mexico City slum where street gangs made and enforced their own laws. Merv was from Benrey and had been enticed into service with Cash Bailey by the prospect of buying a life somewhere a lot more interesting. But publicly executing a bag man was a little *too* interesting. Now Hector was mad at him for criticizing the operation. Merv got along with Hector well enough when he had to, but as they neared the border Merv suspected him of deliberately taking the most teeth-rattling washboard road he could find.

Back in Benrey, Hackett's brown truck was already cruising in the opposite direction. Just before the explosion, Hackett had taken the scope back from Coker. He had the crosshairs trained on Jack Benteen's forehead when the blast hit. For a moment, Hackett half expected a bloody, grapefruit-sized hole to replace Benteen's left temple, but then the shock waves that rocked the truck were unmistakable. He and Coker looked with amazement at the billowing smoke two blocks down the street and the debris falling everywhere like dirty rain.

Cowboy McRose sniffed the air. "Cyclonite," he said in his quiet Sun Belt drawl. "C-four plastique. Must've used a kilo-and-a-half." Hackett drove the brown truck to the Yellow Rose, a roach-infested residential motel on the outskirts of town.

Jack and Hank rushed from the cafe to the site of the explosion. A woman and child were trapped inside the car that had been blown across the street by the force of the blast. It had come to rest angled on top of a parked car that had caught fire. The fire was growing and the flames were licking at the gas tank, so Jack didn't wait for the approaching fire engines and forced the door open himself, then pulled the two victims out. He and Hank dragged them a safe distance away. Moments later, both vehicles exploded. Hank tried to comfort several injured bystanders as the paramedics arrived. As firemen battled to keep the flames from spreading Jack angrily surveyed the devastation, correctly predicting that the evidence would show that it was no accident.

5

Night and rain flooded in as the Gulf storm returned. The headlights of Benteen's cruiser cut into the darkness like a dull knife through black velvet. Jack leaned close to the windshield and boosted the wiper speed. The poor visibility gave him something else to concentrate on besides the bomb and Cash Bailey.

Chicken Champ had been the last straw. Jurisdiction or no, Jack passed word to Mexico that he wanted a meeting with Cash. His M.O. was simple. Right after the fire was under control and a call to the boys from the state lab had been made, Jack, Hank, and Deputy Cortez shook down one of Cash's dealers, a young Mexican man who lived in Benrey's ample barrio, an area of rundown two-story apartment houses and ramshackle garden bungalows crowded together.

The man struggled as Hank and Cortez kept him pinioned.

"Tell him I'm gonna bust his *cajones* for selling dope if he doesn't do like I say," Jack ordered Cortez.

Cortez translated, staccato-fast. The man shouted and spit furious denials, swung at Hank trying to get away.

"Hell, I'm tired of waiting," Hank said. "This may not be too legal but—" He grabbed the man in a hammerlock. One squeeze and there was no further trouble.

"Tell him to go across the border and get word to Cash, his brother's boss . . . Tell him I want to meet Cash on his side of the river . . ." Jack hesitated for a moment, then plunged in headfirst: "Tell him to meet me tomorrow noon. Tell Cash I'll be waiting at the blind where we used to hunt quail."

A sudden wind—ominous, harsh—began to blow dust around the four. Cortez kept translating. Hank kept squeezing.

Afterward, Jack went back to his office, called the Treasury Department, and suggested an audit of Clarence King's bank.

As Jack rolled into the parking lot at Jalisco, a mile or so outside Benrey, the big roadhouse's wet parking lot glistened with reflections of the flashing beer signs in the windows. He pulled his poncho over his uniform and headed inside.

On the stage, which was festooned with tacky, blue sequined curtains, Sarita Cisneros crooned a Spanish love song. Her voice was throaty enough to distract the hooting, boozed-up, Anglo and Chicano roughnecks and farmhands away from the jiggling breasts of the bar girls. Jack kept his eyes on Sarita as he pushed his way through the dim, smoky club and looked over the heads of the couples on the dance floor. Her eyes met his as he took a seat at a table near the stage. His presence had a potent effect on her, which she tried to hide as she kept singing. She liked it when he came to hear her sing. It anchored her performance with an emotional reality.

Her sexy delivery was also a turn-on for Jack. He didn't get out to hear Sarita enough. Too soon the song was over.

Sarita moved off the stage and joined Jack. Her demeanor changed abruptly as she remembered a broken promise.

Jack flashed her his best smile. "You sound real good up there."

"It took you long enough to get here. We were gonna have dinner between shows, remember?" Sarita wasn't letting Jack slide tonight the way she usually did. It was time to let him know she was dissatisfied.

"It's been a hard day. I'll buy you a beer instead and tell you all about it."

Jack's day was the last thing Sarita wanted to hear about. He'd been spending too much time thinking about work and not enough on their problems as a couple. Their love life had deteriorated sharply in the last year or so. But Sarita knew in her heart there was something worth saving in their relationship. She would have to tell Jack what was bothering her instead of hiding her resentments. An awkward silence passed between them as Sarita wondered where to start.

As the beers arrived Jack watched Sarita, gauging her anger. He wondered why she held on to him. He didn't understand his women, but he assumed he had something they wanted, something that made it worth putting up with a man married to his job. Sarita, easily holding on to her good looks and slim figure in her early thirties, could do better, Jack figured, but he didn't question his good fortune or his bad. She could do worse, too.

Sarita took a pull from her beer and set it down, her eyes boring into Jack in a way that made him squirm.

"What's wrong?" he asked, giving her a feel under the table.

"I don't like it when you keep me waiting for hours. I worry about you, Jack. You work late almost every night."

"And it's not doing much good. The town's going to hell."

Sarita shook her head. Getting through to Jack wasn't easy but she couldn't put it off any longer. "So are we, Jack. We've got no life together and we don't have much of a future either."

Jack irritably wondered why she couldn't—or wouldn't—see things from his perspective, and held up a hand. "Can we do this later? Like I said, I've had a hard day."

Jack buried his eyes in the mouth of his beer bottle, watching the CO_2 vapor rise and disappear as Sarita kept going. "Your father's dead and so's your mother. You don't have any brothers and sisters. I'm all you got. You should take better care of me." But she couldn't expect much more out of Jack than she was getting, which was at least *some* stability in her life.

The resignation in Sarita's voice annoyed Jack, but he tried to placate her. "I'm doing the best I can, baby."

Sarita sighed—Jack was who he was. "You're not doing a damn thing different than you ever have. You always avoid the things I want to talk about. I want children and I want you. And I don't mind talking about it right here." The truth was, Jack was far from the worst man Sarita had spent time with and she knew it. At least with Jack she felt like half of a couple —more than she had with anybody before him. She felt comfortable and safe with him or she would have left him a long time before. But that was no longer enough. "I want some kind of life like normal people have, Jack."

The idea of being "normal" didn't appeal much to Jack. The standards were too low for him. Jack stood up, draining the beer. "I came in to tell you that I'm going down to Mexico in the morning. I'll be gone before you get up."

Sarita set her jaw. "Excuse me, but I think I'm missing the point."

"I've got to see Cash Bailey," Jack finished. Unable to open up to her, he turned and walked out, knowing he should stay.

Sarita stared at the door closing behind him as the rain swallowed him up. She finished her beer and whispered "Bye, Jack," to herself, then got back on the stage as the band struck up a song to begin the next set.

6

By late morning, the storm clouds had blown away. The rain-slicked clay streets on the Mexican side of the border quickly baked back to dust, the dust that was everywhere in San Luis, the village Cash Bailey used as a center of operations.

Atop a hill, the three-story Hotel Isabella had a view of the entire village. The hotel was a relic of better times, when 1920s bootleggers had brought an influx of trade to the town. They had built the hotel as a comfortable way station and it had the fading remnants of some of the finer touches the wealthy smugglers had installed there. Broken mosaic tiles still clung to the risers of the once-grand main staircase leading to a broad veranda in front. On each side of the front door, bright-colored parrots were painted onto ceramic inlays. The second story had a balcony supported by four wooden beams evenly spaced across the veranda. Inside was a long cherrywood bar imported from Spain when the hotel was built. The wrought-iron chandeliers were made by Mexico City's finest smiths. However, the peeling beige paint exposed the pinks and blues of an earlier decor. Now the sprawling mass was one of Cash's whore-

34

houses as well as a fortress where he could hole up against anything. In his own way, Cash Bailey was a bootlegger, bucking a different Prohibition.

Cash's bedroom at the hotel was a shambles: clothes and bedding strewn across the floor, the rug kicked aside, drawers pulled halfway open, more clothing dangling from them. A half-naked prostitute slept facedown across the bed. Cash, unshaven for a week, hadn't slept in a couple of days. He sat at a small table near the window, drinking slugs of tequila and looking out over the village—*his* village.

Cash was slim and tall, wearing a soiled white linen suit, gold jewelry, including a Rolex watch and a massive turquoise-inlaid belt buckle, and expensive hand-tooled boots. Like Jack, he was in his late thirties. Cash still retained a boyish charm, which he churlishly blended with a killer's heart.

Belting back a shot and brushing away a nagging fly, Cash leaned back in his high-backed chair, staring vacantly at a pile of marijuana seeds, stems, rolling papers, roaches, and crumpled American and Mexican money. Cash picked up a glass vial and uncorked it, poured some of the nearly pure cocaine onto the web of his thumb and forefinger. He snorted a stiff dose, then another.

The drug sent his heart racing. Contemplating his impending meeting with Jack Benteen, Cash wondered if Jack would try to kill him. Cash figured he was betting his life on being able to buy Benteen off. But Cash always hedged his bets: in the briefcase he always kept by his side was an Ingram machine pistol, loaded, chambered, safety off. Jack would have to be slicker than a handful of snot, Cash thought, to get around that. And even if he did, Cash's guards would make short work of him. If Jack was coming to hang Cash, he'd have to hang himself in the process.

How in the hell did we come to this? Cash asked

himself. He lit a cigarette and inhaled hungrily. He had started smuggling long ago, and back then he wanted Jack to go into business with him. Jack had turned him down and warned him that it was too great a risk, wasn't worth the dangers. But Cash proved him wrong, making fast money and having a wild time of it, until the Drug Enforcement Administration caught him with his pants down. The D.E.A. gave him an easy choice: jail or a job. At first he bragged to Jack and Hank and the other surviving icons of his childhood in Benrey that he had made good in law enforcement.

But soon, rumors followed Cash's own bragging. It seemed to Cash that was when Jack had turned against him. But as a D.E.A. operative in Latin America, Cash made enough connections among the politicians, the military, and the big narcotics suppliers to be able to make a massive leap in stature as a smuggler and he wasn't about to lay off for his old friend Jack. Instead of carrying thirty or forty pounds of marijuana across the Rio Grande on a motorcycle by himself, Cash organized an industry for himself. It wasn't long until he had enough of everything to retire from the D.E.A. and drop out of sight before they could catch up to him. His operations continued in secret as he branched out into gunrunning. The guns were more valuable than money in many of the countries he did business with. They enhanced his bargaining ability. Trading munitions to various Latin American revolutionaries for large quantities of the local recreational drugs parlayed the take to about ten times the price of the hardware, and Cash's empire burgeoned.

He might have taken a different path if his damn mother hadn't committed suicide when Cash was fresh out of high school. He hadn't seen his father in years. Alone in the world, Cash decided to give up on just about everything but Cash Bailey. Jack Benteen was carrying on his family's tradition, and the way Cash had it figured, Cash was carrying on his own family's tradition: playing for high stakes, never worrying about the price. His father had been a heavy gambler and a heavier loser, but Cash saw himself winning big as the foreign bank accounts got bigger and the reins of power stronger.

He and Jack had been on different sides for a while now, but Cash could never quite pinpoint why Jack traded his loyalty to Cash for allegiance to a quaint law-enforcement agency waging a pitifully outmanned crusade against crime and corruption. And because he didn't understand why, Cash felt betrayed.

A noise outside drew his attention—just two Mexican women pounding corn for tortillas under the awning of a makeshift outdoor kitchen in the courtyard below. Nearby a naked child played in the dust. Several prostitutes sunned themselves on the worn stone steps of the cantina, listening to the Tex-Mex border music drifting out the door from the hotel cantina's five-piece band. Near them, a Mexican guard, an enormous, brutal-looking man, his gun and holster visible beneath his open jacket, attempted to play with a yo-yo, making the women laugh. Down the hill in the main village, smoke rose from a few cooking fires.

Cash coughed and took another swig from the tequila bottle. The whine of a sleek French Giselle helicopter's turbine echoed off the streets. Its shadow flitted across the window as it passed overhead, then set down in the courtyard of the hotel, quickly obscured by the tornado of dust kicked up by the rotor wash. Merv and Hector got out of the Giselle, Merv again hauling two large suitcases, the proceeds of another day's collections.

A young Mexican servant girl of fourteen or so crept through the open hall door. She quietly began picking up the mess on the floor. Cash wheeled, startling the girl, who dropped the armload she had just gathered. She froze, waiting for Cash's further reaction, but he waved her away and she scampered down the hall in relief. Suddenly irritated at everything, Cash woke the whore and sent her on her way. She was crabby from being wakened and they traded curses in Spanish as he pushed her out the door, tossed her things out, and slammed the door behind her.

A huge scorpion crawled out of a leather pouch lying amid the trash on the table and began feeding on marijuana seeds. Cash loomed over the table, his face close to the lethal insect as he studied it. He flicked open a switchblade stiletto and began fencing with the scorpion, which attacked the shining blade. Cash mentally superimposed Jack's face onto the scorpion's. He smiled cruelly, enjoying the one-sided duel.

Tiring of the play, Cash dropped the switchblade and laid his hand on the table, coaxing the scorpion to walk onto the back of it. The insect arched its abdomen, poised to strike, but Cash blew softly on it and it relaxed its stance. Cash turned his hand and the scorpion crawled into his palm, trying to stay upright. Suddenly Cash closed his fist, squeezing until it trembled from the pressure.

Cash's face shaded from silent, sweaty agony to bliss and he exhaled deeply. The door burst open and Merv dragged the suitcases in as Cash looked up, startled.

"Eureka!" Merv dumped the suitcases open on the floor, fat bundles of American greenbacks spilling out among the assorted trash. "We'll have three cases tomorrow!"

Cash was expressionless. "Be right with you, Merv." He sounded bored. He opened his hand to reveal the scorpion, or what was left of it, lying in a lake of blood in his palm.

— 7 —

Jack's cruiser sped down a narrow dirt track along the American side of the Rio Grande, a plume of red dust billowing in its wake. Jack's foot was heavy on the gas. Hank Pearson was strapped into the right seat, holding on tight as rocks and ruts pounded at the car as it slid back and forth on the turns.

"Don't cross the border, Jack. You got no jurisdiction. Your granddaddy could do it and your daddy could too. They went any old where they damn well pleased. But things were different then. You can't even *think* about it."

"I've got no choice."

"You sure you want to go through with this?" Hank had qualms about meeting Cash in the middle of nowhere. Cash had all the cards and all the chips. If Cash decided he wanted them dead, they were making it too easy for him.

Jack glanced sideways at Hank. "You ain't scared, are you?"

Hank shook his head, but Jack knew what he meant.

"Yeah, me too," Jack agreed. "But I've got to give Cash fair warning. With any luck, he'll play it smart and retire. If he isn't smart, maybe I'll have to retire him myself."

Jack glanced up at the cut-down Winchester. He'd modified the lever-action carbine to hold ten rounds. Every other round was steel-jacketed, the rest were Jack's personal blend for high-risk situations: hollowed points filled with fulminate of mercury and sealed. When they hit someone, the mercury spread out in a sheet, ripping and tearing through soft tissue in an area about five inches across. When a man took one of those, he died, plain and simple. If the impact didn't kill him, the poison would. The Winchester was an ideal weapon, Jack figured, for holding several men at bay—or sending them to the hereafter, if necessary. He hoped it wouldn't get down to that, but he'd been in tight situations before and was afraid this would be another one.

Jack had had the slow hanging nightmare again the previous night. This time Cash jumped up and broke his neck, and Jack was left to dangle in agony —sometimes it happened the other way around. Jack touched his neck, absently reassuring himself that the rope burn was only in his mind.

The dirt road careened precipitously along the rim of an abandoned gravel pit. The further south Jack got, the stronger his resolve became. Jack knew he could never hope to get rid of all the crime and vice in his district or anywhere else. But, to Jack, Cash was some kind of fertilizer to the underworld, nurturing it and making it grow, raising a putrid crop of decadence and degradation. If anything, Jack decided, he had waited too long to go after Cash, let him get too entrenched, too secure, too hard to get to.

This road was the same road Jack and Cash took as teenagers for their ritual treks to the bars and whorehouses of Mexico. It was the same road Jack's father and grandfather patrolled, fighting back the influx of "wetbacks," liquor, cigarettes, weapons, and all the other usual cargoes of men who crossed borders in the cover of darkness. Jack ruefully acknowledged that he and Cash had brought back their shares of the booty and made a bundle selling fireworks, stroke books, and mescal liquor to their less adventurous friends. But Jack bowed out when Cash branched out into the higher-profit, higher-risk business of smuggling drugs.

The border wasn't as treacherous then. Now any kids who did the same thing had to worry about the bushwhackers that habitually preyed on illegal aliens sneaking in, and anybody else they encountered. Jack knew one rancher with a spread near the border who never drove around with fewer than five guns, including a sawed-off shotgun loaded with slugs instead of pellets. *Los pollos*—"chickens," as Mexicans called those who crossed the border without papers—weren't so well off. Even if they avoided the bushwhackers, they were often preyed upon by the aptly named "coyotes" who led them across. Once, on patrol, Jack had discovered the bodies of a woman and her four children who had died of thirst after being abandoned in the desert by their coyote. When a suspect was arrested, Jack risked his job to deprive the man of water for his first day of captivity.

As the Mexican immigrants living on the U.S. side of the border had dramatically increased in number, the urban areas grew rapidly, evidenced by the expanding *colonias*, the Spanish-language billboards, radio, and TV stations, the businesses oriented to a Mexican clientele, and the currency-exchange stands that took advantage of the peso's instability. But in the rural area Jack and Hank were driving through, the terrain was so desolate and forbidding that they might as well have been on the moon. The native plants had thorns or poisons that prevented man or beast from using their life-sustaining moisture. The only signs of civilization were occasional piles of trash or a shredded tire or a smashed hubcap.

Jack slowed as he came to a jutting rock formation. He stopped behind a stand of mesquite to pull his poncho over his uniform, tuck the Winchester into a hidden pocket of the poncho, and slip a snub-nosed .32-caliber revolver into one of his boots.

Hank slid behind the wheel, and Jack moved around the cruiser to get into the passenger seat. Hank pulled out of the stand of mesquite and carefully guided the car down the path to the river. Jack didn't tell Hank he was going to have a shoot-out, because he wasn't exactly *planning* on it. He was just going to be ready if it happened.

8

Merv bubbled with excitement as he put the money back in the suitcases. "We doubled our volume in one week! And next week, who knows? All the press on this 'crack' stuff has been driving the demand up faster than we can fill it."

Cash blew his nose into a bloody handkerchief, staining it further, then snorted more coke and chased it with another shot of tequila. "Like my daddy always said: 'You get to it, you can have anything you want in the world, plus pussy and beer.'" He looked over at Merv. "You know where to put it?"

"End of the fiscal year," Merv said. "Lot of it'll go to Grand Cayman Island accounts."

"Ain't we having fun?" Cash crowed.

"I don't know if we can rely on Clarence to handle our . . . ah, expansion." Merv was impressed by neat rows of cash in suitcases; the money made him feel omnipotent, invincible. It was the ultimate form of mobility. With enough U.S. dollars, you could go anywhere, do anything. But the fireworks show at Chicken Champ was saltpeter for a money-hungry libido. Merv knew his place at Cash's side and he stood by it, loyal and expediently honest.

"You gave Clarence my message, didn't you? 'Think big,' I said."

Merv nodded. "He's scared, Cash."

"Well goddamn it, Merv, if old Clarence can't pull his own weight, we'll just have to move on without him. I mean, talk is mostly my middle name, but like my daddy used to say, you can't argue with a stupid man."

For the first time, Cash showed appreciation for the fortune on the bed. He picked up a few of the bundles and riffled the edges. "Money, I swear. Will you look at this stuff! We're gonna have to start digging holes." Or give it away, Cash thought as he and Merv walked out to the helicopter.

He figured that buying off Jack Benteen could be a very wise investment, even if the price was three or four times Jack's salary. Jack valued his integrity, Cash knew, but Jack didn't deny himself life's pleasures either. Cash still considered that their common ground. By appealing to Benteen on a level they could both appreciate, maybe he could get them off their collision course.

Cash sometimes felt like a puppy that grew up with a kitten: friendly until they were old enough to realize they were natural enemies, then wondering what the hell went wrong.

Hank stopped the cruiser near the river. There was no sign of Cash on the other side of the Rio Grande. The river was narrow here, hardly a trickle. A man could cross on the rocks without even getting his feet wet.

Hank looked at Jack. "Think he's gonna show?"

Jack nodded. He knew Cash would show up to see if he could make a deal.

There was a faint whine, growing louder, and the

thwopping of an approaching helicopter. Cash's Giselle came into view from the south.

Hank whistled. "Turbine-powered. One of them French jobs. He's spending a little money . . . Looks like he just had it waxed."

The Giselle circled, nearly overhead, crossing the river into U.S. airspace. The helicopter was only fifty feet above the ground, too low for border radar to pick up.

"He's tempting us to shoot him down." Hank shaded his eyes as he watched the Giselle cross back into Mexico.

"He's checking us out, looking for weapons, backups." Jack knew Cash's style—cautious and brazen all at once.

The Giselle settled in a clear area on the Mexican side. Two men, who looked big even from this distance, got out. Jack made out a third figure still inside the helicopter.

"Let's go." Jack indicated the other side of the river.

Hank started the cruiser and plunged it into the river, throttled it across to the other side, where it climbed out onto the steep bank, sliding as its wet wheels muddied the red clay.

"Stop here." Jack opened his door. "Ready?"

Hank clipped a high-powered scope onto a heavy-barreled sniper rifle. "Things go bad, I'm not going to hit much at this range, 'specially if they're moving."

"Things go bad, I want you to put some holes in the helo's turbine and fuel tanks. Give 'em a good show." Jack looked across to the helicopter, still a hundred yards away. One of the men was wiping the dust off the Giselle, the other was holding an automatic rifle.

Jack crossed the chaparral to where Cash was waiting. As he got closer he saw that both guards were heavily armed, a fact Jack noted without surprise.

The guards met him with their rifles leveled. If they

searched him and found the carbine, instant death was a probability. Jack approached them slowly, keeping his hands in view. He smiled and nodded at the guards, but their faces offered no response. One of them, a lanky, muscular Latino named Lupo, waved his rifle. "Give us your gun, man." Lupo's straggly hair and unkempt beard blew in the dry breeze.

"I don't give up my gun. Not without somebody getting hurt."

Lupo's eyes narrowed, his lips tightened. "You don't mess with us, man." He motioned to his companion, a gigantic hulking black with a shaved head. "You remember him from 'Monday Night Football'? He all-star hombre."

Jack turned to the man. "Sure, Monday, I remember you playing benchmark for the Oilers."

"I hurt my knee," the man replied.

"Looks like you hurt your head." Jack sneered.

"Monday" turned to Jack appraisingly. He stood almost a half head taller than Jack and he flexed his long, brawny arms, which could have crushed the biggest lineman in the NFL. "I hurt somebody else's head." His deranged grin said he probably *had* hurt his own head, left himself too damaged to play football, just damaged enough to apply the techniques of brutality he had cultivated in professional football to the service of Cash's organization.

As the two men moved in on Jack, Cash emerged from the helicopter and said, "Back off, boys, let him pass." He waved to Jack. "Hell, come on over here."

Cash looked weary and haggard, but Jack expected that: the pressure of Cash's life-style seemed deadly. Cash smiled broadly. He looked as crazy as the entire Manson family during a full moon.

Cash spread his arms wide. *"Amigo,* welcome to my country!"* Cash affected a bad Mexican accent and laughed.

Jack loathed what Cash looked like, what he'd made of himself, a quivering doper with bloodshot, yellowed eyes, so unlike the Cash Bailey who was star quarterback of Benrey High.

Cash offered his hand, but Jack didn't take it. Cash smiled. He knew the game. "Long time no see, old buddy. Goddamn, how it flies. You look good. Trim. Yes, sir, old hell-raiser Jack and his best buddy Cash. Well, come on over."

Adrenaline pumping, Jack mentally rehearsed the possibility of wiping out Cash and his entourage in a few seconds of murderous rifle fire. Jack had the familiar bad-dream feeling of standing on the board over the wagon bed as the noose was slipped around his neck. This is crazy, Jack thought. If I kill these men in cold blood, I'm no better than they are.

Cash looked as friendly as a poisonous snake. He sought ways to capitalize on their past association. "Still living in the house your granddaddy built?"

"Sure am." Got to watch him and his guards, every move, Jack thought. Got to watch myself.

Cash sat down on a large rock with his worn briefcase beside him. "Make yourself at home." He acted relaxed but was watchful, cautious. "Damn, Jack, I was thinking—whatever happened to old Sally Deegan? Remember when you and me did her up out back of George Fletcher's barn, senior-prom night? Three rounds each, and you never took off your tux. Or gardenia."

"Some people change, Cash." Jack mimicked Cash's familiar manner. "Sally's in Salt Springs teaching third grade." That prom night, Sally was so whacked out on the spiked punch and the over-the-counter Mexican Quaalude Cash gave her that she probably couldn't even tell they were two different men. It wasn't Jack's style these days, but that was his first time and he was eager to take advantage wherever that advantage lay.

Cash shrugged. "She gets tired of that, tell her to come down here and work for me." He spit at Jack's feet. "Come on, Jack, talk to me. I know you didn't come here to tell me how good-looking I am. What's the chief district officer of the Texas Rangers want with poor ol' Cash Bailey?"

"You know why I'm here. Two people dead on Main Street. One of 'em just a kid. Almost killed a mother and her baby."

Cash shook his head. "Don't like it one bit myself, Jack. Nasty piece of business. I heard one of the fellas got killed was unreliable, cheated his partners, held out. Believe it or not, I'm with you." Cash stubbed at a tumbleweed with his boot, watched the brittle ball crack off and roll away.

Jack was wary, he felt the pitch coming on.

Cash's grin spread wider. "Yep, I don't like the noise and I don't like the mess. I need enforcement by local authority, so that nothing like this will happen again. I need you, Jack. We could work together. You ought to pick up one of these." He waved to the Giselle. "Turbine-powered, hundred-forty knots, Austin or Dallas in forty-two minutes. It's just a side benefit. Great for lunch. Or you take and mount a cannon on her, even rack you up some bombs and go hunt pigs, if that's your thing. A lot of things in this world you can buy with a little cash." He smiled at his pun.

Cash paced. "Hell, Jack, I know you're mad, but this is me and you. We got history. We rode the river together. Nothing would make me happier than to see you with a little grubstake of your own. Maybe a hundred thou a year, off the top?"

Jack snorted derisively. "Hell, Cash, you can buy me. You always could. But you can't buy the badge."

"Well, what in the hell else are we gonna do? Shoot each other?"

Jack tensed, ready to make his move. Was Cash on to

him? Jack noticed that Cash kept his right hand only inches from the top of his open briefcase. Probably an "equalizer" in there, he realized. Jack deliberated for a few seconds, letting tension accumulate before he replied in firm, measured tones. "I say you close up shop and haul ass while you can. I'm telling you that 'cause we were friends."

Cash shook his head and scratched an ear. "You still ain't took that tux off yet, have you? Or gardenia. Maybe I should give more to charity. Boy Scouts, United Appeal, Houston Symphony Orchestra, your choice. And maybe you should quit trying to be the only Texas Ranger left with a spit-shine heart. You gotta understand that people like to get high. I do it myself on occasion." Cash tried to catch Jack's eye. "We're old friends, Jack. I miss you."

It was obvious to Jack that Cash was playacting. He spoke softly. "I catch you in Benrey, Cash, you're dead. Hear? You cross that border, your ass is mine."

Cash's eyes went cold, his voice steely. "Don't push me, *friend*. You're on the wrong side of the river and your badge don't mean shit here."

Jack saw his opportunity. He suspended his thoughts, his actions became purely instinctive as he whipped the Winchester from under his poncho and leveled it, pointing it back and forth between Cash and his goons. But his finger froze on the trigger, leaving him in a standoff.

Cash's "barroom tan" drained from his face. His hand moved toward the briefcase, but only made it as far as the wrist when he changed his mind and slowly drew his hand back out again. The faces of Monday and Lupo showed fear and mortification. Probably they're less afraid of dying than what Cash will do to them if they live, Jack thought grimly. He decided to turn this into a grandstand play and hoped that it wouldn't cost him his life.

"If I pull this trigger, you'll all be bloody ribbons," Jack snarled. "Does that mean shit here?" He savored the moment, keeping the three men covered and at bay. Then just as suddenly as he had produced it, Jack turned the rifle aside, but still kept it ready. He looked straight at Cash. "Just remember, Cash, all the time you're living from now on is a gift from Jack Benteen. Don't expect any more favors."

Cash grinned, despite the cold, beaded sweat on his hands and forehead. "A spit-shine heart *and* brass balls. You're the last of a breed, Jack."

"I'm going back to my side, Cash. I'll be waiting for you."

"Think about it, Jack. Tax-free, did I mention that?" Cash persisted.

Jack shook his head and headed for the cruiser.

Cash called after him. "Just out of curiosity, who you got with the rifle?"

"An old friend. Hank Pearson." Jack kept walking.

"*Sheriff* Hank Pearson? Ain't that a hoot. Still getting elected. Remember when he beat our asses for drinking your old man's whiskey and shooting insulators off power lines? Who'd have thought you two would be working together. Shit, tell that old coyote hello." Cash waved at the cruiser, excited, as though Hank were a long-lost friend. "By the way, how's old Sarita?"

"Fine, Cash. She's okay."

"Still singing pretty as ever?"

"*Better* than ever," Jack asserted. Her singing never brought her much, but she was damn good at it. Jack sort of resented Cash even bringing it up in this context. The rifle felt warm and ready in Jack's hands, but, he told himself, you don't kill a man out of jealousy —usually.

"I sure miss old Sarita. Sometimes I think I should

have married her, even if she is a Mexican." Cash darkened for a moment, reflecting on other paths he might have taken, but then he brightened up. "But I got plenty of Mexican poozle right here."

Cash's shoulders slumped. He looked soggy and tired in the stained white linen suit. Jack almost felt sorry for his old friend, but . . . everyone made their choices and had to live or die with them. "Chuck it, Cash. Take the money and run."

Cash shook his head. "Can't do it. Too late."

Jack turned and, with measured steps, walked back to the river.

Jack and Hank were barely a mile from the rendezvous when Hank began to get on Jack's case. "In Texas, the Eleventh Commandment is 'Thou shalt not pull a gun if you're not going to use it!'"

Jack knew brandishing that rifle for show was stupid and dangerous and went against every instinct.

"Live and learn, or you don't live long." Hank was thoroughly disgusted.

Maybe Cash would think twice, but Jack doubted it. He was too far gone to do the rational thing. Besides, Cash was profiting fabulously from Mexico's unstoppable population boom, using illegal-immigrant traffic to mask his own smuggling operations. As Mexico's birthrate soared there was only one place where the human overflow could be absorbed: *el Norte*. Jack didn't blame anybody who sneaked across the border to feed his family—a man had to live, didn't he? But more than two-thirds of the crime in his district involved the illegal-immigrant population, either as perpetrators or as victims. Cash's operations helped swell the ranks of both. So Jack kept up a tough front, letting the Latino community know he was far less corruptible than the lawmen they were used to.

Hank said something that struck Jack to the quick: "The smartest crooks always know how to get a man on the inside. Women too, as far as that goes." Jack wished Sarita had never slept with Cash.

Jack clenched the steering wheel in white-knuckled frustration. Why had his nerve failed him? He had blown his best chance of getting Cash and crippling Cash's organization. He had thrown away the possibility of surprise, his best ally. And Jack had a feeling that the coming weeks and months would multiply his searing regret. As Jack crossed the border back into the good ol' U.S. of Texas he was too wrapped up in his thoughts to notice the rainbows spread out in the mists from the irrigation sprinklers in the afternoon sun.

After Jack's car was out of sight, Cash grabbed a truncheon and knocked out a few of Monday's and Lupo's teeth, which he described as "the most eloquent way" he could express his displeasure at their bungling search of Jack Benteen. Monday and Lupo, the most primitive of thinkers, associated their pain and humiliation with Jack, not with Cash, and hatred welled up inside them. Cash wouldn't let any of his men see his own fear, but he was contemplating his "life insurance policy," several ledgers he kept in a safe-deposit box in Clarence's bank. They might buy him a very cushy asylum in Cuba or Nicaragua if things got too crazy where he was. Maybe it would be simpler just to have Jack iced, but Cash figured that could have unpredictable consequences. His network of political connections was set up to *buy* lawmen, not kill them.

Besides, Cash mused, death didn't really seem a fitting punishment for Jack's breach of their friendship.

Maybe a dose of his own medicine would bring Jack around. Sarita was a soft spot. Cash watched Jack's anger rise when he mentioned her. If Cash could entice her to come back to him, he'd have a hold on Jack. He smiled to himself as the scheming side of his brain clicked into gear.

9

It was dark by the time Jack and Hank returned to Benrey, but they went straight to the Sheriff's Station. Jack couldn't deal with Sarita's gripes yet, not after his meeting with Cash.

The Sheriff's Station was vintage 1940s: tan linoleum floors, scarred oak desks, dark wood filing cabinets, a row of dented olive-drab lockers, wobbling overhead fans, yellow jail bars. Deputy Cortez was still on duty when Jack came in, and he gave the discouraging news that George Corliss, the mayor of Benrey, had called to say the Treasury Department would not be investigating Clarence's bank at this time. Corliss went on to express his dismay that Jack was causing trouble for "an asset to the community" like Clarence.

Jack knew Corliss as a small-time ward healer, cradle snatcher, and graft artist, not somebody who could wrest favors from the Treasury. Hank suggested that it was Cash, not the mayor or Clarence King, who prevented the T-men from following up on his complaint. Cash sure behaved like he had the goods on everybody: he did whatever he damn well pleased.

Jack asked Hank to shake a few trees, see if they

could learn more about the high-level contacts Cash had bought.

"Eight-tenths of my sources are dead and gone," Hank complained, "the rest diagnosed terminal or just drunk from noon on." Hank shook his head as he went into his usual nostalgic reverie. "Used to be I could track a man on hard rock three days gone. It's a new world, son, and Cash Bailey's at the top of a new pecking order."

"Not if we can help it," Jack responded, and spent the next few hours combing the files and compiling a list of people to call or write. The Texas Rangers took a dim view of fancy, high-tech ways of processing evidence, but Jack felt no shame in using the phone or the mails to save legwork. If he could catch Cash Bailey in bed with some VIP, Jack might have the leverage to wipe out Cash's power base.

As it turned out, Hank had been keeping a file on Cash, which was started by Jack's father after Jack and Cash were arrested as teenagers for drunken vandalism. Joaquin Benteen had also started a file on his son then, but Hank couldn't find that, and figured it had been trashed after Joaquin's death.

Hank's file on Cash Bailey contained several articles from gun-nut magazines that described Cash as the D.E.A.'s biggest embarrassment, a munitions supplier to various banana-republic honchos. From what Jack could tell, Cash's loyalty always went to the highest bidder, even if it required what the legitimate business world called a conflict of interest.

One photo showed Cash in Chile, embracing one of Pinochet's field marshals, with the caption HELP FOR OUR SOUTHERN NEIGHBORS. Another was a fuzzy shot of Cash delivering rocket launchers to an El Salvadoran rebel commander, under the headline REPUTED ARMS SMUGGLER.

As Jack studied the dossier he sensed Hank looking

over his shoulder. "Funny. I keep thinking of ol' Cash Bailey as just a kid, back when you were both throwing interceptions for Benney High in between pranks."

"Spare me the wise-ass remarks," Jack replied tiredly.

"Funny ain't it . . . how it all comes 'round?" Hank intoned, scratching his belly. "Right way's the hardest, going wrong's easy. Water seeks the path of least resistance—rule of nature. Makes for crooked rivers and crooked men."

"Spare me the poetry too." Jack sat up and looked his mentor straight in the eye. "I need facts. I can't undo the past, but if I know Cash's support system, I can close him down, and might even nab some bigger fish."

Hank gave him a look that implicitly questioned Jack's sanity. "You're talking about a man who's bought off every politician in Mexico, probably a few up here, has a private army and arsenal, and is crazy enough to use them," Hank said as he gestured expansively out the window. "He's more of a fact of life that you reckon with, than something you can control."

Jack debated whether or not to talk with Hank about his missed chance with Cash, but he thought better of it. Going down there might not have been such a great idea, and it wasn't Jack's style to dwell on his major errors. Years ago Hank had told him how General Sam Houston caught the main forces of Mexican President Santa Anna asleep in midafternoon, thus winning Texas's freedom from Mexico. Jack decided not to give Hank the inside laugh on his personal Waterloo, or San Jacinto. The best thing he could do was prevent Cash from establishing any more beachheads in Benrey.

"Hank, I want you to call the mayor tomorrow and get access to the business licenses on file at city hall. Make sure all the ownership info holds water."

"Good idea, Jack, will do." Hank looked at his

watch, got up, and bid Jack good night as he ambled out the door, warning him, "Keep an eye out for Chub Luke. That trash is gonna try and backshoot you or I ain't half as smart as I think I am."

After adding a few more names to his list, Jack strolled into the main office and poured himself a cup of acrid coffee. Deputy Purvis put down his copy of *Penthouse* and resumed typing a report. Deputy Cotton was on the phone. When he hung up, Jack asked him, "Where's Cortez?"

"Out chasing wets," Cotton laconically replied. Jack had spent many a night on similar duty, always feeling hopelessly outnumbered, but he'd given up pursuing the fence-jumpers long ago.

"Has he got backup?" Jack asked.

Cotton nodded. "Border Patrol is responding now."

Jack retrieved his poncho from the well-worn coat rack and headed out the door. "Anybody needs me, I'm at home," Jack told Deputy Cotton just before the door closed behind him.

What bothered Jack the most, he decided, was that on some level he still counted Cash as a friend. Much as he hated to admit it, he still liked the bastard.

10

Jack emerged from the Ranger Station, still preoccupied with thoughts of Cash Bailey. As he paused to light a cigarette his face was illuminated by the match. An instant later, Biddle pulled the West-Tex truck to a halt on the opposite side of the town square.

"It's the head Ranger," he said to his passengers.

"Jack Benteen," Hackett confirmed. "You should check out his file." Hackett held up the dossier that had been prepared by Jack's own father.

Luther Fry, another Special Forces sergeant assigned to Hackett's mission, adjusted an Afro wig over his close-shaved scalp then poked his head into the front passenger compartment. "Why?"

"The sonofabitch and Cash Bailey were best pals. Maybe still are. They played on the same football team, smoked dope together, stole a couple of cars, rolled the same women—"

Fry interrupted him. "That turncoat bastard probably has Benteen in his hip pocket."

"Could be," Hackett said. "Intelligence reports that Benteen just met with Cash down in Mexico." Hackett's brow wrinkled. "Maybe we should arrange an 'accident.' Break his leg. Or worse." The three men were silent as Jack drove past the truck in his cruiser.

"We need an effective diversion," Hackett said. "Something to keep him out of the operations area."

Fry finished adjusting the wig and posed in mock seduction as if kinky sex might be the diversion Hackett specified. "How do I look?"

"Queer," Biddle replied.

Hackett laughed softly.

"Not true." Fry smiled. "Faggots prefer short hair." He ran his hand over Biddle's crewcut.

"You're the expert." Biddle winked, pulling Fry's hand away. They bantered in light tones, but there was no mistaking the danger that these men carried with them. Their camaraderie was disciplined, professional, well trained.

The brown truck pulled into an alley adjoining Clarence's bank and Biddle turned off the headlights. Fry, wearing coveralls bearing the logo for a bogus alarm service, slipped out of the truck, silently closing the door. Clutching a small toolbox, he kept in the shadows as he made his way to a utility pole, which he climbed using a telephone lineman's safety belt and spiked crampons strapped to his boots.

At the top, Fry opened the rectangular metal circuit box and used a telephone handset to call Clarence's private office number. A car approached and Fry hugged the pole tightly to avoid being seen. After it was gone, Fry consulted an electronic sensor that showed him which phone wire to hook the wiretap into. He knew that Clarence used a bug detector, but Fry was putting a simple inductive pickup on the line. The pickup sensed and amplified changes in the electromagnetic field around the wire without drawing more than a fraction of a milliamp itself. The device was virtually undetectable.

* * *

Jack wasn't ready to turn in, so he decided to cruise the streets of Benrey for a while. He brooded about his problems with Sarita. They had been together for three years—"a while" as Jack put it. Sarita sometimes asked Jack to "introduce me to Jack, Jr.," meaning she wanted to have his kid. But Jack didn't feel ready for the responsibility. He didn't know why. He was well enough situated in his career. Maybe he was afraid he would die in the line of duty and didn't want to leave any widows and orphans. And Sarita hadn't fully given up on her singing career yet, so she didn't press the issue because she wasn't sure herself. Kids meant the end of the dream, or trading it for another one.

Jack's thoughts were interrupted by the sight of two men crouching in the shadows of Clarence's front yard. He switched on his spotlight, illuminating Larry McRose and Buck Atwater, the sixth and final member of Hackett's team. Atwater wore a baseball cap turned backward. He looked like a hayseed. His dirty T-shirt and jeans were stretched by a beer belly, but despite his disheveled appearance, he was a man who could be counted on under fire and he was an expert in explosives, electronics, and counterinsurgency operations.

McRose softly told Atwater, "Play drunk."

Atwater raised his arms above his head, pulling his baseball cap down in the process. A toothpick protruded from his mouth. "Hold everybody, Larry," he slurred. "Evenin', Officer. How's every little thing?"

Jack got out of the cruiser, keeping his hand close to his revolver. The two men froze.

"Shit, Buck, it's the Texas Rangers," said McRose in a voice that boomed, then belched. "Best thing is to confess."

"Against the wall," Jack ordered. "Move it!" Atwater and McRose complied silently. "Who are you boys?"

Atwater pointed to McRose and said, "That's Larry.

Larry Call. I'm Buck Schoonover. Just drifted down here from Dallas. Looking for work."

"Don't mean no harm. Just had a little to drink," McRose added, as Jack frisked them. He didn't find any weapons, but he removed a tape measure from McRose's pocket.

"What's this for?"

"I stole it," McRose said. "From Clementine Construction in Houston. But I feel real bad about it . . ."

Atwater picked up the ball. "He can't help it with measures, he's crazy about 'em. Listen to this: Tell him, Larry, how many inches in two-hundred and seventy-eight feet?"

It took McRose a few seconds to say "Three-thousand-three-hundred-and-thirty-six. But I can't get hired. No sir. Not for shit."

"Just need a job, Captain." Atwater swayed, looking comically pathetic.

Jack studied the men for a moment. Something wasn't right about them, but Jack felt like giving somebody a break. "State employment office opens at eight. It's on Third and Douglas. In the meantime, stay off private property."

McRose moved off Clarence's lawn and onto the sidewalk, motioning Atwater to do the same. "Thank you, Officer."

Jack got back in his car, rolled down the window. He eyed McRose. "I wouldn't be doing any more drinking tonight. Liable to get you boys in trouble." He started the motor and drove off.

When Jack's cruiser was out of sight, McRose said, "Come on out, Coker."

Sergeant Coker emerged from behind a parked car, flicking on the safety of the M-16 he'd kept trained on Jack throughout the encounter.

——— 11 ———

Jack got home just before 2:00 A.M., and though he knew Sarita would be back soon, he immediately climbed into bed and went to sleep.

Sarita hadn't seen Jack since the previous night at Jalisco. As promised, he had been gone by the time she woke up that morning. Driving home, she was still mad that he was so cold and distant, and the notion of his meeting with Cash made her uncomfortable. After all, how would Jack like it if she met with some of his old girlfriends to compare notes? She was feeling uncharacteristically insecure, like everything that had occurred in the past few days was a conspiracy to undermine her relationship with Jack. At this point what she wanted more than anything else was for Jack to stop avoiding her, and to resolve the hard questions she needed resolved about their future together. She put the top down on her MG and let the wind buffet her anger all the way home.

When Sarita got home and found Jack asleep, she took it as a personal affront, and she promptly commenced a program of door slamming and drawer banging. To her greater frustration, it failed to rouse Jack. When he awoke at 7:35, Sarita was lying next to him, glowering.

"Morning." Jack smiled, unaware of her mood.

"Sleep well?" Sarita asked, as if Jack didn't deserve to.

"I was out cold. Hard day yesterday. Sorry I didn't wait up for you, but . . . How was your day yesterday?"

"Not so good," Sarita said, resisting Jack's attempt to snuggle up to her. "You beat up one of us and word gets around quick. People were yelling curses at me in the club last night when I was trying to sing."

"But we barely hurt him at all. Just gave his arm a little twist."

Jack's understatement only made Sarita angrier. Being Jack's woman made her something of an outcast among Benrey's Latino community and she wished he was more sensitive to that.

Sarita's eyes searched Jack's as she asked, "So? What happened with Cash?"

"He said his piece, I said mine. We left it at that."

When Jack failed to provide more details, Sarita decided to lay more cards on the table. "He say anything about me?"

Jack wasn't surprised she asked. He was worried she still carried a torch for Cash, even after all this time. He figured the safest reply would be "Nope."

"Nada?" Sarita asked, raising her voice.

"Nothin' at all," Jack said, his face clouding. He had been in a good mood when he opened his eyes, but it looked like his day was rapidly turning sour.

Sarita studied Jack's expression for a moment. "You're lying. I can tell. I want to know what he said."

It angered Jack that Sarita could see through him so easily or would presume to call him a liar, even if that happened to be true in this case. His voice took on a hostile edge as he covered his ground. "Just like I told you. *Nada.*"

Sarita still didn't believe him. She jumped off the bed and went into the bathroom.

Jack heard her turn on the shower. The best way around this situation was to concentrate on getting ready for work. He didn't want a fight and he knew she didn't want one either. They were in an avalanche situation: once they started arguing, neither of them was able to stop it. Jack slid out from under the covers, pulled on some jeans and his boots. He went into the bathroom to brush his teeth, buckling on his two belts, the one for his holster and the one which held up his pants. When the shower turned off, he tossed Sarita a towel, but she remained hostile.

"Cómo que el chingado no dijo nada?"

"Say again?"

"What the hell do you mean, he didn't say nothing? I know how Cash is, he loves to brag. He must have said plenty so you don't forget he was with me first."

Sarita was goading Jack to get a reaction out of him, which came in the form of a burst of anger and outrage and shoving her against the wall, then a struggle to control it and Jack saying through clenched teeth, "I don't want to talk about it." Jack pictured the avalanche sweeping them away from each other. He felt powerless to reach out for her. Their relationship had always allowed each of them to share problems with the other, but Cash Bailey was too close to both of them and Jack couldn't expect Sarita to be objective about him. But if he didn't talk it out with her, he was shutting her out. Either way, he was losing.

Sarita remained defiant. "I talk to you, you got to talk back, even if you don't want to," she said, attempting to wiggle out of Jack's steel grasp, her anger increasing as she failed. *"Creido!* You think you are so big and strong you *have* to be good! *Y otra cosa!* What do you know about right and wrong? You've never been down and hungry without enough money to keep off the streets . . . Me and Cash, we know all about that."

As suddenly as he had grabbed her, Jack let Sarita go and moved away from her. He picked up his shirt and put it on as Sarita continued her diatribe.

"Cash helped me. He got me started as a singer. He encouraged me more than you ever did."

"Maybe you should have stayed with him." Jack sneered, turned away, immediately regretting his words.

Sarita followed him back into the bedroom. "You sonofabitch! You're the center of my life, *entiendes?* But I hate not knowing where you and I are going, and when we're going to get there. You're an hombre of your word, *sí*, so what is the word?"

The avalanche was shaking Jack's ground, but he stood up to it and told her the truth: "I love you. That's the way it is."

The words melted Sarita for the moment. Then she felt manipulated. "Is that the way it's always going to be?" she asked accusingly.

"We can't get into that now," Jack said with finality. "Don't push me."

When Jack wordlessly walked out of the bedroom, Sarita slammed the door hard enough to rattle the jamb, partly because she still didn't know what Cash had said to Jack and partly out of general frustration.

As he drove through the early morning mists on Benrey's streets Jack wondered why the Latino community was so upset over Cortez and Hank twisting a young cholo's arm to get his message to Cash. A lawman needed information to do his job, and Jack's methods for gathering it were a lot tamer than those of his predecessors. Glancing at the pair of handcuffs he kept dangling from his emergency-brake handle, Jack thought of Reggie Anduhar, the man who had been his first partner and best teacher in the Texas Rangers.

Jack's confidence had been at a distinct low point even before his parents' death in a car accident. Prior to that he had bummed around Dallas, Chicago, Houston, and God knows where else, never finding a line of work that suited him. But Reggie took him aside at the funeral, told him the Rangers needed another Benteen in the lineup. The training instilled in Jack the self-assurance that he needed so badly.

Reggie showed Jack a pragmatic approach to law enforcement that he had adopted for himself. Reggie told Jack about a murder suspect Jack's father had brought into custody, whose accomplice was still at large and who they feared would kill again. Joaquin Benteen took the suspect to an old ranch house where two jaguars and a tiger were being kept by an animal trainer who worked for a circus. Their keeper repaid a favor he owed Joaquin by making himself scarce. Joaquin drove the suspect out there in the middle of the night, then frog-marched the prisoner—whose hands were cuffed between his legs—to the pens where the carnivorous cats were kept.

Joaquin looked his prisoner in the eye and said, "When one of these jaguars attacks you, he grabs your head between his forepaws, then sinks his jaws into your face to hold you. Then he sort of reaches up with his hind legs, puts 'em on your belly, sticks out his claws and just gives you a good push, guts you clean as a dressed deer. *Then* he kills you."

Joaquin smiled as his prisoner went pale. Joaquin turned on his "confiding" act. "I'd hate to watch something like that. Shouldn't happen to a nice guy like you—prisoners' rights and all that—but if they found you out in the desert all torn apart, there wouldn't be much to do about it. Can't prosecute a wildcat for murder, now, can you? But I'd hate even worse to find another woman who's been strangled with her own panties."

Joaquin regarded the man. Judging by the stain in the man's trousers, things were going just as Joaquin planned.

The young man told Joaquin enough to get both himself and his partner strapped into the electric chair, but the mood of the times was easy, so instead they got lifetime berths in the graybar hotel. This revealed a side of his father that Jack hadn't been aware of, but he would bet that Joaquin Benteen, Sr., hadn't lost much sleep over violating the suspect's civil rights.

Like his father, Jack valued the respect of his constituents. It was okay if certain people were afraid of him as long as they thought he was fair. He certainly hoped Sarita saw him as impartial, but if she was taking flak for his actions, that probably didn't matter. She was torn between her love for him and her need for acceptance in her own community. It was just one of many problems Jack knew he should give more attention to, but there was always something more pressing when he tried to pick a day to begin doing so.

12

Jack drove past the employment office just as it was opening and was vaguely pleased to see "Buck Schoonover" among the mostly Hispanic crowd waiting outside, but he wondered why McRose, the man he knew as "Call," wasn't there. Despite "Call's" absence, Jack felt he had made the right decision in not hauling in the duo last night.

Benrey's employment office was a typically dreary government agency, staffed by people who considered government service to be even easier and more profitable than taking welfare themselves. Just like a post office or a D.M.V., only a few of the available windows were open, and the lines moved more slowly than cold roofing tar. The crowd of applicants filled up most of the available space, sitting on benches, standing in line, or just moping around.

Atwater waited off to the side. People gave him a wide berth; his unwashed clothes and five-for-a-dollar cigars were offensive—just like Buck wanted it. When he saw Luther Fry get in line, he immediately took the spot right behind him, though the two men gave no sign of knowing each other. A skinny man chewing tobacco

68

got in line behind Atwater, who turned around and spoke to him.

"Hey man, what's everybody trying for?"

The man was put off by Atwater's slobbish appearance but made an effort to be friendly. "How you mean, buddy?"

"Like what kind of jobs?" Atwater said, stepping forward.

"I dunno," he said with a shrug, trying to keep his distance. "I was working on the new highway bypass until they laid me off."

Atwater nodded sympathetically, and turned to Fry, blowing a cloud of smoke around him. "What about you?"

Fry turned and squinted at Atwater. "You talking to me?"

"Yeah, I mean what kind of job you trying to get?"

"Brain surgeon, asshole. Why don't you mind your own goddamn business?"

Atwater's voice rose to a level that nearly everyone in the office could hear. "You calling me an asshole?"

Twitching uncomfortably under the stares of people around them, Fry spoke even louder than Atwater. "Hey man, I'm just doing my day until you come along and jump my shit, so if I call you an asshole, it's only because you don't give me any choice."

They now had the attention of all the job seekers and clerks, and Atwater couldn't resist showboating, sounding even more like he had a mouthful of marbles than usual as he played Southern racist cracker. "Well, where I come from we don't take to no nigger faggots calling us assholes."

Fry tossed aside the leather sport coat he had been carrying. "You're calling who a nigger faggot?"

Atwater disdainfully glanced around the room, then zeroed back in on Fry. "I'm calling *you* a nigger faggot!"

By now the space around Fry and Atwater had been vacated by everyone except the man Atwater had spoken to first. The clerks watched, stupefied. A woman stormed up to a desk and demanded the person behind it call the police.

"What you gonna do about it, *boy?*" Atwater stubbed out his cigar on Fry's shirt.

Fry balled up his fist and bellowed, "I don't take no racist shit!"

Atwater leered and easily ducked Fry's roundhouse punch. The thin man stepped between them and got Fry's next punch in the stomach. It knocked his wind out, then Atwater decked him with a left hook. Atwater jumped at Fry, tried to put his hands around Fry's throat, and the black man shot back with a punch in the mouth that sent Atwater sprawling on the floor.

"Fight! Fight!" yelled an overweight woman who sounded gleeful. A social worker finally dialed the police as Atwater got up and flailed at Fry.

Hackett, dressed this time in a summer-weight dark suit and wearing a wig, watched the commotion in the employment office from behind the wheel of a rented station wagon. When the sheriff's cars started arriving, Hackett drove to the bank. He carried a large legal briefcase inside and asked to speak with the president.

King was nervous as he approached Hackett, thinking the briefcase contained records of transactions that didn't jibe with Clarence's own records. Hackett had an air about him that made King suspect the man was some kind of bank examiner. Clarence King's apprehension increased when Hackett asked him, "Can we speak in private?"

"Concerning what?" Clarence had visions of a nasty inquiry, culminating in a trial and a jail sentence.

"Your safekeeping facilities."

"Let me show you the vault." Clarence breathed a

sigh of relief that his paranoia was unfounded. The increase in his business with Cash Bailey was generating too much pressure on his bookkeeping and on his peace of mind. He relaxed a little as he led Hackett past a wall decorated with photos of old Texas banks where a few customers waited in line for an available teller. Hackett said he was a collector. King asked what he collected and Hackett smiled.

"Valuables. I need one of your largest safe-deposit boxes for some of the more precious elements of my collection."

Something smelled fishy, but despite the double-talk Clarence was too intimidated to say no. Besides, Hackett might represent a large legitimate account, something that the books of Clarence's bank needed desperately. And in any case, Clarence was just relieved that Hackett wasn't the banking version of the Grim Reaper.

Hackett paid three months rent on the box in cash, then refused an offer of assistance as he placed the briefcase in the metal drawer. He pretended to be concerned with how gently the contents were handled, but Hackett's real reason was to keep any of the bank employees from knowing that the case was empty.

When Hackett walked out of the bank, Biddle was waiting for him outside of the station wagon. "How's the commo setup going?" Hackett asked, palming the safe-deposit-box key as he opened the door for Biddle.

"Bugs all over the place. The mayor's office, the Sheriff's Station . . ."

Hackett pulled off his wig and started the car.

Biddle continued as they pulled into traffic. "We've tapped all the lawmen's home phones."

"How did you manage that?"

"I told them the taps would save sixty percent on their telephone bills and allow them to get cable TV through the phone lines, and they treated me, Coker,

71

and McRose like long-lost family. Everybody hates Ma Bell—even more since deregulation." Biddle chuckled condescendingly.

"What about other phones . . . remotes?"

From his shirt pocket Biddle pulled a galvanized steel disk, roughly the size of a lady's compact, that had four electrical leads sticking out of it. "Silver box. I've installed three of them in the exchange switchers— probably two more than we'll need. We can monitor two dozen phones simultaneously on each of them, as long as we know the numbers. I've got twenty-four voice-activated recorders here running around the clock. And if there's a special problem, like someone outside the exchange, I've taught McRose how to use one of those new AID kits."

Hackett nodded approvingly. "All right. Sounds like we're in business."

13

When Jack walked into the Benrey Sheriff's Station, his plan to spend the morning diligently sifting through suspect business-ownership records was dashed by the intense activity inside. There were more prisoners than available cell space, so a half-dozen new suspects, long-haired, scraggly types, were manacled to a bench.

"Where did these boys get picked up? They're ruining the decor," Jack sarcastically said to Purvis as they walked past the bench.

"Lone Star Motel. They'd been holed up there all week. The manager got freaked out and called us. We found a little dope, and there was fifty thousand dollars hanging around that nobody wanted to talk about."

Jack peered at the disheveled group once more and shook his head. "Just more of the goddamn same."

Jack looked up and saw Benrey Mayor George Corliss glaring petulantly at him. Corliss was the kind of man who got upset a lot more often than he got angry, but today Jack thought he looked both.

Corliss made a token attempt at sucking in his beer belly as he approached Jack and said, "I've got a serious bone to pick with you about releasing that publicity on the accident."

"What publicity? What accident?"

The mayor reached inside his jacket and pulled out a section of that morning's *Benrey Messenger*. "In the paper, Jack, right here. The Chicken Champ. Saying a bomb is suspected instead of just propane. Now that's a damn fool thing for you—"

"Propane my ass! The lab found traces of cyclonite plastic explosive in the wreckage."

"You can't be *sure* that's what it was." Corliss lowered his voice as he unctuously tried to cool Jack down. "I think it was propane, which accidentally leaked and blew up. Hellfire, Jack, this town has a bad enough image already without having terrorist-type stories in the newspapers."

Jack was searching for the appropriate way to suggest Corliss attempt the anatomically impossible when a deputy escorted a handcuffed Atwater behind him, along with a black man Jack didn't recognize.

Looking chagrined, Atwater flashed a toothy smile at him, and said, "Good morning, Officer. It ain't right what they're doing here."

Jack was disappointed but tried not to show it. So much for his good judgment. "Hello, Buck. Looks like you went and got yourself into some trouble." Jack addressed Purvis. "Where'd you find him?"

"Employment office, sir. They was beatin' up on each other. Got another fella in the middle of it as well. Real ugly incident. Yes, sir, real ugly."

"I got *my* side to the story," Atwater protested. "I didn't start nothing. I just drifted down and was looking for work."

"What the hell? This honky picks a damn fight and *I* get arrested? What kind of shit is this?" Fry loudly complained as the two were led past the communications center into a corner of the Sheriff's Station.

74

There, they were lined up against a height chart for mug shots, weighed on an ancient upright scale, and then fingerprinted. Fry and Atwater managed to alternate each other's fingerprints on the cards when nobody was looking.

Purvis led the two prisoners to a pair of adjoining holding cells that were just being cleared of four high school seniors who had been arrested for mooning a Baptist church social. After locking the two men in separate cells, Purvis was immediately distracted by a rush of incoming phone calls that were overwhelming the other officers on duty.

The file clerk, a primly beehived blonde in her early twenties named Donna Lee, caught Atwater's eye as he stretched across his cell bunk. Atwater licked his lips, then stuck his tongue out so far that it almost touched the tip of his nose. Donna Lee blushed, turned back to her work, but smiled to herself.

After canvasing his deputies, Jack learned from Cotton, a soft-faced man whose bushy black eyebrows contrasted sharply with his snow-white hair, that Chub Luke could most likely be found at his mother's house. But the address wasn't on file and the Luke family wasn't listed in the phone book, so Jack asked Purvis to run it down for him, then flipped open a copy of the Benrey business directory looking for ownership irregularities he might trace to Cash Bailey. Hank was not in the office yet, and Jack wanted to have some leads to show the sheriff when he arrived.

When they were sure nobody in the cramped station was looking at them, Atwater and Fry slid open the hollow heels of their boots, and each removed microphone-transmitters. Atwater unfurled a roll of connecting wire and sullenly passed one end through the bars of the cell partition.

"How you doing, nigger?" he hissed.

Fry didn't reply until he saw Atwater flash his tobacco-stained buckteeth. Smiling back at him, Fry said, "Oh, I'm doing fine, Buck, how about you?"

"Not bad, considering you almost broke my fucking jaw, asshole. You were just supposed to make it *look* good." Atwater spoke in a low grumble, but his voice had a demented quality, like he was on the verge of losing control. As he finished hooking up the connection Atwater motioned to the bloody bruise on the left side of his mouth.

Fry kept on smiling. "Yeah, made it look real good, didn't I?"

Atwater poked his face right through the bars of the partition. "Only reason I didn't kick your ass is you would have landed in the hospital instead of jail."

"Yeah, right, Buck. Anything you say."

Fry had wanted to take a shot at Atwater for a long time, but judiciously waited for the perfect excuse. They had met in Vietnam, during the final phase of the "Phoenix" program, in which a variety of means were used to assassinate suspected enemy agents fingered by the C.I.A. The experience gave Fry contempt for "the Company," though Atwater always claimed, to Fry's annoyance, that he liked the dirty side of things.

Atwater was a self-described "swamp rat" from rural Florida who took pride in his defiantly bigoted attitudes. He constantly repeated a handful of ethnic jokes he had probably heard in grade school that Fry had gotten pretty damned sick of.

Ironically, both men had ended up assigned to Werewolf Ops, an elite squad of fighting men, whom the army used for its most sensitive missions. These men were listed on army personnel records as dead. Their next of kin had been notified of their demise, death benefits had been paid. The men on the Dead List had no ties left to anyone except the army. All the commandos on Hackett's team, including the major himself, were, as the army euphemistically referred to them, "zombie" personnel. Werewolf Ops was a slush-funded, supersecret squad with almost total autonomy. In order to preserve the security of those who gave the zombies their orders, orders were cut by a coded computer dispatch. Major Hackett was one of the few men who had the necessary passwords.

Fry thought Atwater's reason for volunteering to be on the Dead List was insane: Buck's father had been a moonshiner who was too fond of his product, and from the way Atwater told it his childhood was something he wanted to put as far behind him as possible. The epiphany of his life had been watching *To Hell and Back,* the movie in which Audie Murphy reenacted the heroism that made him America's most decorated soldier in World War II. From then on Atwater had recurring daydreams of wiping out enemy battalions single-handedly. Whenever he had a few too many drinks in him, Buck would repeatedly act out his favorite scenes for anyone he could get to watch.

To Fry, Atwater was a glutton, plain and simple, a man ruled by his appetites for food, drink, sex, and glory. Fry much preferred men like Hackett, whose instincts for survival seemed to transcend his wish for personal pleasure. Fry had gone for the Dead List because it was the only thing he could do to help his two children survive. He had become violently estranged from their mother during his first tour in Vietnam, and his "underground" assignment meant fifty thousand dollars he could earmark for his little boy and girl. It had been more than a decade since he'd seen them, but Fry still often looked at the baby pictures of Luther Jr. and Cicely that he kept in his wallet. When he got some time, he planned to get some fresh pictures to satisfy his curiosity and his longing.

A scruffy group of Latino prisoners passed in front of their cells, prompting Atwater to say, "Hey, Luther, how does a Mexican know when he's hungry?"

Fry shook his head indifferently.

"When his asshole stops burning," Atwater crowed.

Fry contemptuously narrowed his eyes and turned away from Atwater, who quietly responded to a soft beep from his transmitter. He plugged in a flesh-colored earphone.

"Hey, Charlie, how they hanging?" began Atwater's broadcast.

Biddle responded from inside the West-Tex van. "Loud and clear, Buck. Go ahead."

Hackett, sitting beside Biddle at the control console, monitored Atwater's transmission while Biddle typed into a computer keyboard as Atwater talked.

"Okay, here we go. They got ten canisters of tear gas, but no masks visible. Telephones on sixteen extensions, centrally switched. A weenie-looking deputy named Arnold Purvis is now on the police call radio, tuned in at twenty-three-forty. Toilet facilities: one roll, and a hard seat—"

"Cut the levity, Atwater." Hackett keyed in on the conversation.

Fry nudged Atwater through the bars as Deputy Cortez approached the cell. Atwater shut up and pushed the little squelch button until Cortez passed by and was out of earshot.

"Visible firepower excepting sidearms: five twelve-gauge pump shotguns and ten carbine rifles, thirty-two caliber. One M-sixteen and a couple of oversized clips. No night sights, no scopes, no shields, no flak vests, and no tank in the car park. Ammunition is in a thin green metal locker bearing one yellowed pinup of Jayne Mansfield, circa 1954. This is my summary of impressions and observations: if a cowboy gets drunk, they're ready."

14

The commandos' mission had started a few weeks earlier: Hackett had driven an olive-drab Government Motor Pool sedan through a dismal night rain along mile after mile of electrified barbed-wire-topped chain-link fence dividing government land from the ranch land around it. It was the southern border of a parcel of cracked, forlorn desert bigger than Connecticut known as Fort Bliss Military Reservation. It was home to the U.S. Army's euphemistically named 361st Corps of Engineers.

The windshield wipers clacked and thumped back and forth but merely skimmed over the deluge obscuring the windshield. Inside, Hackett had to lean forward to actually see the road. The 361st's headquarters were more than two hours outside of El Paso—a long way to go in a blinding rain.

Finally, he had turned north at an opening in the fence and pulled up to a gatehouse where a pair of brusque MP sentries, clad in dark slickers, armed to the nines with M-16s and newly issued 9mm Beretta semi-automatic pistols, flagged him down. One of the MPs stood guard as the other leaned into the driver's window, matching the picture on Hackett's ID with the face behind the wheel. The rain poured off the brim of the guard's sou'wester hat and dripped into the car. Satisfied, the guard raised the barricade and waved the sedan inside.

It was another mile before the Quonset huts and low concrete office buildings were in sight. The 361st was a top-security installation, hidden from prying eyes by a rise in the desert floor that came between the buildings and the road. Except for the gatehouse and the fence, there was no sign of its presence to a passing vehicle.

Hackett threaded his way through the disciplined grid of security bunkers and stopped in front of Building C, which housed top-secret personnel records and an A-Priority communications computer that was satellite-multiplexed to similar computers the army maintained worldwide.

Hackett ran through the rain into Building C's vestibule, where a desk sentry checked his ID again, then signed him in and unlocked the door that allowed him into the command center.

Once inside, Hackett quickly went to work. He punched a series of commands into the nearest terminal, then typed:

WEREWOLF OPS

The screen immediately prompted for a password. For further security, the computer didn't display Hackett's typed response on the screen, as it checked its files, then returned:

ACCESS GRANTED

Hackett knew exactly who he wanted. He needed six men including himself. The other five were men he had worked with before. He started typing and the computer quickly gave him the current stations for McRose, Coker, Atwater, Fry, and Biddle. One by one, Hackett cut them new orders. The metal golf ball on a telex printer hammered out:

```
FLASH PRECEDENCE,
071605 SEPT FM HQ,
173RD AIRBORNE DIV,
3RD BATTALION,
FT. BLISS, TX.
TO SGT MAJ.
LARRY N. MCROSE
389502372USA
3RD ARMORED DIVISION,
FRANKFURT, FRG.
TOP SECRET //A01500//
ASSIGNMENT
TEMPORARY DUTY
ZOMBIE UNIT ACTIVATED,
WEREWOLF OPS,
EL PASO, TX.
REPORT NO LATER
1700 ON 09 SEPT.
MAJ. PAUL HACKETT
SENDS.
```

Hackett sent similar assignment orders to the other four.

Less than thirty-six hours later, Hackett, dressed in civvies, had hung out near a view window overlooking the runways at the El Paso Airport, watching the flights take off and land. His men were coming in from all over the globe. He was taking the biggest risk of his career to bring them in.

Larry McRose had moved easily through the airport corridor crowded with overdressed business commuters. He towered over most of them. His crazed intensity instantly set him apart from the rest of the airport cowboys. He spotted Atwater from a few hundred feet away.

Atwater was in the middle of a large passenger lounge drinking rum and coke from a paper cup and taunting a chic young woman in a Laura Ashley dress who was walking by.

"What's your name, honey?"

The woman ignored Atwater.

"Can I buy you an ice cream? A scoop of praline delight maybe?" Atwater continued.

With a haughty toss of her moussed hair, the woman quickened her pace. Just before she was out of earshot Atwater yelled, "Hey, baby, long as I got a face you got a place to sit."

"Buck!" McRose tapped Atwater, who wheeled, surprised and glad to see McRose. They traded punches to each other's shoulders, then grabbed each other in a bear hug. "How you been, you uncouth asshole?"

"What are you talking about? I'm couth as hell." Atwater had traveled first-class wearing his dirty T-shirt and jeans.

"Where you in from?"

Atwater showed off his tan forearms. "Panama. You?"

McRose showed his comparative paleness and laughed. "Germany. They had me in Cologne for the last six months."

"Getting sick of the parking fee for German pussy?"

"Some of us don't *have* to pay for it, Buck."

Across the airport lobby, Luther Fry and Charles Biddle spotted each other. Fry called Biddle's name and held out his hand, which Biddle met with a resounding slap as they clasped hands.

"How you doing, man?" Biddle, dressed out of *GQ*,

sharp, immaculate, checked out his friend. Fry was wearing khaki trousers and a bright blue aloha shirt.

"Ah, you know. Doin' good. Same old shit."

"Where you been?"

"Subic Bay." Fry grinned. "Before that, Manila. Had me up in the hills cutting heads. How about you?"

"Turkey, can you dig it? Ran a whole recon-intell setup and shakedown for their turkey asses." Fry spotted the youngest of Hackett's operatives. "Jesus, lookit what just made an appearance."

Fry followed Biddle's look to see Coker swaggering over, pretending he was unhappy to see them. Coker then vaulted up onto Fry's back, clinging tight.

"Hey, a grease-monkey convention. Don't this beat shit."

Biddle replied first. "What are you doing here, Coker? Must be nobody else available."

"You kidding? Guess you didn't hear about the sweet little number I pulled down you know where and starts with *N*."

McRose and Atwater drifted over. "Been socking it to the peasant farmers, Coker?"

"Making the world safe for democracy," Coker agreed.

"You got it easy this time, Coker," Fry spoke up. "You can just watch how I operate."

"What's he gonna learn from you?" goaded McRose.

"How to stay alive," Fry shot back. "Who'd you have to service to get invited?"

"They had to have somebody keep their eye on you, Luther. So they went out and got the best below-deck honcho they could find."

The five men were still ribbing each other when Hackett came up to them.

"Everything A-okay, men?"

"No problem. Just getting sorted out," McRose told him.

Hackett looked over his men, then flashed a quick smile at McRose. "Been awhile, Larry."

"Sure has, sir." McRose nodded cheerfully. "Where we headed this time?"

"About a hundred miles east of here. You'll never believe the ops. Not in a million years."

Hackett then led his men to the station wagon and drove them to Benrey. He had picked an unpretentious, fairly run-down motel on the Anglo outskirts of Benrey as his team's base of operations. The Yellow Rose was somewhat faded, but its low profile was exactly what the men needed. And, as Atwater had remarked, it beat the fleabags he called home in Bangkok, or Managua, or a dozen other political hotbeds he'd done business in.

Hackett's room was painted a tacky lime and tan and the furniture was a fifties Swedish Modern nightmare. In Los Angeles and New York, people were paying high prices for the minimalist furniture that filled the room. Here in Benrey, though, the furnishings hadn't achieved classic status; the consensus was that the stuff was just shabby. Hackett had laughed inwardly at the irony.

The commandos' deployment on Hackett's mission was now several days behind them. So far their infiltration operation was right on schedule. But Hackett still hadn't told them the whole story.

Biddle parked the West-Tex truck up the street from the motel and he and Hackett walked the rest of the way to their rooms.

Coker was waiting for them. He told them McRose was in the bathroom, still developing the bank surveillance photos with portable darkroom equipment.

A few minutes later, McRose emerged, blinking in the light. He held a stack of wet eight-by-ten prints shot by Coker and Hackett. They showed the sight lines between the municipal buildings of Benrey and the bank, only a short block apart. In addition, there were close-ups showing crucial utilities junctions: phone lines, power lines, switching boxes. Finally, there were numerous detail shots of the bank's interior.

Hackett spread the photos out and began filling the other three in on the bank's layout and their operation.

"They just have five tellers, all on the left side of the building. The counters are open, and an emergency exit visible behind."

"How many guards?" McRose asked.

Hackett grinned at the memory. "One. Wears glasses. Could be as young as fifty. Carries a thirty-eight Colt Python. Video only activates on alarm. Just two cameras, one at the front entrance and one at the vault doors. They've got two Chambers-Reilly vaults, one on the right has the safety-deposit boxes, vault on the left has the money."

"What about the downside?" Biddle wanted to know.

"Both vaults are on a time lock. If we go in at night, we'll have to blast."

"Fuck that! We'd wake up the whole town."

"*If* we go in at night."

That stopped the conversation dead.

Biddle had responsibility for logistics and communications. He was appalled by the idea of robbing the bank in daylight, but Hackett had trained him, brought him into Werewolf Ops, and he trusted Hackett's judgment. In the blighted Chicago neighborhood where he had grown up, Biddle had endured persistent abuse from big kids with room-temperature IQs, knowing he had more brains and agility than any of them. After getting beaten up for his lunch money a few too many times, Biddle became a dedicated martial-arts student. It took him two years until he was able to pummel one of his tormentors into a six-hour coma.

After a lifetime of taking shit for his diminutive size, Biddle had finally met in Hackett an authority figure who respected his capabilities. And although the mission had not smelled right to Biddle from the beginning, if he couldn't trust Hackett, there was no higher authority he felt comfortable turning to.

"What the hell are we doing in Texas, sir?" Charlie Biddle's question was on all of their minds.

McRose chimed in his thoughts as well. "Major, I'm not complaining about being in the old U.S. of A., but I wonder what ComOps has in store for us. This isn't exactly our usual stomping grounds."

Hackett turned to Coker. "What about you, Coker? Got any questions?"

Coker just grinned and shrugged. He wasn't long on small talk—you gave him a mission and he did it. If he needed more information, he did his own recon, figuring you would only tell him what you wanted him to know anyway.

"Okay." Hackett turned to all three of them. "This mission has top priority; national security is at stake. The ops will unfold on a need-to-know basis. As we get further in, you'll understand why we're here." Hackett was hedging, but the need-to-know part was true.

"For now . . ." Hackett spread a map of the town on the bed. "We own this town. As usual, we do not have official status and the information we gather will not be used for purposes of prosecution. It's purely strategic. We are operating here under the same rules as we operate under anyplace else—"

"Meaning there aren't any," McRose joked.

Hackett clenched his jaw and snapped, "Wrong, Larry. Dead wrong. There are always rules. And rule number one is that the mission takes top priority. Rule number two: there are no friendlies excepting the immediate family."

Coker grinned. "There's always the Golden Rule, Major."

They all turned to Coker, who was stretched out on an old Barcalounger.

"Do unto others whatever it takes to get the job done."

Hackett smiled coldly. "You've got the right idea, Coker. For now, we have to forget where we are and do business as usual." He turned to the map. "These are the civic buildings: the Sheriff's Station and jail, the courthouse. Up the street here is the City Bank of Benrey. As you know, these are primary objectives. We need to establish total monitoring of communications in these locations. We want to know who comes and goes and when they do it. Tomorrow we'll get Fry and Atwater out of the holding tank and from there . . . It's full-tilt boogie."

Hackett was selling his men a snow job, but they didn't have to buy it for too long. He was taking advantage of the fact that the chain of command was ingrained deeply into a soldier's psyche: taking orders was a hard habit for a trained operative to break.

15

Deputy Purvis took statements from the witnesses to the unemployment office fight. The only person who put any blame on Fry, whom Purvis knew as "Luther Robeson," was the thin man who had gotten caught in the middle. But the man refused to swear out a complaint, so Purvis had no choice but to forget about pressing charges against Fry.

Judge Frick was called in to give "Schoonover" (Atwater) a hearing. The DA laughed out loud when "Schoonover" insisted he be released without penalty. Frick set his fine at five hundred dollars against a ten-day jail sentence and "Schoonover" just clammed up, mad as a blasting cap in an electrical storm. He glowered as Fry was released, and after Atwater made his allotted phone call he said nothing when Purvis asked him if he was going to pay or stay.

Fry picked up his wallet, belt, shoelaces, and pens, complaining to Cortez how he'd *told* them he'd done nothing wrong. Atwater caught Fry's eye from inside his cell and gave him a thumbs-up when nobody was looking, then flashed his middle finger and a grin.

On his way out, Fry passed Hank on his way in. The

sheriff marched into Jack's office, just as the Ranger's irritated voice came roaring over the intercom.

"Will somebody find out where the hell Chub Luke's mother lives?" It had been nearly an hour since his initial request.

Hank knocked on the office door and walked in before Jack could grunt his usual one-syllable invitation to enter. Jack looked as defunct as the fourteen-pound steelhead trout mounted on the wall behind his desk. Pictures of other Texas Rangers, most of whom were now dead, stared down from the surrounding walls.

"Morning," Hank said as he plopped down onto the sofa next to Jack's desk, lighting a cigar.

Jack's eyes burned, and not just from the smoke. "What's good about it?"

Hank kept his voice low, even. "I just said 'morning,' I didn't say 'good morning.' What put you in such a fine mood?"

"Just the same old same. The lab reports from El Paso are being sent overland by covered wagon, I need more manpower to handle the district, and the damn state bureaucrats are just sitting around with their thumbs up their butts!" Jack rattled off as Hank blew smoke rings.

"All you can do is try to set a good example." Hank laughed. "What else is bothering you?"

"Look, I've been here twenty minutes and already I'm having a terrible day." Jack swallowed a deep breath. "I had a fight with Sarita." He debated for a moment whether to tell Hank more, decided against it, then banged his intercom button. "Will someone out there tell me where Chub Luke's mother lives?" His voice was so loud Donna Lee jumped out of her chair. Purvis came out of the men's room still zipping his fly, and Donna Lee goaded him into finding the address before Jack could yell again.

Hank gave Jack a minute, then gently pried. "Tell me about it."

"Hell, it seems like Cash Bailey's screwing up every part of my life, the low-down sonofabitch."

Hank was really getting sick of the subject. "Now Jack, the way I remember it, you knew Cash was with Sarita before you ever asked her out—makes it kind of hard to hold against her. 'Course, it ain't none of my business . . ."

Jack's facial expression told Hank that he wasn't out of line, that he could keep going.

"Remember the night we all went out for drinks after Cash had been in the D.E.A. for about a year? How frustrated he was at knowing who the big traffickers were but having no right to arrest them?"

"Yeah, so he swore out some warrants and hired the Mexican police to kidnap some of them, take them to the border, and hand them to him through the fence trussed up like Christmas turkeys."

"You'd do that to him if you could."

Jack slapped his palm on the desk so hard it rattled his copper statuette of a Texas Ranger. "The point we're talking here is motivation. That night Cash gave us a dog-and-pony show about how he'd decided to bend the regulations for the sake of getting his job done. So he did just that and put some evil scumbags out of business. But why? So he could replace them."

Hank nodded thoughtfully. "Like your daddy used to say, 'The world is a muddy place. If a good man don't try to clean it up, a bad man will make it a swamp'—or something like that."

Deputy Purvis knocked on the door and entered on Jack's command. Purvis walked into the office sheepishly, carrying a sheet of notepaper which he read from.

"Chub Luke's mother lives down past the John Friendly Ranch on one-oh-two. Also, we just got a tip there's some new faces showed up at some place called Arturo's."

Jack sat up straight in his chair. "The old filling station near Sharpe's Crossing?" Arturo's had been a source of complaints throughout Jack's tenure and Arturo had once been busted for promoting dogfights nearby.

"That must be the place, sir," replied Purvis, slow to make the connection.

Wrinkling his nose in distaste, Hank asked, "Who called in the damn tip?" When Purvis said it was Arturo, Hank shook his head suspiciously. "First time that fat bastard ever did us a favor."

"Cotton took the call," Purvis stammered. "Arturo told him the hombres made him real nervous."

Hank looked at Purvis as if the deputy had just broken wind. "The only kind of people who ever made that lard-ass nervous are the ones that carry badges."

"Smells like a buy going down," Jack declared. "Cash's boys are doing business, and the action got too heavy for Arturo." He stood up and grabbed his hat, heading for the door, his eyes asking Hank if he was game.

"Let's head on out and stick our nose in," Hank said, though his doubts still lingered. "We put enough heat on Mr. Bailey, and maybe he'll find another town to fuck with." As they headed out the door Hank told Purvis, "Hold down the fort." The young deputy glowed with pride at being left in charge.

After dropping Biddle off in the brown surveillance truck, Hackett waited in the station wagon. He and McRose parked across the street from the Sheriff's Station, and when Hank and Jack got into a cruiser, Hackett told McRose to follow them.

McRose looked at Hackett questioningly.

"These two cowboys seem to be the top lawmen

around here," Hackett said to him. "So we watch them, fill out their profiles. That way, we'll know what we've got to deal with, and what to expect on D-day."

The cruiser headed out of town. McRose dropped way behind when the traffic thinned out. He still didn't see the point of the excursion, didn't like the way it made them conspicuous. "We go in at daylight, we're going to need a stunt to distract them."

"Sure. We just blow something up."

Hackett's attitude seemed dangerously cavalier to McRose, but he wasn't in the habit of disagreeing with his superiors. "Any ideas?"

"A building, a house, a barn—"

"A school, a church," McRose interjected sarcastically.

Hackett gave him a dirty look. "Anything that doesn't have people inside. What are you, particular?"

"Nope. I guess I'm kind of whacked out about working at home."

He had anticipated this moment long before the team was assembled, and Hackett was in fact surprised that none of his men had brought it up earlier. His response was automatic: "Truth is, so am I. It's hard to believe that national security demands robbing a bank to cover appropriating the contents of a safe-deposit box."

"Damn straight," said McRose, somewhat relieved that Hackett wasn't as gung-ho about the ops as he had seemed. "What do you think is in the box?"

Hackett's tone became harsher. "Like I said before, that was left on a need-to-know basis only."

McRose quickly realized he had asked the wrong question. "I get it. In case I'm captured and tortured by unfriendlies, I won't be able to divulge sensitive material. Makes sense."

"Yeah, welcome to the army," Hackett said, flashing a tight smile. Jack's cruiser had pulled way ahead of him, and was little more than a speck in the distance. "That goat roper is really moving."

"Damn near one-twenty." McRose bore down on the accelerator. "This guy's a menace. Maybe he should work for us."

As the cruiser got within a few miles of Arturo's Hank tensed up noticeably and tried to hide it as he took out his .38 revolver to check the loads. He put a cartridge in the usually empty chamber he kept the hammer resting on.

"You nervous?" Jack asked.

Hank shook his head indignantly. "Hell, no." He pulled the shotgun from its rack. "It's just, I never used to throw this old pump on nothing but quail. Maybe three times a year I'd pull my .38 on an armed robber or a rustler. Never had to shoot 'em though; they knew when to give up. Used to be you could reason with a drunk, a kid on loco weed, or a couple that was fighting. Once they got cooled down they'd thank you for it. Not now, boy. They get wired and stay wired, french-fry their brains with smack, snort, pills, chopped up inner tubes, you name it. Take T.C. Luke and his brother Chub; hell, I used to fish with their dad. They were sweet kids, not mad dogs trying to take a bite out of your ass."

Jack slowed down as he observed a ramshackle compound in the distance. "My dad and grandpa had to deal with psychos, too. Hell, Gramps was in the posse that killed Bonnie Parker and Clyde Barrow. They weren't much like the kids in the movie. They killed in cold blood for the fun of it, and both of 'em would fuck anything that moved. After they had killed more than a dozen people, most for no discernible reason, a posse led by Texas Ranger Frank Hammer surprised Bonnie and Clyde in a roadblock ambush in Louisiana. The one thing the movie got right was the hail of slugs that hit them. The official count of rounds pumped into Bonnie and Clyde's car was a hundred eighty-seven. That was how they dealt with mad dogs in 1934."

Hank nodded in assent, but then sighed and complained, "Life is a jumble to me now, son. This old horse just can't pull the plow no more."

"Want to call in your deputies?" asked Jack.

Hank's indignation returned. "Hell, no. Cortez is pretty good in a tight corner, I guess. Cotton might still have some of his old piss and vinegar. But them others, ever since they come back from that special 'community interaction' training in Austin, they ain't worth a bucket of warm spit!" Hank hawked at the indignity of it. " 'Be nice' overeducated runts."

"You're gonna have to get more tolerant, Hank, seeing as it looks like the state legislature is mandating female Texas Rangers."

"Hell, I know some women are tough. That Parker gal, for instance. I don't care as long as they're mean as snakes and six-foot-six. Goddamn state legislature, the only thing worse than a politician is a child molester."

Arturo's Gas and Beer was a wood-and-stucco junk heap, surrounded by old chicken coops and wooden shacks that looked about ready to blow away, baked halfway to oblivion by the desert sun. Junk cars and old appliances were gathering rust all around the building. The gas pump dated back to when Exxon was called Esso, and the stacked tires in the front had half an inch of dust on them. Dozens of hubcaps were nailed like post-apocalyptic armor to the front and sides of the building.

It was located near Sharpe's Crossing, a border trail that was watched none too carefully by the immigration and naturalization people. Arturo's small but steady business depended on his reputation for not being very chummy with the law. But there he was, all 280 pounds of him, nervously walking out of the main building's back door as Jack's cruiser pulled in. Jack saw more cars in the parking lot than he expected, so he radioed for some backup. Arturo walked up to the driver's side of the patrol car, and Jack rolled down the window.

"What's doing, amigo?" he asked tersely.

Arturo suddenly seemed to have gotten cold feet about calling them out there. "I think maybe nothing."

Hank cracked open the door on his side. "Get to the goddamn point, Arturo. You called us . . ."

Arturo looked behind him, seeming to deliberately avoid standing between the building and the two lawmen. "I don't know. Four guys inside my place. I think maybe they could be mules."

"Mex or white?" Hank asked.

"Mexicano . . . they been waiting here all morning, drinking beer. Now two gringos come, one skinny and one fat. The big one they call Chub."

Upon hearing that name, Jack jumped out of the car. "For Christ's sake, Chub Luke is just who I want."

Hank emerged from his side and looked around for cover. "You just gonna walk right in?"

There were so many possible escape routes that Jack didn't want to wait for backup, fearing that Chub would get away again in the meantime. "Aw hell, Chub and I were in third grade together. I'm gonna mosey on in and have a beer with him." Jack's voice reflected exaggerated calm as he grabbed his Winchester.

Hank didn't like the idea. "Sure. You can just put your feet up together and talk about how you drilled his brother night before last."

Jack looked chagrined. "Well, I was planning to go in by way of the *back* door."

"I don't know, Jack. Something doesn't smell right."

"I can handle this. You just have a little chat with Arturo, here, and keep an eye out to make sure nobody leaves by the front." Before Hank could protest any more, Jack began walking around the building toward the back.

Jack wasn't halfway there when somebody poked a shotgun through a window behind him. Hank yelled out, then tore the man apart with two quick blasts of buckshot. Jack pressed against the wall and took a few pellets as the dying man fired once. From inside, and from gunmen hidden in the junk cars, several automatic weapons opened fire, and Hank blew out the gas station's windows until his shotgun was empty.

Jack was next to the back door when it exploded into splinters from gunfire inside. He rolled behind a rock, emptying the Winchester into the building. Jack then made his way back toward the car, jumping from any object that could provide a bit of cover to another, squeezing off a few shots with his pistol each time he moved.

While Hank was crouched down to reload the shotgun, Arturo pulled a pistol from the back of his trousers and quickly fired three slugs through Hank's western-cut wool suit. The impact lifted him off his feet, but he didn't fall down.

"You cowardly shit . . ." Hank gasped, and used the pair of shotgun shells he had so far inserted to blow Arturo end over end as if he were a tin can. After he hit the ground Arturo flailed around in circles like a hooked fish, his limbs jerking spastically as crimson spread out beneath him. Hank was caught again by a shotgun blast from the building that tore his suit to bloody shreds. Reeling, Hank emptied his .38 into the man who had fired.

Firing to cover himself, Jack lunged forward and pulled Hank behind the cruiser. "Hank!"

No answer. Hank was stone dead. A rain of slugs peppered the sedan, blowing out all the windows, showering glass down on Jack as he stared at Hank. Jack slid over to the trunk, unlocked it, and keeping his head down, rifled through the tools, ammo boxes, and CS grenades until he found what he was looking for: an R-18 fully automatic machine gun. It was against regulations for Jack to carry such a weapon, but headquarters unofficially sanctioned its use by Rangers who were going up against similarly equipped wrongdoers, and always gave the Rangers fifteen minutes notice before inspections so they could remove anything questionable. Jack dodged several bullets as he grabbed the gun and all the clips he could carry.

Jack heard Chub yell, "How do you like this shit, Jack?" Another burst of gunfire erupted from the station. Jack slid under the car's back door and sprayed the building from underneath it. The two tires facing the building were instantly shot to pieces, and Jack had to slide back quickly to keep from being pinned under the car. Several men ran from the building and took cover behind a stack of oil barrels. Jack blew the men off their feet with the R-18, but he took a few more pellets of buckshot fired from inside.

Hackett and McRose were driving up the dirt road behind Arturo's when the shooting started. McRose pulled the station wagon behind a knoll and the two men scrambled up to look. McRose pulled a silenced Ingram MAC-10 machine pistol from under the seat. They saw Jack hunched behind the cruiser, bullets flying around him, Hank's and Arturo's inert bodies lying nearby. A red-tailed hawk circled overhead and the buzzards were probably on their way.

"Jesus Christ!" exclaimed McRose, clicking the Ingram's safety off.

"Let's move!" Hackett barked, moving back to the car. When McRose didn't follow, he added "Sergeant, I said *come on!*"

"Hey! We could save this guy!"

"Save him! Are you crazy?" Hackett was already in the car, slamming it into gear. "This place will be wall-to-wall cops in about five minutes! Now let's move, Sergeant."

McRose couldn't argue with a direct order, so he climbed back in, barely getting his feet off the ground before Hackett cut the wheel and tore out of the area as fast as the car would go.

Jack emptied the R-18's magazine with a long burst across the windows of the building. He heard at least one man inside the building screaming in pain. "You have thirty seconds to come out of there with your hands up!" Jack yelled. The instant reply was another burst of gunfire. "Well, it was worth a try," Jack muttered to himself as he put a fresh magazine in the R-18 and reloaded his handgun with a clip from the eyeglass case he kept tucked in his left boot.

Holding his fire to draw Chub out, Jack kept out of sight. The withering leaden hail kept up for a few more minutes, then Chub cautiously emerged from the building. Two mean-looking cholo punks, packing shotguns, came out behind him. A third man, an Anglo, stayed behind, lurking in the shadows of the doorway. Thinking Jack was out of action, Chub began to gloat.

"You can dish it out, but you can't take it, Ranger? How's this for a surprise party?"

Jack saw two pairs of feet heading toward him as he peered from under the car. Jack slipped the R-18 down low, blew the left foot off the man closest to him, then jumped up and shredded the other cholo. Chub rushed back to the door and inside. Seconds later, Jack heard an engine fire up. An old blue pickup truck screeched from around the back of Arturo's, headed straight for Jack. The R-18 was empty again, so Jack pulled his pistol. Chub was in the bed, waiting for the ideal moment to spray Jack with his Uzi. But just as the range was ideal, the man with the missing foot hopped between Jack and the truck, and Chub accidentally blew him to pieces.

The truck peeled away, just as Jack began to hear sirens approaching in the distance. Jack instinctively took inventory of his own wounds and judged them not to be serious. There was pain, but it was minute compared to what shot through him as his eyes came to rest on Hank's mangled corpse. Jack's emotions progressed swiftly from shock to regret to guilt to anger to frustration to sadness. Jack knew he had nobody to blame except himself . . . and Cash Bailey.

Hackett tried to avoid the oncoming emergency vehicles by circling wide. Because of this, he and McRose found themselves face-to-face with Chub and his last surviving henchman. Jack had hit the truck's radiator a few times, and the vehicle was parked alongside the dirt road, badly overheated, steam billowing out from under its hood.

"It's the bad guys," McRose said, tucking the Ingram under his coat.

"Act dumb," Hackett whispered. "If they want the station wagon, we give it to them. Anything else, we get mad."

Chub pointed his sub-machine gun at the station wagon, motioning to Hackett to pull over, or else.

"Hi," Hackett said to them as he emerged from the car. "We're not trespassing. We're on the survey crew for the new county assessment."

"I don't give a fuck who you are"—Chub sneered—"we need your car."

Hackett held out the keys. "Take it. No problem, no arguments."

"But you're going to tell people about us, that's the only problem," said the other man, pulling a machete out of the truck.

"No, you're wrong, we won't tell anybody," Hackett said, trying to catch the man's eye. But the machete continued swinging upward until the man was distracted by McRose sawing through Chub with a burst from the Ingram. Hackett vaulted forward, knocking the machete away and locking the man's head and arm in a half nelson.

"I'm the quiet type, amigo," Hackett whispered into the man's ear. "Believe me, this is just going to be our little secret," then broke his neck with one powerful jerk. Hackett pushed the body over next to Chub's. McRose was picking up his ejected shell casings when they heard the thumping of an approaching helicopter engine. Hackett ordered McRose into the car, and they sped off.

II
SPECIAL FORCES

16

The county Sheriff's Department helicopter landed first at Arturo's, where three more bodies were found inside the building. Paramedics pronounced Hank dead at the scene. Jack was the only person they could be of any help to. After the pellets, which were all close to the surface, were dug out with tweezers and his wounds bandaged, the helicopter took off and soon radioed a message about finding the truck and the two bodies. Jack insisted on being taken to the site to investigate. The deputies expressed amazement that Jack survived when they saw how shot up his car was.

Feeling stiff as hell, Jack walked over to Purvis, who was marking ten kilos of cocaine that had been found in the truck. He told the deputy to seal the perimeter of the area until at least nightfall. Cortez showed Jack a plastic bag containing the shell casings he had picked up. Jack pocketed a few of them.

"Excuse me, sir, but shouldn't we send all this stuff up to Austin?"

"We'll send half to Austin. I want to keep the rest."

Jack's tone was dismissive; he wanted to be alone with his thoughts. As he turned away, Cortez cleared his throat, awkwardly seeking a way to preface what he had to say. "I . . . sir . . . me and the guys, I mean about Hank—"

"I knew him since I was a kid," Jack said, cutting him short. "He was a really fine man."

"Yes, he was."

"Like a father."

The reality of Hank's death took root in Jack's mind, gave him an awful feeling of being disconnected from the rest of humanity. Hank had been the last surviving link to his childhood, and losing him made Jack a man alone, without forebears or descendants, the last of his line. As much as he loved Sarita, Jack felt himself moving inexorably away from her. What she had said about Cash that morning made Jack question her loyalty. Hank had been the only person left on Earth whom Jack could really trust. The void his loss created was filled with a single-minded determination that Cash Bailey was a dead man. Jack could no longer think of Cash as a human being, and the rules of civilized conduct no longer applied.

Hector had watched the entire battle through field glasses from a ridge about half a mile away. After Lupo told him what happened when Jack met with Cash, the two of them decided that Jack Benteen must die. With the U.S. military moving into the drug enforcement business, Lupo could no longer rely on the pseudo-army he had created with Cash to protect the majority in their village who lived outside of the law.

Since Cash refused to order Jack's death, even though the Ranger could provide the antidrug militia with all the information they needed to mount a full-scale war against them, Lupo stepped into the breach. As he told Hector, "We can't let them use us as whipping boys for the Yankees who like to get high. Those bastards won't police their own people, so it all comes down on us." So they promised Chub a price for ten kilos he couldn't turn down, plus a chance to avenge his brother's death.

Hector and Lupo were only after Jack, who they knew was more respected than liked in the Benrey community. Hector was a bit sorry that Hank had been hit in the fray. He knew that Hank played Santa Claus each year in the children's wing of the local hospital, was a churchgoing family man, and many a Benrey resident swore they slept better knowing that Hank was looking out for them, as he had for decades. But those were the breaks, the fortunes of war.

Hector waited until nightfall to cross the border again, and this gave him ample opportunity to consider the backlash that would inevitably result from Hank's death. Hector also used some of the time to wonder about the two gringos who killed Chub and the other man. He was sure he had seen one of them before. It was almost dark before Hector recalled seeing the balding man with Merv a few weeks before.

Jack refused to enter the morgue until Hank's body had been taken to the local funeral home. He arrived in the tiled, echoing room as Cortez was taking fingerprints from the body found with Chub. The Benrey Sheriff's Station had recently gotten a facsimile machine that allowed them to send fingerprint composites to Washington, D.C., which in turn would dispatch the subject's criminal record back to Benrey in a few hours. But in this case that wouldn't be necessary. Jack recognized him as Ricardo Hudson, a onetime nationally ranked rodeo cowboy whose wife had run off with another man while he was out on the circuit. From there Ricardo had gone to pieces, taken a bad spill, then begun hanging out with the sleaziest lowlifes he could find after his release from the hospital. Jack had drunk with Ricardo a few times before things went bad, and found him to be a better man than most, but things had changed.

As he contemplated Ricardo's still-whipcord-thin body and prematurely graying beard Jack bitterly remembered how dignified Ricardo had been before the mixture of painkillers and booze proved too much for him. His death was caused by a broken neck, but as far as Jack was concerned, "death by poisoning" would be perfectly appropriate to put on the certificate.

How long, Jack wondered, before the individuals poisoning themselves would grow to such numbers that they would poison the entire community as well? How long before the huge sums of money being spent on illegal drugs did permanent damage to the nation's economy, to the world's economy? How long before the government decided that the "common good" was more important than individual rights? Jack figured the answer to all three questions was "They already have," and he felt the worse for it.

Despite his sympathy with their intentions, Jack was deeply worried by the federal government's decision to bring the military into drug enforcement. People trained for combat were not exactly famous for being civil libertarians. Benteen family lore included many horror stories about the Civil War years, when Union soldiers had the power to arrest civilians, which they did frequently and violently. The terrorizings got worse during Reconstruction and led to the so-called "posse comitatus" law, which forbade military involvement with civilian law enforcement.

But why should U.S. armed forces be allowed to raid drug cultivators and traffickers in foreign countries like Bolivia if they couldn't or wouldn't do the same on their own soil? Jack ruefully acknowledged that it would be easier to argue against the unprecedented steps Reagan and Meese were taking if there were any, more obvious alternative ways to deal with the drug plague.

Jack's train of thought was interrupted when Purvis came up to him, bearing a white enamel–painted metal container full of slugs that had been dug out of Chub's body. "Sir," he said tentatively, "I would just like to hear a simple explanation of what in the hell is going on around here. Every damn day or night lately there's been a shooting, killing, explosion, something terrible . . ."

"It all comes down to Cash Bailey," Jack said.

Cortez joined in the conversation. "What I don't understand is, why would Chub set up such a big dope deal at the same time he was planning to ambush you? And why would the people who killed Chub and the other guy leave fifty thousand dollars' worth of cocaine behind?"

"Hard to figure. Maybe they got scared, got run off by the helicopter," Jack replied. "I'll tell you one thing for goddamn sure, Cortez, and that is Cash is starting to lose his grip on his operation." The only explanation Jack could figure for the ambush, and the killing of Chub and Ricardo, was that Cash's peons were splitting off into different factions.

The morgue was located in the Benrey County courthouse, and as Jack walked into the building's lobby after viewing the corpses of the Hispanics that died in the shoot-out, he was clearly in no mood to temporize. But Hackett emerged from the shadows and buttonholed him anyway, flashing government identification that depicted him as a D.E.A. agent named "Frank Ralston." Hackett wore wire-rim glasses, as he did in the ID photo. He was dressed in a light suit and a tie. Jack squinted at Hackett, waiting for him to speak.

"Ranger Benteen, I'm Frank Ralston, Drug Enforcement. I'm here as point man on a task force investigating the drug traffic around this part of the border."

Jack would have been friendlier if Hackett had

identified himself as an I.R.S. man there to audit his return. "Good luck," he said tersely, continuing for the door.

Hackett tagged along. "Just a minute . . . I need some information."

"Call the phone company."

Hackett's military mindset broke through the act he was putting on as he barked, "Wait a minute, mister. I'm here on official U.S. government business, and I expect you to cooperate."

Jack's cobalt-blue eyes drilled into the lenses of Hackett's spectacles with withering intensity. "And I expect you to get the hell out of my way, Mr. Ralston." Before Hackett could react, Jack was past him and out the courthouse door. Jack then drove to Jalisco, with Hackett trailing behind at a discreet distance.

17

Merv was entering the day's receipts into his portable computer, stacks of twenties, fifties, and hundreds sitting on his desk awaiting placement in the double-doored iron safe that took up a large part of one wall. Merv's office was on the second floor of the Hotel Isabella, and it was always an effort for him to concentrate over the rowdy yelling and mariachi music that came from the bustling cantina—not to mention the moans of sexual ecstasy that came at all hours from the whores' bedrooms nearby. The names of Cash's various North American "subcontractors" scrolled across the computer screen as Merv fastidiously copied them and the weekly take of each into a small green ledger.

At least his window faced the back of the building, instead of looking down into the courtyard, where lights were strung and the ragtag "soldiers" of Cash Bailey's army had food served to them and drank tequila, occasionally firing off their guns in revelry. When Merv first started working for Cash, the hotel had been a fairly peaceful place. But now there were machine-gun nests on either side of the building and two more in corners of the courtyard overlooking the village below. Perhaps fifty heavily armed men roamed around at any given time, most of them in no condition to be handling automatic weapons.

The whole setup was starting to make Merv pretty nervous, but the knowledge that he was only two years away from being solvent enough to retire bolstered his resolve to stick it out. As he finished copying the data and tucked the floppy disc into the ledger's front pocket, Merv ironically reflected on the distance between his present activities and his childhood in Benrey and the accounting classes he had taken at the local junior college.

Hector elbowed through the crowd packing the Hotel Isabella's cantina and made his way to the table where Cash was holding court, Lupo and Monday by his side. Hector stopped a few feet short of the table, managed to catch Lupo's eye. Lupo slipped away and, after learning what transpired at Arturo's, agreed with Hector that the news should be kept from Cash until they saw how Merv responded to their questions about the man Hector had recognized.

Cash was sitting on the upper level of the cantina, near the band. He thought of the raised platform as a dais from which he could survey his minions. It appealed to his sense of "empire" as well as making him less vulnerable if he kept himself apart from the hoi polloi. It bothered him that sometimes he couldn't tell if he served them or they served him, so he cultivated an aloofness that reassured him of his superiority.

The crowded bar took up the whole back wall of the lower level. The rest of the floor was jammed with rickety, crudely hewn wooden tables, many of which bore rough patches where they were restored after one of the frequent brawls. Cash noticed a scuffle at the bar, where two men argued over the favors of a teenage whore.

Cash tossed back another shot of tequila and grinned. He knew what Solomon would do were he in his shoes, so he leaned over the railing and bellowed, *"Oye!"* The Spanish word for *listen* cut through the rude cackling that usually swallowed any attempt to communicate. The two men looked up, fearful, for they knew Cash to be unpredictable, sometimes caring and wise, other times despotic, crazy.

Cash pointed with his tequila bottle at the young whore and he grinned. "Cut her in half, amigos!"

Cash laughed coarsely at his King Solomon joke, and as if on cue, the rest of the hall laughed with him, then went back to the business of drinking and whoring as Cash went back to his own bottle and his isolation. He watched Lupo cross the lower level and go up the stairs to the second floor close behind Hector, but he didn't give it another thought. After all, Lupo and Hector were executives to whom he had delegated the various phases of his operation. They took care of the details so Cash was free to consider the big picture.

Merv was deep in thought, poring over the dollar figures and examining the distribution patterns and traffic flows of Cash's enterprise—New York was up, L.A. and Chicago were down, and he had to decide whether to station some new people in the down markets. A loud knock startled him. The door handle rattled and Lupo called, *"Abren la puerta!"* Merv didn't like the edge in Lupo's voice. As he anxiously unbolted the door Lupo burst past him, followed by Hector, who corralled Merv back toward his desk.

The two Latin men often tried to cow Merv. They resented Cash's special treatment of him and the fact that, as a relatively sophisticated Anglo, Merv was able to do a lot of things and go to a lot of places Lupo and Hector could not. But Merv was a big man and not a pushover. He bore the responsibility and power Cash had vested in him with the confidence of someone who has found his calling. Merv recognized Hector and Lupo's bullying tactics for what they were.

They tried to back Merv into his desk chair so they could stand over him, but Merv held his ground.

"Why the hell do you come crashing in here?" Merv asked in English. He spoke Spanish, but he knew that Lupo's English wasn't very strong and that it irked him to have to speak it.

"Chub Luke was killed today," Hector said accusingly.

"He thinks one of your *vatos* did it." Lupo sneered.

Merv was stunned by the news of Chub's death coming so close on the heels of T.C.'s. Both brothers were an important link in the Texas border network and their loss meant a complete local reorganization. The fact that Hector and Lupo imagined complicity on Merv's part added to the problem. He figured he could reason with Hector. But Lupo's deranged demeanor always suggested he'd rather cut your throat than give you the time of day. His reputation backed up the first impression. It was one of the reasons he was admired by Cash's motley army and why they looked up to him as a natural leader. Lupo was a crucial part of the delicate balance Cash maintained. Cash's ability to control and command loyalty from such men was, arguably, his most important asset. But now, Merv saw Lupo as a potential threat to the harmony of Cash Bailey, Incorporated.

Merv shook his head in disbelief. "You think I had Chub killed? It's the worst news I've had this year."

Lupo moved close to Merv, stared him in the eye. "You've been keeping secrets from us, hombre. Maybe your bald friend, *el cicatriz*, he's working for you now, not Cash."

El cicatriz, the scar. Merv racked his brain, wondering who Lupo was talking about, then: Paul Hackett. Merv was stunned. "How did Chub die?" he asked, stalling for time.

"There was a shoot-out at Arturo's, the Ranger showed up while Chub was passing through. Chub killed the Benrey sheriff, tried to do it to the Ranger, then drove off. *El cicatriz* was watching from a hill, then he and another hombre drove off. Then I heard that Chub was found dead." Hector was stretching the logical relationship between events, trying to support his conclusion. Who else could have done it?

But to Merv it didn't make sense. And besides, he realized that the bad news was greater than Chub's death. If Hank Pearson was dead, they would get a lot of heat. "Chub killed Sheriff Pearson?"

"And wounded the Ranger," Lupo asserted. "Too damn bad it wasn't the other way."

"Does Cash know?" Merv didn't want to deliver the news.

Hector shook his head.

"Why was Chub shooting it out with those guys?" Merv demanded, though he had a pretty solid idea of Chub's motivation.

"I think he had a debt to repay." Lupo smiled, revealing his gold tooth.

"So now he and his brother are dead and we're going to be hotter than a sunburned lizard," Merv stormed. "The sheriff's death is going to cause Cash a lot of trouble. We'd better tell him now."

Lupo saw his information coup slipping away from him, so he maneuvered to stay in position. "I tell you what. We give Cash the news together, like we heard about it at the same time."

"Bueno," Merv replied, after taking a moment to consider his options. He didn't care about Lupo's petty power plays, he just wanted to keep things on an even

keel. They could ride out an enforcement crackdown if they had to, *if* their ship was in order. Cash would have to decide how to smooth things over.

Cash was angry when he learned of Hank's death. "Hellfire, if I wanted Hank Pearson dead, I'd have given the order years ago. Better to stay with the adversary you know than invite a new one in. Chub Luke was too stupid to live."

Lupo exaggerated his eager nod of agreement. He decided to bring up the impounded cocaine later, when Cash had forgotten about the sheriff. Since they were able to lay responsibility for the killings solely at Chub's feet and it was impossible to punish him further, Cash quickly dropped the matter.

But Hector came up with the name of a low-level operative, Garcia, who had recruited the hired guns on Chub's behalf, and it was decided that he shared responsibility for their deaths. A courier known as "Cueball" to most, but whose given name was Jesus, arranged to take a package north of the border similar to the one Cash had Hector take to Chicken Camp. After dispatching him, Cash found himself gazing at a young girl lounging in a hammock slung next to a pre–World War II Coca-Cola cooler that now held the cantina's beer. She reminded Cash of the younger Sarita, especially in her determination to use means other than her body to make her way in the world. The young woman was an island of freshness amid the sweaty, used-up-looking people crowded into every corner of the cantina.

For a moment Cash considered taking the girl under his wing, but what he yearned for most was the closeness he felt with Sarita, the result of much time spent together. Cash didn't feel up for repeating such a process at this point in his life, because every survival instinct told him to stay hidden. Intimacy of any type made him vulnerable. But if he could just pick up with Sarita where he left off . . .

Not too damn likely, after the way he ditched her for a curvaceous blond cocaine whore, whose vapidity Cash had swiftly tired of. After getting the Sarita bug again, Cash had scoured his many entertainment-business contacts, and learned that for $100,000 or so he could press twenty-five thousand copies of a record, and a like sum could buy rudimentary national distribution. It seemed a bit stiff, and the money going into it would be harder to launder than usual, but it might be worth it to excise Sarita's memories of her past humiliation. And after all, thought Cash, what was the point of having large sums of money if you weren't prepared to spend some?

18

Sarita was singing "Ay! Jalisco No Te Rajes," delivered as a sardonic tribute to her place of employment, as Jack walked into Jalisco. She was pushing her vocal cords to their limits, rendering the chorus in a supercharged tone halfway between a scream and a growl. Sarita prowled across the laid-flat phone-booth-size stage like she was ready to jump off and belt somebody. It took her a few moments to spot Jack, and when their eyes met, he deliberately turned away from her and took a seat at an empty table. It placed him under a decorative "loft" adorned with farm tools and Spanish blankets draped over bales of hay.

Jack ordered a beer, and just as it arrived Hackett took a seat on the other side of the table, which ticked Jack off. "I didn't hear myself giving you an invitation. I'm particular about who I drink with."

Hackett loudly set his vodka and tonic on the table and met Jack's withering gaze. "Let's cut through the horseshit. I've got a job to do here, and I need your help. Chances are better than good that you could use some of mine. I've got juice in Washington."

"Juice in Washington," Jack mimicked. "D.E.A. bureaucratic fat-asses fluffing their duffs on my requests for information. I'll bet my file of unanswered queries is as thick as a phone book."

"Look, we're like you, civil servants, overworked and underpaid. There's only a few thousand of us to fight the entire war on drugs. And just like with your people, sometimes things fall through the cracks."

"Yeah. Cracks the size of the Grand Canyon."

"I can see to it when I get back to Washington that you get top priority on everything you send up," said Hackett, figuring this empty promise might prompt Jack to confide in him. "In the meantime, I could use every bit of evidence you have relating to those drug dealers who were killed this afternoon."

Jack pondered how much to tell Hackett as Sarita began another song, then decided to do a little fishing himself. "I can give you a sure lead. Ever heard of Cash Bailey?"

As Jack studied his reaction Hackett said only, "His name is in our files."

"He's behind most of the drug traffic around here. Those were his boys that got killed today. Last few days, it's all his doing. A restaurant was blown up, which killed an innocent kid along with the drug dealer that owned it. Cash Bailey was also behind the ambush at Arturo's that killed Hank . . . Sheriff Pearson." Against his better judgment, Jack began to tell Hackett what was on his mind. "They never had a better sheriff here, and never will. Hank died falling forward. That means something down here."

Jack finished his beer in one long draw, then continued. "Me and Cash go back a long way, but times change . . . turn a friend into a showdown enemy. One way or another, I'm going to run him down."

Hackett sensed the determination in Jack's vow and

wondered how he might turn it to his advantage. "Any way I can help, you just let me know."

"Maybe you can lend a hand," Jack said, after taking a moment to consider Hackett's offer. He then fished in his shirt pocket for one of the Ingram shells Cortez found near Sharpe's Crossing, and a slug that had been removed from Chub's body. "This is a sample of what killed Chub Luke. I don't recognize the case markings. I sent a few to Austin but don't expect a report for weeks. How soon could you get these run down in Washington . . . with your juice?"

Seizing the opportunity to send Jack down the wrong trail, Hackett replied, "Twenty-four hours, maybe a little more."

Jack flipped the slug and casing to Hackett, who nimbly caught them. "Try to make it twenty-four hours. That will impress me."

"Will do. For whatever it's worth, I think I know how you feel. I've lost friends in the line of duty myself. From what I hear, Sheriff Pearson was one of the best."

Jack thought it was a patronizing thing for Hackett to say. He rose and tossed a five-dollar bill on the table just as Sarita ended her song and sought him out.

"Yeah, I'll go home tonight, drink whiskey, and think about Hank." Jack then walked away, leaving Hackett sitting alone. Sarita left the stage and rushed after him, catching up just before Jack stepped outside. The band played an instrumental to cover her absence.

"You come to watch me sing, then you don't even take a minute to say hello. What's going on?" Sarita's tone was more plaintive than angry.

"Just came by to have a beer on my way home," Jack replied, avoiding eye contact.

"You want to talk about Hank? I just heard about it an hour ago. I don't know anything about how it happened. Were you there?"

"Yeah, I was there." Jack saw Hackett watching

them through the glass window of Jalisco's anteroom, and edgily moved closer to the door.

"You want to tell me about it? Is that why you came? I know how much you like him, how close you were . . ." Sarita then noticed the dressings on Jack's wounds and tenderly ran her hand over them.

"I don't want to talk about it, Sarita. I want to *do* something about it."

"You've got to let it out, Jack. Like with you and me. It's better if we talk."

Jack became suspicious of her sudden appetite for information. "Sometimes a man has to keep his cards to himself."

It was an insulting remark, and that was exactly how Sarita took it. "You crazy? For three years we are lovers, and now we don't talk?"

"I didn't think you had anything else to say to me after this morning."

Sarita felt herself being shut out of Jack's life. "What's the matter, *amor*? I know you like a husband. We have fights before, but this time it's not like you, it's real bad."

"Yeah, well maybe we should give it a rest. The talk, all of it."

Sarita felt the way she had felt when Cash had replaced her with that shag-head bimbo. A different sort of rivalry was involved here, but the effect was the same. Sarita wasn't backing down yet. "Look me in the eye and tell me you don't want me no more, if that's what you're trying to say."

"I'm not saying that." Jack looked directly at Sarita. "I just said you and me should give it a rest. That's all. This stuff with you and me and Cash is just too hard, too goddamn complicated."

Now Sarita was really angry, appalled at Jack's selfishness. "Too hard, huh, too complicated? For you, Jack? I give you three of my best years, and you give me this shit about hard and complicated?" Sarita turned away from Jack, furious, and opened the anteroom door, looking back at him for a parting shot. "Someday you're going to want me, Jack, but I won't be there when you look. I'm down the road. I told you before you don't know a good thing when you got it."

Jack said nothing as he watched Sarita walk through the door and back to the bandstand. She had in effect told him that he was burning his bridges, but Jack rationalized that he was trying to save their relationship. The thing with Cash had to be resolved before they could get on with planning their lives together. And if Jack decided otherwise, Sarita had unmistakably told him it was time to walk away. If Gramps or his dad was still around, they would have violently objected to the idea of Jack marrying a Latina, giving them "halfbreed" grandchildren. On the other hand, they might recognize how the barriers between the people of Texas and those of Mexico were irrevocably coming down, for better or for worse. As prejudiced as his forebears were, they might appreciate that Jack's creating a family with Sarita would be a powerful message that the better outweighed the worse.

All Jack could do now was hope that Sarita would ride out the time during which he resolved the situation with Cash. He would miss her, but having Sarita out of his life for the time being would give him freedom to deal with Cash in whatever way he saw fit. Jack wanted his life set up so that Cash couldn't hurt anybody except him if he decided that Jack was pushing too hard.

Jack drove his cruiser home. As he pulled into his dirt-and-brush "yard" his headlights caught several golf balls studding the yard. They were left over from when Jack and Hank had practiced their swings together at a barbeque the weekend before. While he was in the Sheriff's Station he had spoken to Hank's widow, Jeanette. The news had already been broken to her, so it was left for Jack to fill in the details, judiciously leaving out the grimmer ones. Jack wondered if he should call her again, deciding not to when he couldn't figure out anything insightfully comforting to say. Hank and Jeanette's three kids had all grown up and moved to other cities, but each had made arrangements to return to Benrey for the funeral, which was to take place Saturday morning two days hence.

Jack shouldn't have been surprised by the absence of Sarita's orange MG convertible from his driveway, but on the trip home he'd allowed himself to forget her for a moment. Jack felt a flash of the same searing regret he'd experienced after letting his chance to kill Cash slip by.

Jack turned his attention to the sky. It was the first clear night all week. His house was far enough away from the lights of Benrey so that Jack had a spectacular view of the heavens.

Looking up at the cupola his father had added to the roof of the house, Jack saw the moon dimly reflected in the green copper roof. His eye wandered to the carved oak owl that was permanently perched on the cupola's wooden railing. Beyond it the stars glimmered. Jack watched until he saw a shooting star and imagined Hank having a wild ride on it.

Upon entering the house, Jack avoided the kitchen and bedrooms, walking straight to the living room. He grabbed a bottle of Jack Daniels from the bar. The living room/study was dominated by a stone fireplace, which had shelves on either side that contained Jack's books and memorabilia. On the tops of the shelves were shooting trophies won by Jack or his kin, and the walls were full of stuffed and mounted animal victims of their prowess with firearms. Walking past a cowhide-covered sofa, Jack went to the desk in the far corner. Prominent on it was a Texas Ranger mug that held pens and pencils. Jack dumped them out and poured himself a few eighty-six-proof ounces of the Jack Daniels without bothering to rinse out the mug.

The sour-mash bourbon, graphite dust, and pencil shavings scoured his throat and scorched his stomach lining. Gasping for breath, Jack leaned against the edge of the desk, eyes watering, then went into the kitchen, added some water and ice to his drink, and walked out onto his patio. There were only three or four other houses in sight of Jack's, all of which belonged to farmers or ranchers. Many a morning their roosters had awakened Jack and Sarita, and between getting up and deciding it was too late to go back to sleep, they often made love with a fervor that jump-started each other for the new day.

Jack recalled the time that a well-respected farmer's son, who was strung out on heroin, had shot up the family home and threatened to kill his parents. Bringing Purvis along, Hank had found the boy standing by his parents' pool, having shot out the lighting system. A large-caliber automatic was sticking out of his waistband. Some other lawmen would have shot the boy down like a dog, but Hank just walked straight up to him without pulling a gun. The last few feet were very intense, but Hank had managed to disarm the boy without a shot being fired. However, upon noticing that Purvis had left his gun in the car, Hank had a screaming fit, furious at the lack of backup.

Sitting down in the wooden porch swing he had made himself, Jack thought about a discussion he and Hank had not long ago about the war on drugs. That Hank, who had favored a more realistic and pragmatic approach to drug enforcement than most of his colleagues, was its latest casualty was a cruel irony.

"They say there's forty million pot smokers in the country now, and that number has stayed pretty level since the early 1970s," Hank had declared. "And while I've seen hayheads do plenty of goddamn stupid things, they don't worry me anywhere near as much as the five million cokers we're supposed to have. The real damage being done by dopers is monetary. The consumer demand is there, so why shouldn't the government legalize and tax pot, and use the money to fight the really dangerous drugs? Hell, have you ever heard of anybody dying from pot?"

"C'mon, Hank, think of the political consequences. Other nations would condemn us as irresponsible. For Christ's sake, we want them to keep their antidope laws on the books."

"Maybe so, but if marijuana was legalized, then the tax revenues from it could be spent on letting the D.E.A. go after the hard stuff, 'stead of always making the easy busts. Shit, in 1977 they estimate about five tons of cocaine total came into this country, but they got more than that just in the big Pennsylvania raid last year. I don't know if the D.E.A. is corrupt, incompetent, or just plain underfunded."

Hank had gone on to insist that drug traffickers had effectively become captains of a multibillion-dollar industry, and had to be treated as such, if the drug problem was to be truly dealt with. The real enemy wasn't people like the Luke brothers, but those who had successfully isolated themselves from the actual commerce. Even Cash still had to get his hands dirty in that end of it. Jack decided that if he were running the D.E.A., his first priority goal would be putting a wedge between the drug millionaires and their assets. But that was one job Jack knew he was not meant to fill.

Garcia disliked being ordered to the Benrey bus station at three o'clock in the morning, but nothing had been said about the bloodbath at Arturo's, and he was grateful that Jesus still deemed him trustworthy enough to perform a presumably important errand. Garcia looked with contempt at the downtrodden people huddled on the benches, actually spitting at a teenage girl with a mixed-race baby. As he neared the row of lockers he was looking for Garcia nearly kicked the swollen legs of an elderly woman out of his way.

Using his body to shield the locker contents from the prying eyes of the waiting passengers, Garcia opened it with the key Jesus had given him. An angry coral snake leaped out and bit Garcia near the jugular. Jesus had chosen that particular locker because the height was perfect. Garcia desperately grabbed the snake and tried to toss it away, but that only made the serpent clamp its jaws down harder. As the poison sped to his heart he sank to his knees, and the snake slithered away from him just as everything began to turn black.

The snake raced through the lounge, sending people scrambling up onto the benches. All one could hear was screaming, until the security guard killed the coral snake with his cane.

19

Biddle had the brown truck parked near the City Bank of Benrey when it opened, and he used headphones to listen in on a conversation between Merv and Clarence King. Biddle also tape-recorded it for Hackett's later perusal.

"Hidey, Clarence, Merv speaking, how're things?"

"No problems. How's everything down south?"

"Lots of sun. That's all we get down here, lots of sun and lots of money. Speaking of which, we're coming in on Monday morning, about ten o'clock, with two big suitcases full of the stuff."

"Jesus Christ! Didn't I tell you that I'd had my fill for the month?"

"I heard you, but our business doesn't adhere to any cash-flow quotas, and Cash doesn't see why yours should either."

"I'm telling you, and I'm telling Cash Bailey, I can't handle two suitcases now."

"Aw, save it for the judge, Clarence. You're in up to your fat ass, and you don't have any other choice. I'll see you Monday, have a nice day."

Biddle involuntarily groaned at Clarence and Merv's

125

lack of concern for the possibility of wiretaps. If the feds wanted to nail them, it would be easier than killing a rat in a jar. His attention then shifted to the armored car pulling up to the bank. As Biddle studied the videotape he was making of the driver's routine Fry climbed into the back of the truck, pulling an audio-tape cassette from his shirt pocket.

"Check it out, Charlie. Seems the mayor has a new honey," Fry said as he inserted the cassette into one of the tape machines. On the tape, Corliss could be heard ushering a girl he called Cheryl into his office and locking the door. Cheryl sounded like she was sixteen or seventeen, and quite awed to be getting it on with the mayor of Benrey. Then came the sounds of Corliss hastily clearing his desktop, struggling out of his clothes, and mounting Cheryl with the audible finesse of a bull elephant. Fry found it amusing, offering a mock sportscaster's play-by-play—"And the wide receiver is getting it in the end zone . . ."—but Biddle quickly tired of the grotesque rutting noises.

"Enough of that shit," he said, reaching to shut off the tape machine.

"Be cool, Biddle, this dude only takes a few seconds."

"What the hell business is it of ours who the man is humping?"

Fry thought Biddle was being a prude. "C'mon, Charlie, didn't they ever train you to hit your enemy where he's exposed?"

"Since when is the mayor of an American city the enemy?"

"I'll bet he's on Cash Bailey's payroll like everybody else around here," responded Fry defensively. "We're looking at one dirty town, bro."

"But it ain't our job to deal with this kind of thing."

"Maybe it should be." Fry was thinking about his

own children, and the hazardous temptations they would soon be exposed to, courtesy of men like Cash Bailey.

"That's how it was when Dred Scott got returned to his master." Biddle was talking about the infamous pre–Civil War case of a black man who had escaped from servitude and settled in a "free" state. Federal troops had escorted him back to the slave state he'd run away from, and the U.S. Supreme Court had ruled that Scott could not sue his captors for illegally seizing him, declaring blacks to be "beings of an inferior order and altogether unfit to associate with the white race, either in social or political relations; and so far inferior, that they have no rights which the white man [is] bound to respect."

For Biddle, learning about the case had created a strong incentive to put himself on the side of authority, but he maintained a keen awareness of the capabilities of authority to be wrong, and do wrong.

But Luther Fry was not familiar with the case, as evidenced by his asking Biddle, "Dred who?"

"Forget it. If you don't know your history, I don't have time to teach it to you." Biddle archly turned his attention back to the video monitor. His earlier suspicions about the operation had been intensified by how shaken up McRose had been the previous night. Biddle tried to find out what had upset the normally imperturbable McRose but had been told in no uncertain terms that it was none of his business, which was also unlike McRose. Biddle didn't know that Hackett and McRose had been forced to kill Chub and Ricardo.

"Talk to me, Charlie," prodded Fry. "You having trouble with the job?"

"Never. Just in this situation, we shouldn't be taking so many initiatives. One step over the line and we're raping the Bill of Rights."

"As if she ain't never been violated before."

Maybe Fry knew about the Dred Scott decision after all, Biddle thought. "Not by us. Let's keep it that way."

"Well," Fry muttered, as if chagrined, "you and me are the linebackers on this squad, and I think we need a running back. Our QB may have some screws loose."

Biddle relaxed a bit, renewing eye contact with Fry. "I know, Luther. But in this situation, we've got no room to punt."

At about the same time, McRose was using just those words to tell Coker why it had been necessary to kill Chub Luke and Ricardo Hudson. Hackett had euphemistically described it as "double contact inadvertent" when he first explained to Coker why it would be necessary for the team to acquire some "clean" firepower.

"Jesus! Prejudicial?" Coker had asked.

"That's right," McRose said. "Terminal."

"Clean," emphasized Hackett. "It was their choice. Drug runners. Cash Bailey's team."

Coker had turned to McRose for confirmation, and he said, "They had us cold. No room to punt. If I hadn't opened fire when I did, Major Hackett would have been decapitated by the one man's machete."

"Or he would have forced me to shove it up his ass," said Hackett, miffed at the implication that he couldn't take care of himself in combat.

"Couldn't you have made tracks when the shooting started in the gas station?"

"Yeah, and we could have gone down another road, too," interjected Hackett. "It was bad luck all the way around."

"What about the fallout? Couldn't we get into deep shit for killing people on American soil?"

"It was the only course of action, Sergeant!" declared Hackett. "Anyway, we're fighting some of the world's highest-level drug dealers, and they certainly aren't cutting anybody slack."

The discussion ended with Coker being given his marching orders, but Hackett could see that his men couldn't stomach having to treat their fellow countrymen as the enemy. They weren't programmed to think that way. This was a factor he had only briefly addressed while planning the operation. It impressed him the way McRose had kept his cool up to this point, but Hackett wondered how long this would last. It was Friday, and all he had to do was keep the team together for less than one more week before he wouldn't have to worry about such things ever again.

Jack allowed himself to sleep two hours later than usual. After checking in with the Sheriff's Station by phone and cursing out Purvis because he wasn't immediately told about the Garcia killing, Jack drove to a cinderblock store on the outskirts of Benrey. Its owner was Bill "Bear" Jacobs, a gunsmith who was a few years older than Jack. Bear had bought his life membership in the National Rifle Association at the age of sixteen and was the type of person for whom the term "gun nut" had been devised.

Bear's firearms store was the only one in the county that was licensed to deal in Class 3, or automatic, weapons. Jack suspected that Bear had been awarded that plum because of his outspoken bigotry, as he almost never sold machine guns to nonwhites.

The flamboyantly eclectic decor of Bear's store always puzzled Jack. The security system was so elaborate it seemed as if Bear was mocking his own paranoia. The walls were covered with a strange assortment of icons: a surfboard painted in camouflage colors, a Dillinger-era sub-machine gun, several assorted fur traps, a hangman's noose, a samurai sword crossed over a Middle Eastern scimitar, and a Soviet flag with muddy footprints all over it, among other things. There were also a number of bumper stickers, with slogans like POLAND HAS GUN CONTROL and REGISTER MATCHES —PREVENT FOREST FIRES pasted on the cash register. Several model tanks and helicopters were scattered around, the toys presenting an odd contrast to all the truly deadly firearms on display.

As Jack sauntered through the entrance an electric eye activated a jarring buzzer that brought Bear scurrying from the back of the store. He was a slight but paunchy man with a precisely trimmed beard and beady eyes that appeared ideal for looking down gunsights. On this day he wore a black T-shirt that depicted a skull wearing a green beret and the warning SPECIAL FORCES —MESS WITH THE BEST, DIE LIKE THE REST.

Bear seemed both glad and surprised to see Jack. "I'm damned sorry about what happened to Hank."

"You and me both, Bear. You don't see many people who give more than they take, but that was Hank, and we'll never find another like him."

"I hear you were damn lucky not to be laid out on a slab alongside him."

Jack pretended to take offense. "You don't think skill had anything to do with it?"

"Sorry, partner. I heard they found an M-two-oh-three combination M-sixteen and forty-millimeter grenade launcher all loaded up. You're goddamn lucky those fuckwads were too stupid to figure out how to use it, otherwise they would have fragged your ass to kingdom come."

"How come you know more about it than I do?"

"Because it's my business. I need to stay on top of the needs of law enforcement agencies. Hell, if that's the kind of firepower you're up against now, then the Rangers and the sheriffs ought to be equipped with rocket launchers. Think how handy one of those would have been at Arturo's."

"I'd rather not," Jack said with a grimace. He then removed a pair of the mysterious slugs and shell casings from his shirt pocket and handed them to Bear. "What can you tell me about these?"

Bear first examined one casing, studying the head-stamp mark. "That's odd. It says 'forty-three on here, but I don't see how they can be that old, because, see these little marks here?"

Jack squinted and saw the abrasions Bear pointed out.

"If I'm not mistaken," Bear asserted, "these are from the extractor on an Ingram sub-machine gun."

"We thought it was an Uzi, that's what I saw Chub with. It would have been poetic if they used his own gun on him."

"What's even more interesting," Bear said, looking at one of the slugs through a magnifying loupe, "I believe these marks here came from a factory Ingram silencer. Only one outfit in the country uses those: the Green Berets."

Jack was about to comment when he saw an unfamiliar figure standing in the doorway between the display and the gunsmith workshop.

Bear quickly sensed the source of Jack's discomfort and said, "Jack, I'd like you to meet my new assistant, Paul Kenner." Declan Patrick Coker then shook hands with Jack. "Paul is fresh out of the Marine Corps," Bear continued, sounding both proud and envious.

The introductory handshake became a test of strength, each man inflicting bone-bruising pressure on the other.

Jack laughed, lightly acknowledging the machismo contest. "Why did you hire a stud like this, Bear? You still thinking about that damn fool crazy idea of putting a volunteer border patrol auxiliary together?"

"I'm not like those Civilian Military Assistance lunatics who are going into Mexico and shit like that, Jack.

131

We're talking strictly domestic ops here. I'm just a good citizen trying to avert a catastrophe, which is what I see brewing with all these unchecked hordes of wetbacks swimming the river." To illustrate the point, Bear gestured to a newspaper photograph of a Latino shantytown outside of Benrey, which he had taped to a display case.

"What's the harm done to you, Bear? You afraid some *bracero* is going to marry your sister?"

"No, Jack, I'm worried about this country turning into one big barrio."

"You should live so long." Jack turned to Coker. "So, where are you from, Paul?"

"Billings, Montana. My daddy took me hunting every year since I could walk, and I developed kind of a knack for firearms."

"That so? Well, just don't let this reactionary kook talk you into doing anything illegal."

Jack motioned to Bear that he wanted to speak to him privately, so they stepped out of the front door of the shop. "How can I confirm if these slugs were fired from a U.S. Army weapon?"

"Real simple. Just make up some hundred-fifty-grain loads in the shells and send them to Austin for a chronograph. If it turns out they go less than twelve hundred feet per second, it was an Ingram, because the silenced one has the lowest muzzle velocity of any automatic weapon. But I'm surprised this didn't come up in your training, *Ranger* Benteen."

"It did, Bear, I just sometimes enjoy hearing you carry on like a pompous ass. In small doses, of course. Anyway, I want you to keep this on the cuff with Kenner."

"He's okay, Jack. Hell, it only took the federal Treasury boys forty-eight hours to clear his license to sell Class-3 weapons."

"This is still just between us, clear?" Jack walked to

his car. "Otherwise you're going to have a world of hurt."

"Never a kind word for anybody, huh Jack?" Bear laughed coarsely as he headed back into the store.

Coker had not resented the two men leaving him alone because it gave him a chance to continue compiling his "shopping list" of items his colleagues would need. He had mostly told the truth about his upbringing, except that he really grew up in Provo, Utah. Coker loved his family, but found the local life-style far too dull for him. After getting in trouble with church authorities a number of times, he was caught poaching a ten-point buck out of season. It would have made a fine trophy, but instead it got Coker's family a stiff fine, and he got the choice of reform school or the army. The opportunity to join the Dead List gave Coker the assurance he was seeking that he would never cause his family shame or hardship again. Indeed, his reported demise in the Nova Scotia chartered-plane crash had made his folks local media celebrities for a week or so.

Coker had very mixed feelings about his whole situation. He cherished the freedom to carouse around and not get called into the deacon's office for "attitude readjustment" administered with an oak paddle. He loved being anonymous, away from the scrutiny of a clannish community that kept score on even the most minute transgressions. Just being able to drive above the speed limit was an intense pleasure for Coker, blessed relief after years of deprivation. But he had replaced his old shackles with a new set. No wife. No family. No place to call home. But Coker had grown up in a sometimes oppressively familial atmosphere and he considered the restrictions that came with being a "zombie soldier" a fair trade for the ones he had before.

At about eleven-thirty that morning, a blue Dodge

Lancer, the second rental car in the commandos' operation, pulled up to the Sheriff's Station. Fry and Biddle remained in the Lancer as McRose went inside to pay Atwater's fine. They had arrived a few minutes behind Jack, who had gone into Hank's office before doing anything else.

Jack studied Hank's work space, knowing it would be dismantled in a few days. There was no good reason why it shouldn't be. Jack's office looked out on a scuzzy part of downtown Benrey, but Hank had finagled a view of the nearby hills. The rolltop desk had been Hank's grandfather's, and except for the TV and the typewriter, most of the furnishings dated back to the turn of the century. The clock inset in a wooden covered-wagon carving might have been from the 1920s, but the black leather desk blotter, lined with metal studs, was probably a relic of the Teddy Roosevelt era. Same with the wooden filing cabinet, the longhorns mounted on the wall, and the hand-assembled pine gun rack. One of the more telling things about the room was the absence of pictures of Hank's wife and family, the result of a career-long superstition. But at eye level behind his desk chair was a picture of Boomer, Hank's favorite coonhound. The dog was getting very long in the tooth, and Hank had fussed over him a lot. To Jack it was a cruel irony that the dog had outlived his master.

Emerging from the cramped office, Jack noticed McRose talking to Purvis at the booking desk and wandered over to listen in on the conversation.

Purvis motioned contemptuously to Atwater, who by now had grossed out every employee of the station house and was indiscriminately scowling at everyone who glanced in his direction. "You know this drifter, huh?"

Smiling affectionately, McRose replied, "Yes sir, he's my buddy."

Purvis made his "I just smelled something bad" face and said, "He isn't making too good an impression around here, starting fights and talking dirty in front of womenfolk."

"Some kind of hormone imbalance, I think. Nothing anybody should take personal." McRose flashed a disarming grin. "So, what happened to the guy he slugged it out with?"

"We let him out this morning because our investigation was concluded and the witnesses concurred, the colored fellow didn't start nothing. Mean-looking mother, though, I'll tell you that."

Jack walked over to the holding cell and looked dolefully at Atwater, who was dressed entirely in black, including his defingered gloves. "Should have known better than to cut you a break, huh, Buck?"

Atwater whistled through the gap between his front teeth. "A man's gotta stand up for himself. That's what dignity is, ain't it?"

"Buck, I think you're allergic to dignity, so you might be well advised not to talk about it. Purvis, is this boy's fine paid?"

"Yes, sir, his friend showed up to help him out." Purvis went over to the holding cell and unlocked it, then led Atwater to the front desk to sign the release form. "Good thing you got a friend, cowboy."

Atwater wished he could tell Purvis how easy it would be to mop the floor with him. Every aspect of McRose's demeanor said "keep your mouth shut," so Atwater contented himself with just fantasizing about beating the shit out of Purvis. Atwater had used most of his captive time to daydream. He'd concocted an elaborate scenario in his head of him and the other commandos storming the jail, using surgical strike techniques to render the police impotent.

But all he said was "Damn right. Nothing's better than a friend when you need one." Atwater signed the form, and Purvis handed over the envelope containing his valuables. Atwater gave Jack a big grin that went unreturned.

"Don't let me see you again, Buck." There was a threatening edge in Jack's voice.

Atwater arched his back and ran through a routine in his mind of knocking the wind out of Jack with an elbow to the solar plexus, and then pummeling the Ranger's head with his fists. McRose seemed to read his mind and motioned that they should get the hell out of there. Besides, the Ranger had really treated them okay when you got right down to it.

"No, sir," said Atwater, in a tone heavy with menace. "You can color me gone." He punctuated the sentence with a sinister leer, and McRose practically dragged him out of the Sheriff's Station before Atwater said something that would get them in more trouble.

When Atwater saw Fry in the car outside, he protested that it would look very suspicious if any lawmen saw them together. McRose ignored them as the two made faces at each other. As the two climbed into the car Biddle said, "Guess what, Buck, we've been reprogrammed. It's a daylight hit."

Atwater went livid. "My ass."

Fry nodded in affirmation. "ComOps special, Buck."

"What kind of horseshit is this? Who does command think we are, Jesse fucking James? It's crazy, they'll get somebody killed!"

"Hey Buck," said McRose, "don't tell us, tell Hackett."

When Jack went into his office, the first thing he did was get out his cartridge headstamp catalog to double-check what Bear had told him. It didn't take long to establish that the ammunition that killed Chub was different from any of the shell casings he found at Arturo's. As he searched fruitlessly for a reference to the shell, marked "BRM" by where the year was stamped, Jack felt the presence of another person in his office. He looked up to see Hackett standing in the doorway.

"Perhaps I can help you," he said.

"How's your juice in Washington, Ralston?"

"You asked for twenty-four hours, Jack, but it only took me fourteen to get a report back. The ammo is nine-point-three millimeter out of West Germany via Montreal. BRM, distributed here by H&R. It's special, but not that special." Purvis passed by, and stopped to listen in on the conversation.

What "Ralston" said did not jibe with what Bear had told him, but Jack decided to play along like Hackett had done him a favor. "It figures. Cash is buying foreign arms and ammo for that private army he's supposed to have, and supplies some of them to the boys he sends across the border to do his dirty work. Might be some good people for you to go after."

"I think our objectives are a lot more similar than you realize, Jack. You've really got it in for Bailey, don't you?"

"Ralston's" presumptions of intimacy prompted Jack to cut the conversation short. "Yeah, you might say it's personal. Thanks, *Frank*, I need all the help I can get."

Hackett realized he was being dismissed and got up to leave, bumping into the oblivious Purvis on his way out.

"Real nice fella," Purvis remarked after Hackett had gone.

"Yeah, clumsy though," replied Jack, as if Purvis had been talking about himself. He then called the crime lab and asked them to prepare one of the cartridges from the site where Chub and Ricardo's bodies had been found for a chronograph test in Austin. Cotton then brought in the rap sheet for Garcia, the man killed in the bus station by the coral snake. Garcia and Chub had once been arrested in the same drug raid and had a long association together on the wrong side of the law. Was his death punishment for what Chub had done, or had Garcia double-crossed Chub? It was starting to look like Jack had an all-out gang war to contend with, on a par with Chicago in the 1920s.

If he didn't get it under control quickly, he'd have to deal with all sorts of outside interference. Jack took pride in being able to handle his own territory and resented it when the D.E.A. or F.B.I. or anybody else was brought in to step on his toes.

The stunt with the snake reeked of Cash Bailey and his enforcers, but the key would be learning who killed Chub. Perhaps a new contender, unknown to Jack, had entered the arena. The shells were undoubtedly the most valuable clue he had. Jack picked up the cartridge headstamp catalog and looked for a listing on the 1943 BRM 9.3mm bullet, but found none. Neither Bear nor the book was infallible, but if Hackett was blowing smoke up his ass, it could mean that a paramilitary wing of the D.E.A. was using U.S. Army equipment. Jack was aghast at the idea, but he realized that if this was so, there wasn't a hell of a lot he could do about it.

20

The A-team commandos gathered in Room 204 of the Yellow Rose Motel for an anxiously awaited briefing. Hackett, still wearing his Frank Ralston getup, arrived last. He noticed that McRose was seething about something, so he took him aside in the cubicle kitchenette, which consisted of a two-burner stove, shoebox oven, and like-sized refrigerator, all in one compact unit.

McRose steeled himself, knowing that this would be his only opportunity to express his qualms to Hackett, but the major began by saying something that overrode the objections McRose planned to make.

"I've been giving this a lot of thought, Larry, and decided to make you my second-in-command for D-day ops. You'll share responsibility with me in planning all the key logistics."

"Like on how we take the bank?"

"Affirmative." Hackett could tell from the subtle movements of McRose's face that his psychological ploy was on target.

"Is there any way we can requisition an armored car?"

Sure, if you don't mind a five-finger requisition, thought Hackett. "I don't see any problem, what for?"

"Well," McRose began tentatively, "I figure we could park it right in front with no suspicion, and if the law gets the alert before we're out, we've got a bullet-proof escape vehicle that will plow through just about any roadblock they put in our way."

"Wouldn't it have to be for the same service the bank uses?"

"No, the bank employees wouldn't see it, and we can use Charlie's recon to make sure there are no other pickups or deliveries scheduled."

Hackett kept his face impassive for a few moments, then reached out and clasped McRose's shoulder, which was his equivalent of a bear hug. "I like your thinking, Sergeant. That will be reflected in your ops evaluation."

Although volunteering for the Dead List had severely limited his prospects for career advancement in the army, McRose retained an ambition to be a squad leader like Hackett. He figured he only needed this operation to get the recognition he deserved. After that day in the desert, McRose had realized Hackett was less than a total asset to the nation's fighting forces. This mission was sort of a Siberia for the major rather than the cutting edge of covert action McRose and his comrades had been led to believe.

McRose had been quietly encouraging rebellion in the ranks during the past day, but he now realized that it would be in his best interest to insulate the major from the other men, to keep the men in line and Hackett from screwing up. McRose might very well be able to present himself to Command as the man who prevented the ops from becoming a disaster.

"Major, I'd like to volunteer to take charge of coordinating supply operations for the ops. I've visualized the needs of the plan I proposed, and if you are accepting it, I believe I can assemble the physical means to make it real."

"Go for it. I'm open to any idea that will get us out of this circus ride alive." Hackett sensed strong comradely feelings for McRose among the men, even though feelings were not part of their programming. Even when things looked outrageously impossible, it felt good to know McRose was on your side. Hackett sighed quietly and for a split second allowed himself to smile. "Now we can move on to the other assignments."

The meeting began with Biddle presenting his final asessment of the bank's security system and how to circumvent it. "Video scan can be shorted out by cutting one conduit here," he said, motioning to a diagram he had drawn, "in case they have a battery backup." Biddle removed that chart and replaced it with another. "Now once the device at the main conduit detonates, that will short out the entire system —it's not tied to a backup alarm. They haven't gotten that far down here."

Biddle rolled up the diagram and handed it to Hackett, who addressed the group. "It's time to cut orders. Keep your eyes nice and sharp. And be sure to keep your radios off until it's time. One stupid beep and it's all to shit."

Atwater waited until Hackett paused for a breath before speaking up. "Not wanting to talk out of turn, Major, but I've been talking things over with the boys, and we all—"

"Knock it off, Buck!"

McRose's vehemence caught Atwater off guard. Hadn't he told him to bring his gripes to the major just that afternoon? But perhaps McRose felt the timing was wrong, so Atwater shut up. Fry grabbed the ball.

"He's saying the job stinks. Security stinks. Our objective is right across the street from the Sheriff's Station. The whole thing smells bad."

"Your orders deal with all possible contingencies, Sergeant." McRose paused to let that sink in, then added, petulantly, "Aw, Christ, Luther, act like a soldier."

"It's okay, Larry." Hackett's tone of voice said, Enough, knock it off. The major then turned to Fry. "This job is different. Maybe we had all better have a heart-to-heart. This job is different, but it's also the same. Yeah, it stinks. But they all do, Luther. When did they ever give us a nice one? We do every dirty job that our country wants done and doesn't want in the paper or on the evening news."

The major's apparent frankness prompted Atwater to resume his original line of attack. "Yes, sir, but I don't understand, sir. Sorry, I don't. Maybe I'm a candy-ass wimp, but this isn't fucking Lebanon or up in the hills in Thailand or some swamp in Honduras. This is Texas, for God's sake, home of the Astros, the Cowboys, and our main man George Bush."

"Buck, our country has asked us to do this job. We are acquiring sensitive material for the sake of national security. Ours is not to reason why. I can tell you this: the world is getting more complicated. All the bad guys aren't over there. Some of them are right here at home . . . or just across the border. Hey, I work for Command just like you do. I respect their judgment. I give them my best, and that's what I expect from you. All of you. Right?"

McRose quickly seconded him. "Right. Don't ask questions, just get it done." Atwater, incredulous, tried to catch McRose's eye, but the burly sergeant avoided looking at him. The other men all stared at one another.

After allowing a few more moments of silence, Hackett asked Fry, "You squared away now, Luther?"

Fry knew that the question was rhetorical. "Check." Atwater quickly concurred, but he gave McRose a dirty look.

Hackett focused on Biddle. "Charlie?"

"Yeah, I'm cool," he said, but was thinking they were in Dred Scott territory.

McRose and Coker quickly added their "checks."

"Good, let's get on with it. Biddle, you're stationed at home base. Atwater, you're partnered with Fry to handle underground surgery on the alarm system. Larry, you're coordinating transportation, and Coker will scout a site for the diversion, on top of his duties as auxiliary armorer. You men have done so well thus far that I think you've earned a chance to blow off some steam tonight. There will be cold beer for everybody at twenty-one hundred hours, right here." This was met with a general murmur of approval.

Jack arrived at Jeanette Pearson's at 7:00 P.M. sharp as promised, bearing a large cashier's check Jack and the deputies had chipped in for. The enclosed card instructed Jeanette to turn it over to whatever charity would best serve Hank's memory. It was also a tactful way of offering a financial stopgap if one was needed.

At the door, Jeanette and Jack held each other for as long as they could without awkwardness. Hank's and her three children, the closest of whom lived in Corpus Christi, kept a respectful distance from Jack, their spouses and children even more so. Sensing this, Jack projected a warmth he scarcely knew he was capable of, expressing Hank's frequent declarations of love and pride for each of them.

Taking over Hank's ritual of saying grace before supper, Jack quoted a line from the Book of Proverbs that Hank was especially fond of: "He that is slow to anger is better than the mighty and he that ruleth his spirit is better than he that taketh a city." To Jack that meant no matter how formidable a foe Hank ever faced, he always had an unbeatable moral advantage.

Hank's eldest, Mike, was a game warden based in Fort Collins, Colorado. The dinner-table conversation skirted the subject of Hank's demise, as there was a lot of other catching up to do, until Mike mentioned a problem he had recently encountered.

"All over the Rockies we're getting illegal-alien families living out of camping equipment. Dozens freeze to death every year when the snow hits. I know it's the only place a lot of these people have to go, but they're screwing up the ecosystem, poaching game, littering—"

Jack, who was on his third bourbon and branch water, felt compelled to interject, "And it's Hank's and my fault for letting them in?"

The remark caught Mike off guard, but he didn't back down. "It was illegals that killed my dad, wasn't it? I support the proposal for counterfeit-proof social security cards, or some other form of U.S. national ID to help us keep track of these illegals. A lot of other countries with that problem have them, and I understand they've done a lot of good."

This was something Jack had paid close attention to, even among the new immigration laws and bills that he studied diligently. Five years ago he had been intrigued by the idea of national identification cards, but too many disturbing implications cropped up for Jack to endorse it.

"In the countries like France and West Germany that have them, the key is the penalties to employers that hire illegals. This 1987 federal bill takes a step in that direction. But until I can arrest employers for taking advantage of illegals, wages and working conditions will continue to go down in some places. If I can't punish people who *hire* undocumented workers, I'm damn well not going to bust the workers themselves. Being that poor is punishment enough."

"You can make them counterfeit-proof with holograms like the ones on new credit cards," said Sue, who worked for a New Orleans bank. "That will offset discriminations if bosses are liable for hiring illegals."

Jack was about to mention the law enforcement axiom that "counterfeit-proof" is always a temporary description. But a more salient point came to mind. "Don't you realize that all those cards are going into an electronic data bank?"

"Sounds like it would be great for keeping track of criminals," said Jay, a Corpus Christi realtor.

"You trust the system a lot more than your daddy did," Jack said. "It isn't just nice people who'll get access to your financial records, personal data, urine test results, stuff like that. You all believe in mandatory urine tests?"

Nearly all of Hank's offspring and in-laws nodded their heads in agreement. Jeanette, however, did not.

"It would sure be nice if they perfected the testing method before they mass-produced it. I keep hearing about twenty and thirty percent inaccuracy rates, which seems like an awfully easy way to put a black mark on a good person's record."

The Pearson clan was uncomfortable with Jack's aggressive tone, but listened raptly as he continued with uncharacteristic passion.

"If your dad was here tonight, he would tell you not to put faith in simple solutions to complicated problems. Whether it's piss tests, English-only laws, national ID cards, or calling in the army to fight the war on drugs, none of that can substitute for standing your ground. All you can do is uphold your moral values. You can't force other people, even your own kids, to subscribe to them. But you can make your children want the same values you have."

Jack had surprised himself with the vehemence of his tirade. The lengthening silence made him more uncomfortable. Jeanette made a few game attempts to steer the conversation back onto safe ground, but there was no doubt in Jack's mind that he had overstayed his welcome.

As he stood up to leave Jack said, "I'm sorry. Hank Pearson was deeply worried that many innocent people will be hurt by the current antidrug campaign, just like the McCarthy blacklist, the Salem witch trials, or any other time leaders need scapegoats. I thought you'd want to know his opinions, but I guess this isn't the proper time or place. I share your grief over Hank's death, and I hope I haven't offended you."

As he took his leave Jack saw from the adults' expressions that he had not made them angry. Despite everyone's urgings, he felt a powerful desire to go home and ponder the question of whether killing Cash would be just what he had condemned: a simple solution to a complex problem.

21

Buck Atwater probed a cluster of wires he had exposed by dismantling a section of pipe and jumped back when one jab with his screwdriver resulted in a shower of sparks. Luther Fry turned his flashlight on Atwater to make sure he was all right. The two soldiers were inside a utility conduit, ten feet under a side street just around the corner from the City Bank of Benrey.

Fry clicked his tongue when he saw what Atwater had done. "Not listening to me again, Buck? I told you that could be hazardous to your ass."

"I thought you said these were all phone lines. Or is this another one of your 'accidentally on purpose' shots at me?"

"Don't be so paranoid, Buck. Okay, now look here." Fry turned his flashlight on the wire cluster that had thrown sparks. "You pop these covers," he said, indicating the metal plates that were bolted over the pipe, "and it releases the pressure gauge on the line and tells them where to come and make a repair. But if you crimp back the line, that maintains the pressure. Then you cut, and they have no idea where the phone line went bad."

Suddenly Atwater started flailing when a large rat jumped off a pipe and ran down his back. He swiftly whipped out a survival knife and skewered the rodent. Atwater watched with vindictive pleasure as the rat wiggled its final moments away impaled on the blade.

Scorning Atwater's panicked reaction, Fry said in an instructional tone, "I'll tell you about rats. For rats you want Managua, you'll get great ones, two and three pounders down in the sewers. Now, pay attention. We could cut here," he continued, wrapping the jaws of his bolt cutter around a thick gray wire, "and electrocute us both to death, which I don't favor, or we could try over here, which would leave the bank with no alarm system . . ."

Twenty minutes later Fry and Atwater were finished, and drove the blue Lancer back to the Yellow Rose Motel, where both were looking forward to kicking back and drinking a few beers. On the way there they passed a black stretch limousine with smoked-glass windows, which the two men would be surprised to learn contained Cash Bailey himself.

The limo, with Monday at the wheel and Lupo by his side, turned down a narrow street in a poor neighborhood, once ethnically mixed but now almost exclusively Latino. By reading the graffiti spray-painted on virtually every available surface, Lupo could tell which gangs were increasing their turf and which were getting beaten back. But the cryptic symbols and Spanish phrases were nothing to Cash or Monday but a disquieting reminder that they were not among friends and had left much of their security back in Mexico.

No sooner had the limousine parked in front of a five-story tenement building when several teenage kids gathered around it. They looked none too friendly, impressed as they were by the car. At the sight of Monday emerging and scowling at them, the kids backed off. They called themselves *los olvidados*—"the forgotten ones"—but their prudent reaction to Monday showed they weren't quite ready to face their ultimate reward yet.

When a path was cleared to the back steps of the tenement, Monday opened the back door for Cash, who got out carrying a bouquet of roses. He was uncharacteristically clean-shaven, and by some miracle of the dry cleaners' craft, his white linen suit was virtually spotless. Cash had even made an effort to sober up for the occasion, but his hands trembled at the prospect of enjoying the liquid and powdered treats the limo bar was stocked with during the long ride home.

Cash walked up the birdlime-encrusted metal back stairway, actually a fire escape, listening cautiously as he ascended to the fourth floor. He heard the typical sounds of people living in crowded quarters: kids yelling, men and women screaming at each other, but a lot of laughter too. Cash could also hear ten or more different recordings of Mexican songs coming at him from different directions. The air was heavy with cooking odors.

It was with some relief that Cash reached the entrance to Doña Isavel Cisneros' apartment, where his contacts had told him Sarita was staying. There was freshly washed laundry hanging just outside, and when Cash walked in without knocking, he saw Doña Isavel stirring clothes packed into a washtub that was steaming on top of an ancient gas stove. Sarita had taken her mother to laundromats several times to show her how much easier the job could be, but ultimately realized that tradition meant more to Doña Isavel than convenience.

Cash slipped on his most charming grin and called her by name, which prompted the wizened but dignified old woman to flash him a gap-toothed smile. Cash only needed two long strides to get through the kitchen to

Sarita's room, pausing to give her mother an affection-
ate pat. The door was slightly ajar, and again Cash
entered without knocking. But he did not feel the
surprise he had anticipated, as Sarita was sitting at the
window, watching the waiting limousine. She turned to
him and said, flatly, "Cash Bailey. It's been a long
time."

The room was as austere as a nun's cell. A pair of
shelves were lined with toys from Sarita's childhood,
and delicate religious icons—candle holders, crucifixes,
and a china figurine of the Madonna and Christ child.
The only furniture was a single bed, chair, and a
nightstand that had a soft-playing radio on it, which
Sarita shut off.

Sarita had become devoted to the Catholic faith
when she was a teenager. Neither of her parents were
churchgoers. Sarita had been inspired by an interfaith
group that was organized by the local Roman Catholic
diocese. It had been the first Benrey community effort
to help the disenfranchised who lived in the *colonias*.
The group had made some charity handouts, but most
of its work was educational, teaching Sarita and José
about rights they hadn't known were theirs as native-
born Americans.

They also helped with English lessons that enabled
them to attend better schools, and job training, but
Sarita cherished the Bible studies most. The nonde-
nominational instructors had not espoused the Christi-
anity of intolerance and exclusion like the gringo TV
preachers she had seen, but one in which sins were
forgiven and all humans were equal in the eyes of God.

Sarita's thoughts in the last day had wrestled with the
irony of a peace-loving woman like herself having two
killers as the most important men in her life. She did
not let the Church dictate her personal life, believing
that birth control was less of a sin than bringing

unwanted children into the world, having seen enough of them. But perhaps, she mused, Jack and Cash's true natures having been revealed to her, there was a more important reason not to bear their children. However, Sarita could not deny the love she still felt for both men.

"Too long, darling, way too long," was Cash's reply to her muted greeting.

"Why are you here?" Sarita asked him.

Cash thrust the flowers at her, as if they ought to explain it all. "Well, why not? You're still pretty as a picture, and I'm still single. It's no fun having all your dreams come true if you don't have somebody to share the spoils with."

Sarita wryly recalled that Cash had never been too demonstrative, and she tried to change the subject. "From what I hear, this isn't a good time for you to be on this side of the Rio Grande, no?"

"Yeah. So let's *andale.*"

At least he wasn't beating around the bush, Sarita thought. "Where to?" she asked, ready to object, whatever Cash proposed.

"I've got a place in Mexico," Cash began, "up in the mountains, way back in the middle of nowhere. Real fine, probably hasn't changed much in fifty or sixty years."

"Sorry, but I'm fond of running water." Sarita glanced around the cheap apartment. It hadn't changed much in the last half century either, but at least it had everything a person needed to live cleanly.

"Hell, I've got wells, pumps, generators. Even a satellite dish. I've got room for a twenty-four-track recording studio if you want. I have servants and bodyguards and even people growing my food. And by God, they treat old Cash like a king."

Sarita shook her head, saying, "You want a prisoner,

a plaything to keep inside the fortress you built with drug money."

Cash opened up his jacket to show that he wasn't carrying a gun—unless you counted the .22 Ruger automatic loaded with hollow points that he kept in his hand-tooled boot. "I've decided to retire, darling. It will be different this time. I came here tonight to get you for keeps. What made me decide was seeing Jack again the other day; it brought back all those good memories. You're the best woman I've ever known, and the way I treated you before wasn't right. I've been a sick man for a long time, but I've finally figured out a cure, and that is spending the rest of my life with you."

Was he serious, Sarita wondered, or just horny? "I was so good you dropped me where your amigo could pick me up," she said, her voice oozing sarcasm.

"I wanted to keep you out of danger," insisted Cash, putting his arms around her. "You were too good for the place I was headed. But I've been waiting all these years to earn a nest egg, make a place where we can both start over. Where you'll be free to come and go as you like. I always knew I'd have to change my ways before you would be my woman again."

Cash had lied to Sarita enough times in the past that she was skeptical, but she wanted to believe him.

"How long will you call me *amor* this time before you get bored? How long, Cash?" Sarita was startled at how good his touch felt, yet she was compelled as if by survival instinct to try to drive him away.

Cash's face became strained and angry as he tightened his grip on her shoulders. "When I was a little kid in my old man's cotton patch, I'd stand there in the goddamn furrows, blisters all over my hands, knowing I couldn't chop enough cotton to keep us from being dirt poor no matter how hard I worked. Whenever we'd get a little bit ahead, my daddy would blow his seed money at the Del Rio horse track, or my mama would decide to spend two weeks in bed. She got so sick of being an impoverished sharecropper that she blew her head off with my shotgun.

"When that happened, I vowed that if I ever found a woman worth having, I'd buy her everything she needed to be happy, and never turn her loose. And I'd never let anybody take her away from old Cash. I'm crazy about you, Sarita, and I have been for most of my life."

The only argument Sarita had left was, "I still love Jack. You've got to know that." Cash backed away and appraised her silently for a moment. She seemed to be wavering. "But he can't love me. Maybe because of you. You were with me first . . . he can't get over that, because of his damn macho pride. It hurts him as an hombre. I think maybe, deep down inside, he wants to love me, but you . . . I think maybe you only love Cash Bailey."

Cash realized that he was getting through to her and bore down for the kill. "Would I come to this side of the river, and maybe get my *cajones* blown off, if I wasn't desperate for another chance?"

Grasping for a way to justify to herself the decision she was about to make, Sarita told herself that if Cash was serious about giving up his outlaw career for her, leaving might be the best possible thing she could do to help Jack.

"Like my mother says, '*Usaremos lo que dios nos dió.*' A girl has to work with what she's got. Maybe I belong in Mexico; I should go there and try to forget about Jack. Can you give me some time down there, before we be lovers again, so I can get my head clear?"

"Anything you say, sweetheart." It took Sarita just a few minutes to pack a bag for the trip to Mexico. Cash used the time to persuade Doña Isavel that her daughter had chosen the best possible course of action, primarily by handing her a large roll of bank notes. Tellingly, Sarita left her flowers behind.

22

The full moon gave Jack a well-lit view of the surrounding hills as he drove home. The huge shadows they cast made him feel very small, and an eerie absence of cars underscored his isolation. There were a few houses lighted and visible in the distance. All owned by family men, Jack reflected, who would be leaving something behind when they died. At dinner that night he could see Hank living in all of his progeny, and that Hank's grandchildren would grow up rightfully proud of him.

Jack gave himself a rare license to visualize what it would be like to be married to Sarita and finally get his house finished. He initially imagined smelly diapers and losing what little privacy he had left. But his thoughts progressed to the upside, the joys of family life, and the realization that he still had some growing up to do. Most of the people his age had only become truly adult after their children were born. But Jack deplored the way a lot of them raised their kids, neglecting them almost criminally. But like Hank had said, setting a good example was the best influence Jack could hope to have.

While he usually jerked his mental leash whenever such thoughts progressed too far, Jack was only forced off the subject this time by a call on the radio from headquarters. Deputy Cotton reported that Mrs. Enid Walker, the tough young widow who ran the Yellow Rose Motel, was suspicious of some of her guests, had seen them packing guns, and now they were disturbing the peace, and her guests. Jack was less than a mile from home and figured you had to accept some partying on a full-moon Friday. But when Cotton mentioned that Mrs. Walker thought she had seen a machine gun, Jack decided to drive the six miles to the Yellow Rose.

One of the things the Dead List men liked least about their current assignment was being robbed of the opportunity to drink in bars. Together and individually they had caroused in most of the world's major fleshpots, where money was so scarce that parents would coerce their daughters into prostitution. Whether it was in Asia, Africa, or Latin America, women for hire were so plentiful the commandos had always made a point of seeking out the ones who were most adept at pretending they enjoyed themselves.

But in Benrey, Hackett had kept his men under a strict curfew, requiring them to be in their motel rooms after dark unless they had a specific assignment. Fraternization with the locals was strictly forbidden, as was any drinking or doping. Atwater had joked with his cohorts about saying to Hackett, "Sir, requesting permission to beat my meat," but hadn't the spunk to ask the major to his face.

McRose had a scare that afternoon when he ate lunch in a coffee shop and saw a girl who looked much like the fiancée he had broken up with by signing up for the Dead List. He bolted the first time her back was turned, leaving behind most of a meal he had relished as a break from the takeout food Hackett brought to the motel. He watched from concealment until the girl left, and saw the resemblance was not that strong. He later mused that his mistake might have been caused by the guilt he was running away from.

For Friday night Hackett had called an unexpected moratorium on the squad discipline he'd been rigorously maintaining, and the men were taking every advantage of it. Biddle rigged up a "boom box" that blasted a party tape of the 1969 Da Nang hit parade. Fry was strumming a guitar, and over Creedence Clearwater Revival he sang a mock-gospel song of his own devising:

> "I put Jesus in my heart
> When I didn't have no hope
> When I didn't have no shoes
> And I couldn't get no dope
> When I couldn't find a woman
> And I didn't have a dog
> I put Jesus in my heart
> Just to get me goin' whole hog."

Bob Dylan's "All Along the Watchtower" as performed by Jimi Hendrix came on the tape, and Fry was shouted down. The group was partying in the middle room to avoid disturbing the neighbors, but the men were so loud the people in the room below started banging on their ceiling. Hackett motioned for the men to quiet down, but the noise level soon came back up.

Hackett was devoting most of his attention to McRose, aware that the other men now felt less comfortable hanging loose with him. McRose was grilling Hackett about his background, curious as to how he had chosen his particular path.

"I signed up for covert ops after something that happened to me in Nam. The only reason I'm alive today is because of a sergeant named Joey Fisher. We were ordered to follow this guy who was supposed to lead us to a VC arms cache. It was afternoon, and I was sweating so much it felt like I was taking a bath. The jungle practically gave you the shits it was so quiet. We went with the slope for about half a mile, and I sort of dropped back for no reason, leaving Joey walking point. Suddenly he tripped a wire, I guess. Hell broke loose. It was like grenades in the trees, our own claymores all over the ground. I hit the dirt, and from there I saw Joey just get blown apart. Then our sonofabitch guide turned around and laughed. I emptied my M-16 into him. I watched the bullets jerk him around on the ground until he was hamburger."

"Well, I guess I've heard my share of those kinds of stories," said McRose. "None of them have happy endings."

Hackett shrugged. "I'm here, aren't I? I've got a cold beer. Anyway, after that day, I decided that I wasn't going to let any more rear-echelon assholes make mistakes that could put me in a body bag. On one level the duty got more hazardous, and yet I always felt safer because I was calling the plays."

"What about now?"

"I'm still calling them. I just don't get to pick the opposing team." Hackett glanced around the room, as if to show McRose that leadership entailed having all the men who serve under you on your conscience.

It did Hackett's soul some good seeing the men enjoying themselves, knowing that thanks to him, it might be the last time they celebrated anything. If what he needed from the bank turned out not to be there, Hackett would have to commit the group to a "black ops." In military jargon there were two essential definitions of the phrase. First, it referred to a tactical operation devoted to spilling enemy blood through means that most would consider dishonorable. Second, it meant a virtual suicide mission. To achieve the end required by Hackett, both definitions would probably apply.

Coker was talking to Biddle about his infatuation with a girl whose father had taken her with him to Bear's store. She was obviously bored witless by all the gun-nut blather, and had used the time to flirt with him. Coker had gotten her phone number, but had not dared to use it, and asked Biddle what he thought the right course of action would be.

"Cheerleader type, huh?"

"Yeah, kind of an airhead but great upholstery. She really seemed interested, but I'm sure the major would blow his stack if I tried to do anything about it."

"No question, it could jeopardize the ops. But save the number. Call her long-distance from the next garden spot you're assigned to, offer to fly her down for a weekend."

Coker smiled lecherously at the prospect. "I like your strategy, Charlie. Very suave and debonair. You ever done that yourself?"

"Once or twice. But I've grown kind of fond of third-world nookie. Those ladies know what it's for."

"More your size too, I guess. So why did a righteous dude like you sign up for the Dead List?"

Biddle appraised Coker, who had probably gone through a six-pack already. It really wasn't any of his damn business, but . . . "This may sound dumb, but I never bought the explanation that that James Earl Ray peckerhead killed Martin Luther King all by himself. That trial seemed awfully fast, like they wanted to get it over with before somebody stumbled onto the truth. I figured that somebody was behind Ray, and this seemed like my best chance at finding out who."

"So what did you learn?"

"That if my hunch was right, the motherfuckers got away clean, and if another Dr. King comes along, they'll probably get him too."

Fry was picking his guitar again, this time doing a takeoff on the familiar armed forces TV and radio jingle:

> "Bleed, all that you can bleed,
> Find your sutures, in the arrrrrrmeeee."

The thumping on the floor was heard again, and Coker shouted down at the source, "Blow it out your shorts!" Hackett gestured admonishingly to the youngest member of his team. The major realized that the law might pay them a visit and began mentally devising smoke screens in case that should happen.

Biddle grabbed the empty ice bucket and was headed downstairs to fill it when he saw Jack's cruiser pull into the Yellow Rose Motel parking lot. "Shit in hell!" he hissed.

"What's happening?" asked Hackett as he poked his head through the door.

"John Fucking Wayne, Junior," said McRose, right behind him.

The men sobered up in a hurry. Mrs. Walker, a handsome woman in her midforties, was waiting for Jack in the doorway of the manager's office. Jack walked over to her but zeroed in on the men standing on the second-floor balcony. They were backlit, so that Jack couldn't see their faces. Mrs. Walker immediately told Jack why she had called the Sheriff's Station.

"I saw at least two of them carrying guns. And the others were acting really suspicious, lugging big bags—"

"How many are there?" Jack asked.

"Six: four white, two colored. They've got three rooms. They're some kind of gang, I'm sure."

After some fast thinking, Hackett decided that the best course of action would be to identify himself.

"Hey, Jack!" Hackett called down. "How you doing, Benteen?"

"Ralston?" Jack squinted, wondering why the man standing closest to Hackett looked so familiar.

"Hey, the D.E.A. gang is all here, come on up and meet the guys, get stoned." Hackett guessed correctly that Jack would have no inclination to.

Jack turned back to Mrs. Walker. "Are these the people you're talking about?" When she nodded, he offered a reassuring smile. "Those are federal authorities," Jack intoned with mock reverence, "here to fight crime, Mrs. Walker."

"They are?"

"Yes, ma'am. Under normal circumstances they sleep all day and party all night," Jack said with a wink. She relaxed a bit, and he noticed her three children peeking through the office window as he continued. "They can be distinguished from the common criminal by the fact that they do no work at all, even by mistake. But if they do act up any, like throwing chairs or molesting your female guests, you let me know."

Jack and Mrs. Walker shared a good laugh, and by the time he looked up again the men had all gone inside and quieted down. McRose watched Jack walk back to his car from between the curtains of the middle-room window, muttering, "I always did hate cops."

"What's wrong with cops?" Fry asked him.

"Once one hit me."

"Then what happened?"

McRose was deadpan. "He died."

"You snuffed a cop?" Fry wasn't sure whether to be impressed or intimidated by this.

"His mother-in-law backed over him by mistake. In her LTD. Which is why I like Fords."

Fry laughed heartily at this, and soon the drinking, talking, and music were resumed, but more quietly.

Outside, Jack was just getting ready to fire up his engine when he saw a blue sedan hop the curb and lurch erratically into the motel parking lot. It would have been an easy DUI bust, but Jack just wanted to make sure the driver had reached his final destination for the evening. He was unpleasantly surprised to see Buck "Schoonover" Atwater stagger out of the driver's seat, toting a case of beer. On his way to the stairwell Atwater encountered a little boy of six or seven, who seemed proud to have been given the job of filling an ice bucket for his parents.

"Crazy world, I'm telling you," Atwater said, a drunken slur on top of his regular one. "If I was a kid like you, I'd be confused. Are you confused, son?"

The little boy shook his head, showing his nausea at Atwater's rancid breath.

"Well, then you're an asshole." Atwater sneered at him, then walked up the stairs to the rooms where his thirsty comrades were waiting for him.

Jack was baffled by the possibilities this presented. He supposed it was possible that Atwater could be a D.E.A. agent, though it would seem more likely he was an informant. But that made him remember the man standing next to Hackett/Ralston as the man with Atwater in Clarence King's yard, the man who subsequently bailed Atwater out. Jack made a note to call the D.E.A. on Monday and see what more he could learn about this strange operation.

23

As their limousine sped toward the Mexican border Cash and Sarita ran out of small talk in less than an hour. Cash's charm evaporated with each shot of tequila and pretty much dried out after he pulled out a vial of cocaine and tried to force Sarita to snort some with him.

"Cash, I don't want to be with you when you are doing that shit!" she had exclaimed, and demanded that he take her back to Benrey.

"That just ain't in the cards, darling. You needed some time to think, right? Well, you're going to get some."

"I've changed my mind. Tell your driver to turn the car around!"

"Women are prone to doing that, m'love, so I'm assuming that I heard you right the first time." Cash tried to put his arms around Sarita, who then grabbed for the door handle, even though jumping out of the limo at its current speed would be suicide. Monday flipped a switch that made it impossible for passengers to unlock their doors. Lupo leaned over the front seat, ready to restrain her further if necessary.

"I need to make some sort of arrangement with Jack, and I do believe a week of your time is all it will take to convince him. Hell, it's fiesta time in San Luis, and when was the last time Jack took you to one of those?" Cash smiled at her, very pleased with himself.

Sarita was mortified as Cash dropped all pretense of being the earnest suitor willing to mend his wicked ways for her love. It had all been pure manipulation. She now could see that the man who had broken her heart was no more.

Cash's mind had disintegrated into something subhuman, each of his flaws magnified to an evil perversity. If he wanted to use her as bait, why hadn't he just kidnapped her instead of pulling that cruel charade? Sarita knew she would have to escape to save both herself and Jack, but there was no hope of that until the limousine reached its destination. She said nothing for the remainder of the journey.

Jack was surprised when Sarita failed to show up for Hank's funeral the next morning. Just about everyone else Jack knew in Benrey showed up, even Bear, whom Jack had never seen in a coat and tie before. Jack stood beside Jeanette in front of the casket, which was draped with the Texas flag, and fruitlessly scanned the crowd of mourners looking for Sarita.

When his eyes failed to locate her, they settled on the flag itself, the Texas lone star set in a blue triangle, the inward-facing point of which divided the red and white sections of the flag. The white stood for the sky, the red for the blood-soaked ground over which secession from Mexico was fought. Jack could appreciate how well it fit into the tradition Hank was so proud of.

As the honey-voiced choir mistress of Hank's church sang "What a Friend We Have in Jesus," Jack revisited the unfamiliar places his mind had taken him to the previous night. He had pretty much decided to ask

Sarita to marry him, and nothing he thought about threatened to change his mind. Imagining his own funeral, and what a sparse crowd it would attract, Jack adjusted further to the idea of leaving survivors behind him.

But he also realized that marrying Sarita would make them a separate unit from the community at large. They would bridge the Anglo and Latino enclaves, create something new. Only by devoting the time he had left to a future generation could Jack hope to repay the gift of his own life, he concluded, as the hymn did likewise.

Mayor Corliss delivered the eulogy with all the eloquence he could muster. "Hank Pearson was sheriff of Benrey County for twenty-three years. He was honest and tried to do the right thing. Tried to uphold the law even if it meant bending it a little bit. We can all be grateful for Hank's ability to think on his feet, and the lengths he would go to protect us all. He had courage, he had heart, and he died doing his duty, which is the way he would have wanted it. We'll miss him. It won't be the same in old Benrey without Hank."

The resulting sobs and sniffles were momentarily drowned out by three volleys fired with .357 maghum revolvers by six of Hank's deputies.

Hank's preacher, Reverend Hunter, then took the dais, and intoned, "Greater love hath no man than this, that he laid down his life for another. May the eternal soul of Sheriff Hank Pearson rest in peace . . . in the name of our lord Jesus Christ . . . Amen."

The cemetery was located on a hillside with sparse vegetation, and as a bugler played taps to accompany the lowering of Hank's coffin into the ground, a cloud of sand and dust was suddenly kicked up by the wind. A moment before, Jack had folded up the flag that had been draped over the casket and handed it to Jeanette.

She held it to her face, perhaps to shield her eyes and nose from the particles in the air. Jack reflected that the dust storm might be a communiqué from the Fates themselves to express their indignation over the wrongness of Hank's death.

Jack stayed at graveside with Jeanette and the rest of Hank's immediate family until after the sheriff's honor guard and the rest of the mourners had left. After giving Jeanette a tender embrace, he put his hat back on and walked by himself back to his car.

Most of the commandos woke up with hangovers, so Hackett gave them some extra sack time to compensate. After the encounter with Jack the previous night, the major decided it was time for his men to bivouac elsewhere. He had scouted a wooded area about ten miles out of town that would be an ideal place for them to lie low until D-day, about thirty-six hours from then. Living off the land would undoubtedly bring back memories of boot camp for the soldiers and the unquestioning obedience that had been drilled into them at that time. And that suited Major Hackett's purposes just fine, as the next few days would test their respect for his leadership as never before.

The limousine arrived in San Luis shortly before noon as the village began to swelter under the full force of the day's heat. Sarita was surprised at how, despite this, the surroundings were lush and green, thanks to the many oak trees and assorted scrub brush that dotted the landscape. The streets were being set up for a coming fiesta, and Sarita allowed herself to forget her desperate situation for a moment and nostalgically absorb the scene.

As colorful streamers were being hung above them vendors set up their food carts and laid out the handcrafted items they were selling. There were clay piggy banks, woven wool mats, candles, straw fans, toys, hats, bird cages, a miniature wooden ferris wheel. Posters advertising bullfights, boxing matches, and Atlas cigarettes were everywhere. Food sellers set out flat metal warming dishes, jars of pasta and spices, cases of Wink, Orange Crush, and the ubiquitous Coca-Colas. A snow-cone stand was being set up with ten different flavors of syrup for its ices. The whole scene gave Sarita a warm feeling for her native culture.

But she shook with fear as the limousine turned at a rusting Pemex station and passed a small graveyard on the way up the hill to the Hotel Isabella. When Lupo parked behind the hotel, Sarita thought of making a run for it, but he and Monday flanked her, making this impossible. Cash led them into the cantina, which was even more crowded than usual, its air foul with stale tobacco smoke. Sacks of grain and boxes of ammunition stacked in the corners added to the anarchic feeling of the place. Rosa, who oversaw the prostitution side of Cash's business, had imported extra girls for the fiesta, and thus was annoyed when Cash told her to put aside a room for Sarita.

"We'll even put in a few rosaries and crosses, make you think you're back at home," Cash promised her, but at this point the only thing Sarita was grateful to Cash for was the proprietary sway he held over her. This prompted the many sweaty, unwashed men ogling her to keep their distance.

The band ended its up-tempo mariachi number and went into a gushy love song. Cash asked Sarita to dance with him but she refused, asking to be taken to her room. As Rosa led her under the stone arches toward the stairwell Sarita was appalled at the number of machine guns being brandished, cringing at the thought of what would happen if one went off in such a densely populated place.

As they watched Sarita go up the stairs Cash nudged

Lupo and said, "Just you wait, amigo. She'll get used to this place in a few days and take old Cash for the girly ride of his life." Lupo nodded in agreement, not daring to voice his own desire to go for a girly ride on that particular señorita himself.

Rosa led Sarita to a room at the end of the second-story hallway. After assuring her that somebody would be by soon to change the mattress, Rosa left and locked the door behind her. There was a window, but nothing safe to climb down on anywhere near it. Sarita figured that if she was lucky she'd be able to sneak out in the confusion of the fiesta. In the meantime, she decided that she could do some playacting of her own, give Cash a taste of his own medicine. But for the moment, all she could do was ponder her future, just as Cash had suggested.

Jack spent the rest of the day overseeing the boxing up of Hank's office belongings and combing his under-world contacts for any clues to the killer of Chub and Ricardo. Either nobody knew or the culprit had intimidated the informer types into remaining silent. Jack was on his way out the door when he received an anguished phone call from Bear.

"I've been robbed! Kenner must have used his keys and done it, there's no sign of a break-in."

"What was taken?"

"An Ingram MAC-10, a Steyr Aug, pump shotgun, a few pistols. But what really pisses me off, he took my cellophane-wrapped copy of the Madonna issue of *Penthouse*."

After he got the other pertinent details from Bear, it occurred to Jack that one of the men he'd seen at the motel the previous night bore a distinct resemblance to Kenner. He ordered all available units to converge on the Yellow Rose Motel. But the six men had checked out before the troopers arrived.

Jack found himself red-facedly congratulating Mrs. Walker on her intuition after confirming that a man with the same description as Kenner had been among Ralston's group. Jack put out an APB, then disgustedly went home for the night.

When dawn broke over the hills of Benrey the next day, Hackett was already up, finishing his notes for the ops orders. Biddle had stayed in town, sleeping in the West-Tex truck, and the other men had slept under the stars. By midday he would have the other four men split into two teams, each heading for a different destination. The more he thought about it, the more convinced Hackett was that following the bank job, no matter what he found, black ops was the next step.

24

The hydrogen truck was a luck deal. Coker and Atwater were cruising for anything that would burn. They passed through a truck stop about twenty miles east, but there wasn't a gasoline or diesel truck to be seen. Produce and livestock were all they could find, so they headed back to Benrey. When Buck spotted the hydrogen truck outside Big Mama's Roadside Ribs, he lit up like a torch. Coker tried to talk him out of it, but there was no getting around the fact that this was perfect, better than they could have hoped for. The hydrogen would ignite like the Hindenburg all over again. The truck's reinforced steel tank was several tons of potential shrapnel. Atwater reasoned that since what they wanted was just a big fireworks show, the hydrogen would do as good a job as they could ask for: it would make lots of noise, leave very little evidence, and attract plenty of attention.

Once Coker was convinced, Atwater just went about his business and Coker left him to it. After all, he didn't really care what the medium was. Elements and molecules were all the same to him. He had a job to do and

Atwater's own job was part of it. Taking the truck itself was cake: one of several master keys conveniently opened the door and another turned in the ignition. The driver was inside the restaurant and didn't notice the truck leaving without him. Coker, whose special abilities included driving anything that moved, throttled the thing to the floor, pushed the levers through all thirteen gears. The satisfying diesel roar thumped through him as he sped away from the scene of the crime. Atwater followed close behind, victoriously whooping to himself behind the wheel of the blue Lancer, contemplating the success of the operation, burning off nervous energy. He pulled out a bootleg tape of Kinky Friedman's "Asshole from El Paso" and cranked it. They didn't have much time, but they had enough.

Coker pulled the Peterbilt to a halt about a quarter mile from an abandoned warehouse. Atwater stopped behind him, then got out with a briefcase in hand. He looked incongruous: his dirty jeans and ripped T-shirt didn't really belong with the black anodized aluminum attaché. Coker's tractor was hauling a fat trapezoidal tanker filled to the brim with pressurized liquid hydrogen, the simplest element and the one most ready to combine with oxygen for a fiery good time if given half a chance.

Atwater's mind was ticking like the clock that drove the ignition timer. Or humming was more like it —digital devices didn't tick, they just silently counted at high speed. When the number got high enough —BOOM! Buck was running the event down in his mind as he popped open the case that held the six spiders nestled three on each side of the central console. Spiders, as in spider bombs. Cute as hell, six to a pack, each one a baby still slaved to the central control like nursing pups to a bitch. Atwater grinned, running his fingers over the push buttons. To Buck there was an incredible beauty to the machinery of death, an elegance that more mundane machines like cars or planes could never match.

Atwater skittered along under the hydrogen tanker, sticking the magnetic clips to the heavy channeled steel frame. Each spider neatly clicked against the metal, clung upside down, its LEDs winking "Blow me" to Atwater as he activated the timers, setting them for half a second apart. He chomped on his greasy panatela, ignoring the smoke stinging his eyes. He was mad in a regulation sort of way. The army liked his type of crazy. And for Atwater's type, the army was the only place you could draw a regular paycheck for doing what you did best.

For Atwater, this was heaven on earth. As he set the bombs, getting ready for them to blow, the any-minute-I-can-be-blown-to-kingdom-come excitement made him feel alive down to his fingertips, which were now stroking the remote control. A good explosion was the next best thing to the Big Bang, an event for which Atwater had an inordinate fondness. He had his own theory about it too: maybe the universe was formed in the nexus of the biggest explosion anyone ever heard of and maybe not. But if you really wanted to find out, you'd have to hook up all the nuclear warheads you could find with all the conventional explosives on the planet. With any luck you could duplicate the conditions that originated the whole mess. In effect you would be pushing the reset button for the human race and the planet. And if it didn't work out, you could try it again in a few billion years. Atwater chuckled happily to himself as the last bomb went into place. He clicked the remote control a couple of times and the bombs flashed the acknowledge signal: they were armed and ready to go at the touch of a fire button on Atwater's hand-held remote. At the last minute he decided to forgo the timers and use the manual trigger in case anything went wrong and Coker couldn't get clear in time.

He turned to Coker who waited calmly beside the cab. Coker knew Atwater was a mad genius with anything that went bang. He trusted Buck completely. He had to, because now he was going to drive a time bomb: ten thousand gallons of liquid hydrogen on a short fuse.

Atwater rolled along behind him in the Lancer for about half the distance to the warehouse, then he slammed on the brakes. Coker let the truck run half again that distance. It was only an eighth of a mile to ground zero. He stomped down the throttle, set the cruise control, then pushed open the door and rolled out and away from the truck. As quickly as he could, he jumped up and hotfooted toward the Lancer, which looked like it was light-years away, though it was advancing rapidly on him.

The Peterbilt kept on churning toward the sheet-metal walls, as inevitable as death. The urgent padding of Coker's feet churned up the dust behind him. Coker leaned back trying to pour on the speed. Atwater watched him coming, watched the truck moving away. He slammed on his brakes and stuck the remote trigger out the window. Just before the truck got to the building, he pressed the button.

The truck hit the vast barnlike warehouse, tore through the thin facade like scissors through paper, and was swallowed by the building. There was a crunching roar as the Peterbilt bowled down the roof posts. Coker was still running when the first spider flamed to life and the hydrogen started to burn. The explosive acceleration of the hydrogen started to tear the tank apart. Five more sequential explosions served to ignite the rapidly expanding gas evenly. It blew the roof off the building then flattened the walls. The truck was gone in a sudden roar of molten metal. The blast wave knocked Coker off his feet, but he was up and running again in a flash.

Coker tore open the left-hand door of Atwater's Lancer. "Let me drive," he grunted.

Atwater darkened. "What the hell for?"

"Come on, asshole, move over!" Coker shoved and Atwater moved over. There wasn't much time to argue and anyway who cared? Coker was a driver and Atwater was a demolitions man. Not that Atwater minded pushing a gas pedal, but Coker didn't tell Buck how to set a fuse, so Atwater figured he would let Coker drive—as a professional courtesy of course.

Coker slammed the Lancer into reverse, backed the car around. He paused for a second to watch the warehouse burn, then popped the car into drive and slammed down the gas pedal. He cleanly controlled the fishtail and pointed the rent-a-car back toward Benrey. He deliberately swerved to hit an armadillo that was crossing the road, sending it rolling like a bowling ball.

"Ever eat road kills?" Coker asked.

Atwater shook his head.

"Funny, I would have guessed you had."

Atwater flipped him the bird. The only sign that Atwater's blood was racing was the increased pace of his chewing on the cigar butt.

"I do like doing the dirty work," he confided to Coker as he settled in for the breakneck race to stay on schedule.

The West-Tex truck was parked by the courthouse square in Benrey where the hidden cameras had a good view of the city bank. Inside, Biddle was monitoring the operation's timing while Hackett studied the video monitors. The bank wasn't open yet and a number of customers were waiting for the guard to open the doors.

A beeper went off and Biddle flipped a switch to shut it up. "Package one delivered—zero-niner-five-zero," he reported. They had no actual communication from Atwater, but it was nine-fifty on their synchronized clock. Coker and Atwater had their job to do and the mission proceeded on the assumption that all phases were completed as Hackett ordered—on time.

The switchboard at the Sheriff's Station was lit up like the Milky Way on a clear night. It seemed like everybody in a five-mile radius was calling about the big explosion. Purvis finally had to ignore the board while he dispatched some cars and tried to raise Jack Benteen on the radio.

Jack was on routine patrol, doing ninety on U.S. 83. He clicked his mike in response to Purvis's call. "This is mobile one. What's all the commotion, Purvis?"

"Old storage warehouse out on Flaxton Road. Exploded and on fire."

"Who's covering it?" Jack asked.

"I scrambled Cortez out of here a few minutes ago."

"Count me in, too." Jack clicked the mike off and sped up to a hundred and twenty, flicking on his cherry lights and siren as an afterthought.

Purvis started picking up the calls again. "Deputy Purvis . . . Yes, sir, all our units are on the way . . . the Rangers too . . . Deputy Purvis here . . . if you want any more information call the fire department . . . Deputy Purvis here . . ."

Inside the West-Tex truck, the roar of the passing firetrucks and their howling sirens momentarily drowned out Purvis's voice coming over a monitor speaker: "No, ma'am! We have no report on what caused the fire! Call the hospital—they'll know if anybody is injured."

Coker had the turbo-charged Lancer nearly airborne on a rough stretch of back road as he and Atwater circled back to their rendezvous with the other commandos outside the city bank. So far they were on schedule, but it was tight.

Coker had a tight grip on the wheel, fighting its tendency to wrench away as they pounded through the rutted and potholed surface. Atwater had an equally tight grip on his door handle with one hand and the cloth of the seat beside him with the other. He was getting fed up with Coker's showboating.

"Hey, leadfoot, slow it down! You're pushing ninety!"

"Any slower, we'll never get there in time," Coker answered, keeping his eyes on the road, sideslipping to avoid the worst of the ruts.

Ahead of them, the road curved gently toward the straight paved county road that would take them back to Benrey. A turnoff was coming up. It, too, was dirt road. It was the hypotenuse of a triangle formed by it, the road they were on, and the county road. In other words, it was a shortcut across to the county highway in the direction they needed to go. Coker decided to go for it.

"Now what are you doing?" Atwater demanded. "Stick to the road!"

But it was already too late. The Lancer swung in a wide dusty arc onto the side road.

"Shortcut. I scouted it yesterday," Coker reassured Atwater, then sped up some more. "It'll give us maybe four more minutes." But Coker was overconfident.

The car hit a particularly nasty bump and all four wheels came off the ground. As it crashed back to earth the front wheels dug into the soft sand and the car spun around out of control. Coker fought to straighten it out, fishtailing side to side. But just as he got it back in hand he spotted a jagged rock sticking out of the roadway. He spun the wheel, barely avoiding the rock but sacrificing control again.

This time the car slid toward the side of the road. The dirt there was even softer than the road itself. As Coker gave the car gas to try to power-slide his way through the mess the wheels started to spin and just dug themselves right in. The car came to a sickening stop. They hadn't crashed, but they were stuck deep.

Atwater just stewed for a minute as Coker tried flipping the shifter back and forth between forward and reverse. The tires kicked up a lot of dirt, but they were trapped.

"Oh, Christ, what the hell were you thinking? How are we going to let them know we're stuck out here in the boonies? They're counting on us, baby! We gotta take that spic out!"

Coker tried the gears again. The car wasn't even rocking now. He flipped Atwater the trunk key. "Get the jack."

But Coker knew they were in trouble. An operation this tight didn't stand for mistakes. And no doubt about it, this was a mistake. A bad one. Atwater started wishing he had stuck with the timed detonation—and that it had blown a little early.

25

Inside the brown West-Tex truck, another of Biddle's timers warbled.

"Zero-niner-five-eight. Package two delivered, sir."

Package two was Fry's sabotage of the city bank's alarm system deep below the sidewalk. The system went down just like it was supposed to.

Fry stripped off his yellow slicker and hard hat, the costume he wore to fend off prying eyes and questions. Underneath, he was wearing a security service uniform. He had two minutes to be up top and around the corner to meet McRose.

Hackett watched the monitor screens, keeping a vague eye on the front doors of the bank. It was still a couple of minutes from opening for the day. Half of Hackett's mission was in place; now his main concern was precise timing. The ops depended on everyone being in place on time. Hackett was counting on it.

The monitor speakers kept crackling with Purvis's phone calls. ". . . no, sir, we have no further information, sir! Thank you for calling . . ."

Hackett signaled Biddle. "Package three."

Biddle nodded, spoke to Purvis's disembodied voice.

178

"Last phone call, Mr. Deputy." He licked his thumb and brought it down on a switch.

Purvis's switchboard flashed for a moment then stopped ringing. A moment later all the lights came on solid, without blinking. The board starting buzzing —the circuits were overloaded. Purvis clicked his receiver button as the line went dead.

"Hello, sir? Can you hear me?" he asked his caller, but the line was quiet. "Now that's strange." He tried connecting on several other lines, but the thing was jammed. He turned to Cotton. "What do you think could have happened here? One minute I was talking, the next minute nothing works."

Deputy Cotton shrugged. "Trust the phone company to screw it up."

Biddle's timer flashed 10:00. "Ten hundred hours, Major."

He and Hackett turned to the view screens. The bank guard was unlocking the doors and the customers gathered more tightly around the door.

A crowd of sightseers had jammed traffic around the Flaxton Road site. Jack was stuck behind a pickup towing a horse trailer that blocked both lanes while its driver stood on the roof and gawked at the fire. He pulled his cruiser out onto the dirt and sped across to where the sheriff cars were congregated.

The warehouse was no longer raging flame and smoke when Jack got there. The hydrogen had started a small blaze on the dry grassland nearby, which a few firemen were busy turning over with shovels. Mostly, the police and fire teams sifted through the rubble looking for clues to what had happened.

Cortez saw Jack coming. He had put together some of the pieces: A bit of a FLAMMABLE GAS sign and a logo for the hydrogen vending company as well as some half-melted fragments of zebra-striped warning reflectors. "Eighteen-wheeler hauling gas or something came busting through. The acclerator must've jammed—no way the brakes could stop it."

"Registration?" Jack asked.

Cortez shook his head. "No plates. Must've gone up in the explosion."

"How about the driver?"

"Found part of a belt buckle." Cortez smirked humorlessly at the image. "One of the Highway Patrol boys ran it over to the lab, but I can't get a report on it 'cause I can't raise the fort. We've lost touch with Purvis. No radio contact, no phones."

Jack did a double take. "I talked with Purvis not five minutes ago."

"Kinda funny," Cortez confirmed. He scratched his head.

An explosion and three-alarm fire. No plates. Phones out. Jack started stringing the pieces together, wondering how this one would tie into Cash Bailey. Nobody else at the scene was thinking much beyond the immediate business at hand, but Jack was suspicious, ready to look deep for conspiracy, certain this was more than it appeared to be. He was, in effect, right even if he was, for the most part, wrong about who and why. He quickly got back in his cruiser and headed for town, trying without success to raise Purvis along the way.

Atwater, furious and sweaty, finished jacking up the Lancer to get it partway out of its self-made ruts. He braced himself against the back and got ready to push.

"Try it, motherfucker! You got front-wheel drive and you're level."

Coker started the car and Atwater heaved and prayed, "Don't blow it this time, you asshole" to himself.

The car rocked a couple of times as Coker surged it forward, then let it slide back as it started to bog down again. Atwater heaved on each surge, relaxed on each slide. After a few tries it slowly crawled through the soft sand and out onto the firmer part of the road, popping the jack free as it went.

Atwater ignored the jack and hopped in. "Take off! We're four minutes behind schedule."

The car raced off toward the bank zone, still a couple of long, long miles away.

On the view screen in the surveillance truck, package four was just coming into frame: an armored truck with McRose at the wheel and Fry riding shotgun.

"Ten-oh-five. Package four right on time," Biddle sang out.

McRose sat for a few seconds surveying the scene. He was comfortable in the armored truck. The bullet-proof walls and glass gave him a sense of security he usually couldn't find. But he didn't know the truck was stolen. Hackett had found the thing sitting in a storage yard in El Paso. It didn't look like it had been used in more than a year. The kind of "everything is fair game" attitude that Hackett took in his operations made logistics pretty easy. The truck started right up. After that, all it took was a coin-operated car wash to pretty it up enough for his purposes.

McRose was satisfied that everything was in place. The West-Tex truck was parked where it was supposed to be, everything else looked normal. Besides, there was no contingency plan for aborting the mission—a bad idea, McRose thought. He wished there was. He pulled into the loading zone in front of the bank, shut off the engine, and pulled a stocking over his head. Fry's stocking was already in place. He had a cocked .45 in one hand and a big flight bag in the other as he headed out the door. McRose followed close behind.

Hackett, too, put a stocking over his head and pushed his nose and upper lip back with the tension of the sheer nylon, further helping to distort his appearance and giving him a vicious toothy leer. He unsheathed a stainless-steel Smith & Wesson .41 magnum and hit the sidewalk, covering Fry and McRose as they approached the bank.

McRose and Fry approached the bank calmly. Unless you looked closely at their faces, they looked like they were part of any normal delivery or pickup of bank funds. Hackett was dressed casually in khaki chinos, a black windbreaker, and loafers. All of their guns were held low beside them, keeping their presence hidden. Hackett scanned the scene for unwanted intruders who might interrupt their precision maneuvers. So far, the coast was clear.

The three masked men burst into the bank snarling, "Freeze! Hands in the air!" The bank guard, a wiry old cowboy, went for his gun, but Fry whirled and dropped the butt of his pistol on the man's skull and he went belly-up. Fry tossed the man's gun to Hackett, who slipped it into his belt.

"Any more heroes?" Hackett called out. "Then kiss the floor!" He waved his gun. "Now!" The stunned patrons slowly lay down on the floor.

"Heads down!" Fry bellowed. The people were too fascinated not to look, but most of them were too terrified not to obey.

Hackett and McRose spun toward Clarence's desk, where the bank's president was frantically jabbing the alarm button beneath his desk.

"Open the vault," Hackett told him. Clarence was still desperately pressing the button, his face blank, his mouth hanging open, his eyes wide with fear. Hackett grabbed him by the scruff of the neck and pulled him to his feet. "Alarm's cut, fatso. Now open the vault!"

Clarence felt his knees wobble underneath him as he

rose to his feet to comply. He was moving too slowly, so Hackett shoved him in back of the head with the muzzle of his Smith & Wesson, forcing him to stumble toward the vaults across the room, wincing in pain and trembling with terror.

"Move it, sucker!" Hackett kept the rage in his voice simmering neatly at the surface, giving the impression —not far wrong—of a madman with a short fuse who might lash out uncontrollably if not humored. The rabid-dog act was a typical trick in the toolbox of a robber or terrorist. Here it served the army's purposes. The people inside the bank were thoroughly cowed.

Fry was herding the tellers out from behind their windows. "Everybody out where I can see you! Move it! Move it!"

The bank employees moved stiffly but quickly and Fry pointed his gun to the floor. "Down! Get down there!"

The gun came back up. Keeping his prisoners covered, Fry easily dragged the unconscious guard out of the sight lines of the bank's glass entry doors.

Hackett shoved Clarence into the vault doors.

"Open 'em up! Come on! Hurry!"

Clarence could hardly make his fingers spin the knobs. "Don't hurt me," he pleaded.

Hackett pressed the muzzle of his revolver against the back of Clarence's jaw and whispered urgently, "Move it or die!"

Hackett's soft voice contrasted with his earlier snarling to produce greater terror in Clarence's already faint heart. He had the dual vaults open in a flash. Hackett pushed him inside the right one as McRose moved into the left.

McRose quickly jimmied open the sheet metal of the secondary security boxes where the bank's cash supply was kept. He started filling canvas moneybags with stacks of bound bills.

One of the customers, a middle-aged redneck wearing an oversized Stetson and tooled cowboy boots, couldn't resist looking up at Fry. "Hey, mister! You a tairist?" The man's thick accent muted the syllables.

Fry stared at the man. "Me?! A tear-ass?! What're you talking about? I ain't one of them mothers!"

"Well, you look like them tairists on TV," the man persisted.

Fry waved the pistol at the man. "Hit the floor, cowboy."

Hector's rusted old pickup came around the corner at precisely eight minutes after ten. When he and Merv parked across the street from the bank, they had no way of knowing that there was a robbery in progress.

Merv slicked back his hair and smoothed his suit as he got out of the truck. He pulled the suitcases out behind him.

"I'll see you in five minutes."

Hector was agitated and nervous. He didn't like coming to this gringo town with all that money and he wanted Merv to keep things short and sweet. "Five minutes only! No later!"

Merv gave him an easy grin. "Keep it down. Your *puta* will wait."

Hector was intense. "Yeah, but I can't! I've been saving it up for her all week."

From his surveillance truck, Biddle watched Merv cross the street hauling the heavy suitcases. Biddle smiled and spoke aloud to nobody. "Right on time, my good man. That leaves your partner sitting there waiting to get a forty-five shoved down his tonsils by Mr. Buck Atwater." He started the truck and pulled around the corner to get in position for the getaway run.

Merv pushed open the bank door. He was inside by the time he realized that there were people all over the floor. He didn't see Fry standing to one side against the wall until he turned to leave and Fry clipped him hard with the butt of the gun. Merv dropped the suitcases and fell backward.

"Stay down! Get over there!" Fry shouted, and angrily forced Merv toward the rest of the prisoners. "Crawl! Doggie style!"

Inside the right vault, Hackett pinned Clarence against the wall. "Open Cash Bailey's box."

Clarence shrank away. "I don't know what you're talking about. Honest!"

Hackett shoved the barrel of his pistol in Clarence's mouth until Clarence gagged. Then he pulled back the hammer. "You and Bailey are in it together. I know you've got a key. You can keep your brains in your head or in the safe-deposit box behind you. Your choice."

Clarence slowly pulled out a keychain. Hackett let him go to open one of the boxes. He unlocked the door and slid out the box.

"Open it!" Hackett directed.

Clarence fumbled the lid open, showed Hackett the contents. The terror of his immediate predicament forestalled the impending terror of telling Cash Bailey that things weren't going so well. Inside the box were three small black ledgers stacked on top of several fat bundles of hundred-dollar bills.

"Let's have it."

Hackett held out his hand for the box. As Clarence passed it to him Hackett lashed out with the gun and smashed Clarence across the face. The blow laid open a huge gash and Clarence passed out cold and bloody.

"Much obliged," Hackett remarked as he unlocked the box he had rented and stuffed the ledgers inside.

In the vault next door, McRose was still filling the canvas sacks. There was so much cash they would have to make a couple of trips to haul it to the armored truck. So much cash that taking more seemed meaningless, but McRose kept shoveling the stuff into the bags and Hackett helped. Okay, so the money was part of their cover—a bank robbery pure and simple, no funny stuff about government intrigue, official secrets. But McRose kept wondering what the government was going to do with the money. Put it into the general fund? Allot it to the Defense Department? Give the commandos a raise? Probably stash it for secret operations that didn't have congressionally approved financing, he decided.

Outside, Hector was antsy. He knew that Merv was taking his pretty time about things, playing big shot with the banker. But there wasn't much he could do about it, so he just chafed and waited, watching the armed guards hauling bags out to the armored truck parked in front of the bank.

McRose and Hackett hauled the first load and came back for the second while Fry stood guard. But when they grabbed the other bags, Hackett signaled Fry to pick up Merv's suitcases and head outside.

Hector had felt a little funny about those guards. Their faces were weird or . . . something. He was getting really bad feelings now. Where was Merv? He saw the guards come out again. This was too much. One of the guys carrying the money had a uniform, but the other guy was plainclothes. It didn't smell right. It didn't taste right. Then a big black guy in a uniform came out with Merv's suitcases.

Hector spun out of the truck, a gun in his hand. He started moving swiftly across the street.

Biddle was lined up in the West-Tex truck, right where he was supposed to be. He saw Hector move out. He couldn't believe it. Where the hell were Buck and Coker?

Fry didn't know anything was wrong until Hector opened up with his Uzi. Fry dropped the suitcases and tried to turn, half drawing his gun as he fell to the sidewalk dying, blood pouring from a half-dozen bullet holes. His final thoughts were of his children.

Hackett and McRose dropped their canvas bags and returned fire as Hector ran for the suitcases. He managed to grab them and start back across the road to the pickup truck before pellets from McRose's shotgun caught him in the spine. Hackett finished the job with a clean shot to the head as Hector started to fall.

Finally, too late, the Lancer skidded around the corner, Atwater leaning forward, pistol in hand, ready for the melee, knowing that being late was bound to mean trouble. He would soon find out how much trouble. He quickly spotted Hector falling and the two suitcases.

"You fucked us up good, man. We missed our guy—somebody else had to do our job," Atwater said, clenching his fist.

Coker screamed obscenities back at Buck as he spun the car around in the street so Atwater could make a clean swipe at the suitcases.

Hackett hustled McRose into the armored truck and they took off full blast.

Biddle turned the other way. He had watched Fry die. He was stunned. Things were bad. Real bad. None of them had liked doing the ops inside the country in the first place. Now one of them had died robbing a U.S. bank on a mission they didn't understand.

Atwater's mind was going a million miles an hour faster than his body would carry him. He scraped at the street as he picked up the cases and tossed them into the backseat. Coker was already moving as Atwater closed the door.

"Fry's dead, man." Atwater was choking with rage.

"What're you talking 'bout?"

"Shut up and drive, motherfucker!" They could scream forever but nothing would change the fact that they had blown it. They weren't there when they were supposed to be, and because of it their buddy, friend of many missions, had died—in Texas, not Commieland somewhere, but deep in the heart of . . .

Merv had gone to the window and cautiously looked outside when he heard the gunfire. He saw Hector go down. When the various trucks and cars left the scene, he made his own getaway. There was no way he wanted to be associated with this mess.

As Coker took off he nearly sideswiped the blue cruiser driven by Jack Benteen, who was still trying to raise Purvis on the radio. Jack still had no idea about the bank being robbed, but he recognized the car from the motel. He instinctively did a hundred-eighty-degree turn and gave chase, knowing somehow that this was what he was looking for.

He flipped on his emergency lights and the siren, but there was no way Coker was going to stop. He drove over a curb and cut inside a turn on the sidewalk, Jack following close behind but on the outside.

Coker kept turning, figuring that the small car could eventually pull off a turn that Jack's larger cruiser couldn't. But for about a half mile, Jack kept pace.

Coker spotted a narrow alley partway down one block. He accelerated, knowing Jack would follow suit and that it would get Jack's momentum too high to react in time. With Jack right behind him, Coker suddenly swerved, braked, and slipped into the alley as Jack went sailing past, knocking over a DRIVE FRIENDLY —THE TEXAS WAY! sign in the process.

But in the alley was a garbage truck lumbering toward the rapidly moving turbo Lancer. Atwater jumped into the backseat as Coker slipped to one side in the narrow alley. The Lancer came to a rude, scraping stop, jammed between a cinderblock wall and the truck.

Jack had spun in a wide arc and managed to come in

a second or two later. He saw the garbage truck when he sailed by and knew his quarry wasn't going anywhere. He got out of the car, cutoff Winchester in hand.

Coker started to raise his gun, but Atwater held it down.

"Put it away," he hissed. "Don't kill no civilian —ain't gonna do no good. He's an American."

Coker gave up.

Jack could see the two men inside the Lancer. Quickly, Jack smashed out the rear windshield with the butt of the gun, then shoved the muzzle just inside.

"Get out of the car, keep your hands where I can see 'em."

Atwater and Coker slowly brought their hands up.

Atwater tried a weak smile. "Yes, sir. Just me again, sir. Same old same."

"Get out of the car, Buck." Jack couldn't exactly say he was glad to see "Schoonover" again.

"Yes, sir." Atwater meekly began crawling out through the shattered glass. Coker followed suit.

They had lost a man. Two men captured. Hackett's mission was in trouble. And there was no fall-back position.

III
BLACK OPS

26

The Sheriff's Station was in an uproar. Once the phone company had located where Biddle's switchers broke the lines, the phones started ringing nonstop. Too much was happening in Benrey for one day. Too much was happening in Benrey, period. First the Chicken Champ —two dead, three injured. Then Hank dead at Arturo's, followed by Chub Luke and Ricardo. Now the Flaxton Road warehouse was gone; though, luckily, this time no one had been injured. All followed by two deaths during a bold daylight robbery of the Benrey Bank. Jack Benteen took it personally.

Jack inked a fingerprint roller with a certain amount of vengeance as Coker and Atwater, handcuffed nearby, looked on, Smirking, Jack thought, the bastards are smirking. Cortez came up and flashed him a couple of fingerprint charts already filled in.

"You get what I wanted?" Jack asked.

"Yes, sir. I lifted these prints from the two-sixty-fives at the morgue." Cortez fanned the sheets out to display them. "These here are the Mexican fellow's and these are the black's." He glanced over at Coker and Atwater. "And here's the booking slips for the freak show —Buck Schoonover and Paul Kenner."

Cortez left and Jack set aside the charts to begin the task of wresting fingerprints from Atwater, who resisted insidiously. Once Jack got Buck's hand inked and onto the paper, Buck twisted his fingers just enough to muddy the print so it was unusable. Before Jack could finish the job, he was accosted by Purvis, who carried several clear plastic bags jammed with evidence from the robbery.

"This is all we recovered, sir. Ski mask, blood samples, hair samples, handgun, automatic pistol, spent cartridges, and a roll of film I took of tire treads and skid marks around the southwest corner of the bank."

"Tag it, Purvis. All of it."

"Yes, sir. Tag it." Purvis started toward the door.

"Purvis!" Jack called him back, realizing that the bumbling Purvis needed the most explicit of instructions. "Lock it up. And give me the key."

"Right away." Purvis saluted briskly, then left.

Jack shook his head as he turned his attention back to the recalcitrant Atwater/Schoonover, who was grinning as Jack fought over control of his fingerprints.

"Leave him alone! All we done was pick up a couple of suitcases on the pavement without a claim check!" Coker/Kenner shouted.

"Give me your thumb, asshole," Jack growled at Atwater.

"We don't want no fingerprints. It's against the Constitution. Can't take my prints till I have a lawyer."

"I'll loan you a dime. You can call the Civil Liberties Union." Jack forced Atwater's thumb onto the ink pad.

"It ain't right. Goddamn it, it ain't right."

Jack whipped Atwater's wrist with nearly enough force to crack it. No more Mr. Nice Guy.

"Roll it left to right, Buck. Don't smear it."

Finally Atwater realized he was going to lose. He gave up his prints, shrugging to Coker.

Purvis returned just as Jack finished printing his prisoners. "Evidence bagged and tagged and under lock and key, sir. Like you asked."

He dropped the key into Jack's hand, then tossed some rough paper towels to Atwater and Coker. "You boys can clean up with these, then follow me." The two commandos comically struggled with cleaning the print ink off their hands while their hands were still cuffed together. Purvis herded them off to the holding cells and locked them in without waiting for them to finish cleaning up.

Jack gave Purvis the fingerprint cards for Coker and Atwater along with the cards from Hector and Fry that Cortez had brought from the morgue.

"Plug these into the F.B.I. in Washington. Top priority. You let me know the minute they get back to us."

"Right away." Purvis turned to leave, then turned back again. "Oh, and sir . . ."

Jack watched the about-face with a grimace. Purvis never seemed to get everything out in one try.

"Word came in from Ranger ballistics in Austin on the shell casings. You remember? The ones that shot Chub Luke?"

"Yeah, I remember, Purvis," Jack growled. "What have you got?"

Purvis consulted his clipboard. "Well, yes sir. It was army-issue. Special Forces. That's why it wasn't in the catalog; they keep it secret and all. The stuff that got Chub, that batch was reported stolen eight months ago from an army base at Prentis, Oregon. Which means . . ." Purvis wrinkled his brow trying to draw some conclusions. Thinking was an inordinately difficult effort for the man, and Jack could almost smell the wood burning. "I guess that D.E.A. fella must've made a mistake," Purvis finished lamely.

"Either that or he lied to me about it," Jack prompted, realizing that Bear had been right about the ammo all along.

Purvis looked puzzled. "Right. Yes, sir. Probably lied to you." Purvis wasn't very smart and he was naive on top of that. But one thing he had going for him was an innate honesty and straightforwardness. He couldn't conceive of a dishonest lawman. And he didn't grasp that there might be deeper implications when a D.E.A. agent was misleading a Texas Ranger about the source of ammunition used in some kind of a drug slaying.

Jack, on the other hand, had been getting plenty of practice lately in the characteristic thought processes of paranoia.

Purvis turned to leave again, and again did his one-eighty. "Oh and, sir, the F.B.I. fellas that just got here want your Form 407 and your Form 800. They also want your Work History Reports for the last two years, plus they say the Coke machine's empty and the toilet don't flush."

Jack rolled his eyes. "Purvis?"

"Yes, sir?"

"Tell the F.B.I. to kiss my ass."

Purvis deflated. "Yes, sir." He turned to go. "Kiss my ass, yes sir."

Grinning at Purvis's reaction, a bit of lightness in a heavy day, Jack addressed Donna Lee. "Get me through to Washington right away. I want the Drug Enforcement Administration personnel office."

Jack stepped into the sanctuary of his warm, oak-paneled corner office and closed the door, shutting out the racket of voices, typewriters, facsimile machines, and telephones. Thank God for Purvis, he thought.

Without him, I wouldn't have a damn thing to laugh about.

Coker sat moping on his cot with Atwater watching him, boiling over in the adjoining cell, leaning with his back to the bars. They both heard Benteen tell the secretary to get the D.E.A. on the phone. Things were coming to a head. Soon the Ranger would have enough info to put the pieces together and . . . what then? What of the army doing business on U.S. turf in violation of its charter? What of their ops? And what happened to soldiers who did their duty in violation of the law, but in compliance with their orders?

The questions ran through their minds as they contemplated the demise of Hackett's mission. They had failed. It was never this bad. In some foreign backwater, they could do what they were told and always return to the bosom of their motherland. But here they were *in* the motherland. In jail like common criminals. And for God only knew how long.

"Kee-rist Almighty Jesus!" Atwater snarled. "If, if, if!" He looked over at Coker. "But what's done is slop under the bridge, do you know what I mean? Jerking off our conscience don't turn one thing around."

"We fucked up, Buck. We were supposed to cover the spic . . . We fucked up."

Atwater eyed his buddy without fondness. "I'd kill you if it'd bring Fry back, but it won't," he said softly. "He's dead and that's the way it goes when you're soldierin'. Bite the damn bullet and play taps for a brother gone down."

Both commandos were stunned by how badly things had gone, both were looking for ways to make it right. Atwater, for one, didn't see any way. No room to punt, as McRose liked to say. But Atwater had a flair for leadership that surfaced in a crisis. It was that kind of blind optimism that made him tell Coker, "Got to think positive. We gotta find a way to get out of here, get on with the mission."

Coker chortled. "Yeah. Hackett's mission. I can't believe it. Here we are space age high-tech and we got caught by some Stone Age cowboy."

Atwater chomped on his cigar, savoring the bitter juices. "Ain't it a bitch."

In his office, Jack slammed down the phone as Purvis knocked and entered.

"Never heard of him!"

"Sir?" Purvis wondered what was up now.

"Frank Ralston or whoever the hell he is. The D.E.A.'s never heard of him."

"Must be some mistake," Purvis replied. "He was right here in our office."

An awkward silence passed as Jack contemplated what to say. All he came up with was, "What do you want, Purvis?"

"Uh, just reporting back, sir." Purvis smiled disarmingly. "I sent the fingerprints off on the FAX. We should hear word back in a couple of hours."

— 27 —

The West-Tex truck was parked in the middle of nowhere on a dirt road at the end of a box canyon. It was peaceful here, but a little too quiet for Biddle's taste. He and McRose were standing outside the truck, McRose leaning back on it with one boot heel hooked over the bumper, watching Biddle pace nervously.

"How long are we supposed to wait?" Biddle asked.

"Until he gets here," McRose answered softly. He was trying to provide a calm center, a point of reference for Biddle, who was taking Fry's death hard. It wasn't that McRose didn't feel the loss as well; he was just holding it together a little better. He'd been through this enough. So had Biddle. But sometimes you cut a buddy some slack.

Werewolf Ops were dangerous. Sometimes they smelled funny, too. This one stunk to high heavens. Of the commando team, only Hackett seemed not to mind. Biddle was magnifying Fry's death by his distaste for the mission, McRose knew. It was tough, but Biddle would get over it. They all would. They had no choice.

"Until he gets here," Biddle echoed bitterly. "How

long is that?" Hackett's arrogance pissed him off more than anything else.

"I don't know." McRose was curt. He wanted to snap Biddle out of it; being soft wouldn't help. "I follow orders, Charlie. I was supposed to dump the armored car. I did my job, now here I am."

"And here we sit. A lot of money in this truck and every cop in the state looking for us. *I could have stayed in the ghetto to rob banks!*" Biddle cried out. "Why the fuck did the ops call for me to leave my buddy exposed? I should've been on his flank, wasted that spic the minute he stepped out of that truck."

"Are you laying it on Command?" McRose demanded. He had enough of it now. "In case you forgot, the major wasn't the one that didn't show up."

"It was *his* plan that put Fry on a slab in the morgue. Next stop—a body bag. And not in some goddamn foreign jungle operation, but in Texas." Biddle was crying real tears now—just a few, tracking wet and glistening on his smooth dark cheeks.

McRose was moved, too, though not yet to tears. He was second-in-command on Hackett's mission and he had a lot to worry about. The mission was in jeopardy. Military discipline was breaking down when a man like Biddle questioned his orders. McRose knew because his own sense of discipline was failing him. He was questioning the ops more and more himself.

McRose gently tapped Biddle on the shoulder. Biddle looked up at him.

"All right," McRose said. "This mission's got the smell of puke. But the orders come down to the major. Then what's to be done, we do it . . . and take our chances."

By the time Hackett arrived in the station wagon, Biddle had clammed up. He just glared at the major. Hackett had seen the response before. He left Biddle alone. He could take care of the morale problem later.

"You and Biddle follow me," Hackett told McRose.

It was a twenty-minute drive on the back roads to get to the freeway, then another forty minutes to the El Paso Airport. Hackett led them to the long-term parking lot. He pulled into a vacant slot and McRose pulled into another slot alongside.

Hackett got out of his car and went around to the passenger side of the West-Tex truck. As Biddle got out, Hackett made sure the door was locked behind him. He checked the rear doors, then went around to the driver's side. McRose got out and locked the door.

"Give me the parking ticket and the keys," Hackett ordered.

There was something funny about Hackett just now, McRose thought. He hesitated a moment, but he shrugged to himself, thinking this was over his head. McRose dropped the keys in Hackett's outstretched hand, then fished out the parking ticket and gave it to Hackett as well.

Hackett climbed into the station wagon, flipping the central door-lock switch open for McRose and Biddle. McRose climbed into the front seat, but Biddle just stood looking at the truck. Hackett rolled down his window.

"Let's go, Sergeant."

"That's a lot of money in there," Biddle mused.

"It won't be there long," Hackett replied. "It goes right back to the F.D.I.C. to cover the payments on the theft."

Biddle climbed into the station wagon and Hackett started the motor and pulled away. Biddle watched the truck holding what he thought of as Fry's blood money gradually disappear behind him.

Purvis waited by the Sheriff Department's Facsimile Receiving Unit, gulping down some bottled water from the dispenser behind him. The outdated FAX transceiver coughed and slowly etched out four fingerprint cards, each eight inches square, sent direct from the F.B.I.'s National Crime Information Center computers. Purvis grabbed the cards and headed for Jack's office.

Jack looked up as Purvis barged in without knocking.

"Fingerprint reports, sir. From the F.B.I. in Washington." Purvis held out the cards proudly, as if he had matched up the prints himself.

Jack let Purvis do the explaining. "Who are they?"

"Well, sir"—Purvis squinted at the cards—"the Latino one's name is Hector Zuniga. Says here he's thirty-two years old, born in Mexico City. Three arrests, two convictions—smuggling controlled substances with intent to distribute. Mexican national."

"Figures," Jack said. "Probably one of—"

"Cash Bailey's boys, yes sir," Purvis chimed in.

Maybe Purvis wasn't so dumb after all, Jack realized. He's got *me* figured out.

"Listen to this, sir." Purvis read from another of the cards. "Luther Fry. Twenty-eight. U.S. citizen. Born Detroit, Michigan. No criminal record. Served in U.S. Army." Purvis looked up from the card. "That's the black fellow they got down at the morgue."

"What about Buck Schoonover and the other one? Kenner?"

Purvis nodded. "That's the funny thing. Neither of their prints matches up with their names. Schoonover was filed under . . ." He switched the cards around to find Buck's. "Buck Atwater, thirty-five. U.S. citizen. Born Seminole Swamp, Florida. No criminal record. Served in U.S. Army." Purvis switched cards again. "Then Kenner, he's listed as Declan Patrick Coker, twenty-four years old, U.S. citizen, born Salt Lake City. Juvenile conviction for poaching. No adult record. Served in the U.S. Army." Purvis looked up from the cards. "So I guess there's a connection."

Jack nodded. "Anything more about their military records?"

"No, sir. That's all that came through."

On the tip of a ballpoint pen, Jack balanced one of the cartridge casings recovered near Chub Luke's body. The shells were reported stolen from an army base and the only connection between the bank robbers was a military background. "Purvis," Jack said, "I want you to transmit facsimiles of all three of our soldier boys to Army Center, Personnel Section, St. Louis, Missouri. Tell 'em we want a top-priority response."

"Right, sir. St. Louis." Purvis returned to the FAX transceiver, slamming the door behind him. He looked up the contact number in a directory, then punched it in and fed the cards back into the machine.

Purvis stood around and watched the facsimile machine. Nothing happened, but Purvis didn't mind waiting. In fact, he was hardly conscious of waiting at all. He was totally absorbed by the coincidence of three army guys robbing a bank at the same time. He mentioned it to Cortez when the switchboard was slow for a few minutes. Then the facsimile machine started humming again.

"Ranger Jack!" Purvis sang out excitedly. "It's coming in, sir!"

Jack came out of his office to find Purvis and Cortez poring over the personnel reports it was ejecting.

"Sir." Cortez, still reading, addressed Jack. "This report, it's kind of wild. It says: 'The attached information as requested by your agency is forwarded for your disposition. Re your request for service records of Luther Fry, Buck Atwater, and Declan Patrick Coker, please be advised . . .'" Cortez looked up. "You're not going to believe this, sir."

"Just finish reading it, Cortez." Jack was ready to believe anything.

"'Sergeant Declan Patrick Coker, five-six-one-five-six-seven-four-four-one, Fourth Battalion, First Infantry Division killed on leave from Lebanon in chartered flight crash, twelve-four-eighty-four. Unmarried.'"

Confused, Cortez handed the report to Jack. The head shot of Coker at the top of the transferred military record matched Coker exactly. The next record came out of the FAX.

"'Luther Fry . . .'" Cortez read. "'Killed training maneuvers Fort Polk, Louisiana, ten-twenty-five-seventy-seven. Death benefits paid to ex-wife and two children.'"

Jack took Fry's report as Cortez pulled Atwater's report.

"'Sergeant Buck Atwater . . . killed defusing unexploded bomb, Laos, eleven-eleven-seventy-four, buried U.S. Armed Forces Cemetery, Hawaii; posthumous Bronze Star Medal. No next of kin.'"

The facsimile machine ground to a halt. Cortez tore out Atwater's report and handed it to Jack. Purvis peeked over Jack's shoulder as he examined the ID photos.

"You recognize them?" Jack asked.

"Well, I'll be damned," Purvis gawked. "The black guy is the one we had in the tank for fighting."

"You booked these two together," Jack said, holding Atwater's and Fry's reports out.

"Yes, sir. On a Class C."

"The disorderly conduct stuff was a ruse," Jack told Purvis. "They got themselves tossed into jail so they could check out our operation."

"But how can they be officially dead and be locked up here?" Purvis asked.

"Purvis," Jack said. "One of them *is* dead."

Purvis nodded. "Right."

Jack told Purvis to file the material, then crossed to the holding cells.

"Where'd you serve in the army, Buck?"

"Army?" Atwater snorted. "Me? I never made the service. Had a bum knee. Bum heart. Plus galloping VD."

Jack figured that was how Atwater would play it. Covering up the military background was the only thing that made sense at this point. Jack turned to Coker.

"What about you, Coker? I guess you stayed home with your mom. Stole cars."

Coker didn't react to his name. "No, sir. I sold dope. So I bought cars."

His prisoners smiled at him. Jack grimaced back. Looking at his watch, Jack figured the F.B.I. would not get around to grilling the duo until the next day and decided to sit in on that session rather than risk stepping on the agents' toes. Jack did respect the fact that bank robbery was F.B.I. turf.

"It's been a long day, boys. I've got a lot to think about. Tomorrow you better have some answers, because the next person who gets custody of you may be a lot meaner than me."

On his way out of the station, Jack passed Purvis, who was reading one of the reports again. Jack told him to stand guard.

"Sir?"

"With a shotgun, Purvis. From the rack."

"Shotgun ready, sir." Purvis complied, looking worried.

"I'll take care of the keys." Jack pulled the holding cells' key ring off a peg on the wall and carried them with him.

28

Jack's cruiser slowly rolled up his driveway. It was almost a quarter mile from the road to his home. He could see the living-room lights shining through the trees that shielded the house. He hoped it meant Sarita had returned, but when he got to the bare dirt on the back side of his house where he and Sarita usually parked, her ragtop MG wasn't there.

Jack unclipped his Winchester from the roof mount and cautiously got out of the car. He heard the sounds of a boxing match on the television inside. An announcer was feverishly calling the hits. Jack knew Sarita wasn't watching; she hated the fights.

The front-door hinges whined softly as Jack slowly opened the door. He crept down the hallway then quickly swung into the living room, training his gun on a half-lit figure sitting in an armchair. It was Hackett, whom Jack only knew as Ralston, the D.E.A. agent that wasn't.

Hackett raised his hands.

"I didn't come here to get killed, Benteen. I came to talk."

Jack didn't move.

"I'm unarmed," Hackett insisted.

Jack cautiously lowered the Winchester. Hackett slowly lowered his hands and switched off the TV set.

"I'm Major Paul Hackett, One Hundred Seventy-third Airborne, Third Battalion. If you run a check—"

"You'll turn up dead like those other two clowns I've got locked up," Jack interrupted. "What the hell is the military doing robbing banks in Texas?"

"Putting Cash Bailey out of business," Hackett told him. "Have a seat, Benteen, I'll tell you the whole thing."

Jack didn't comply. "My ears work fine standing up."

"Fine. Be a hard-ass." Hackett took a breath and plunged into his story. "Cash Bailey has been using your bank here in Benrey to launder and stockpile his drug money. *And* to store documents which could embarrass our government if they were ever made public."

"You've got to do a lot better than that." Jack sneered.

Hackett continued: "For five years Cash Bailey was the D.E.A.'s number-one deep-cover agent in Central America. Three years ago he turned. His knowledge of contacts and the drug enforcement network gave him all the tools he needed. If he uses too much of what he knows, he could set the whole program back a long time."

"So what? So he's got the D.E.A. and some federal boys by the balls. Why didn't *they* handle this whole thing? Why in hell did they bring the military in?" Hackett wasn't telling him much of anything that justified what had been going on in Benrey.

"Read the newspapers, Benteen. By presidential directive, military force can now be used to stop the narcotics flow across the U.S.–Mexican border. The directive identifies the drug traffic as a national security threat because the profits are used to finance revolution and anarchy throughout Central and South America. Bailey himself is known to be bartering guns, ammunition, and demolitions gear instead of cash to acquire the cocaine and the marijuana he sells. National security depends on finding out where Bailey got those weapons and what their ultimate destinations are."

Cash was reaching farther into Jack's life than either of them had even imagined. And it seemed that the players on both sides of the drug war were people to watch out for. Jack didn't trust Hackett much. He had no way of knowing how much of Hackett's story was true or if he was getting the whole story.

"That's a pretty nifty trick having your boys listed as dead," Jack said. "Why?"

"It helps when we're doing work overseas. These operatives are free to undertake activities which the U.S. government cannot officially sanction, but which must be done. As nonexistent entities, their activities can't be linked to our policies."

"Unless they get caught," Jack taunted.

"Even *if* they get caught," Hackett responded. "Foreign governments aren't as lucky as you are, Benteen. They don't have access to the F.B.I.'s master computer in Washington."

"Well, you boys are real smart," Jack said. "You've done a hell of a fine job."

"We've made a mess of the whole operation," Hackett contradicted.

"No kidding."

Hackett got up and approached Jack. "I need your help."

Jack leaned against the mantelpiece and waited for Hackett's pitch.

"I'm going into Mexico to finish the job," Hackett continued. "I need the two men you've got locked up."

Jack guffawed. "You've got to be kidding, mister. Those boys are in for armed robbery, bank robbery, accessory to murder, assaulting a police officer, possession of automatic weapons—you name it. I'm just going to let them go? I haven't heard that the army's charter allows you boys to go robbing banks. I don't even think it lets you operate legally inside the U.S. borders."

Hackett ignored Jack's ridicule. "I want Cash Bailey. So do you. We can help each other."

Jack shook his head. "Nobody wants Cash more than me, but I don't see that I need any help from you."

Hackett smirked. "Sure, Benteen. You're going to do it like the Rangers did in the old days. Piss on the border—if your man's in Mexico, just go get him and drag him back."

"Matter of fact," Jack drawled, "that's exactly what I'm gonna do."

Hackett chewed his lip and nodded. "Must be a hell of a grudge between you two."

"Old friends is all. Old friends gone bad. I'll tell you the first thing they teach a Ranger. Been teaching it for a hundred and some years. They taught it to my dad and my granddad. 'Say what you mean and mean what you say and cover the ground you stand on.'" Jack paused, then continued, "And I say I'm gonna go down to Mexico and get Cash Bailey."

"Except you don't know where he is," Hackett said. "And I do. By the time you stumble around the mountains for two weeks trying to find him, he'll either have his private army kill you, or if he feels sorry for you, he'll just fly around in that helicopter of his, keep moving from town to town until you get tired and go home. Either way he'll be laughing like hell."

Hackett watched his words sinking into Jack; their effect had been carefully calculated. Hackett knew what he was doing when he came here. He knew, maybe better than Jack knew, how to get a man where he wanted him. In this case, fragments of the truth were on Hackett's side, and it was easy for him to paint the picture he wanted Benteen to see. After a few more moments, Hackett hammered out another fragment of truth. "His private army, Benteen. At least fifty men. Every outlaw, thug, and drug runner in northern Mexico. Plus he's bought off every government official. You'll get no help out of them."

Hackett smiled inwardly as he watched Jack swallow the bait. A man usually gave away his thoughts in subtle facial movements: a twitch of an eyebrow, the slow tightening of a lip or a corner of the mouth, the tension around the eyes or the jaw. Hackett was good at reading the signs. Even Jack's fair poker face was an open book to him. And he knew he had won.

"Okay, Major. What are you offering?"

"You let my men go," Hackett started. "We'll slip across the border. This is Monday. The day after tomorrow we'll slide into Bailey's town. I'll give you thirty minutes with him before I move in. A half hour to settle up with him—it's what you want, isn't it?"

"Yeah," Jack agreed. "That's exactly what I want."

"All I need are some papers Bailey has in his possession," Hackett said. "You kill him, it's fine with me." He smiled. "How about it, Benteen?"

"I'll think about it," Jack said.

Hackett started to leave but turned back to Jack in the entrance to the hallway. "I have to know by tomorrow. Otherwise the whole operation will be blown." He watched Jack, gauging how to deliver his argument's Sunday punch. This was as good a time as any. "By the way, Benteen, my intelligence sources tell me Cash Bailey crossed the border two nights ago. He went back with your girl."

Hackett turned on his heel and left without giving Jack a chance to reply.

Jack was stunned by the news. He numbly heard Hackett close the door on the way out. Then he crossed to his liquor cabinet and poured himself a drink. If Sarita had gone with Cash, did she go willingly? He wouldn't put it past Cash to just come and take her. And he'd be surprised if Sarita wanted to go with Cash, unless she just wanted to get back at Jack. The only way to find out was to track her down.

Outside Jack's house, Hackett's rented station wagon pulled up. McRose was at the wheel, Biddle in the backseat. They had been waiting in the shadows of some trees uphill from the house.

Hackett got in and turned to his remaining men. "I think we're going to have a new partner," he told them.

"You straight?" McRose asked.

"Dead level," Hackett replied.

McRose was impressed. He hadn't thought it would be possible to turn the lawman to their side of the ops; the commandos were in too much trouble. But Hackett had pulled off tough orders before. Maybe he would do it again.

Biddle said nothing. He brooded in the backseat. Hackett could feel him, eyeing the back of his neck. If looks could kill . . . Hackett thought. He didn't need Biddle or the other men much longer, though. All he had to do was hold the commandos together for two more days, until Black Ops got under way.

Jack didn't stay inside long. He couldn't stand waiting around, not knowing whether Sarita had really gone, so he got in his cruiser and went looking for her. He didn't think she was working, but his first stop was Jalisco.

The parking lot of the roadhouse was nearly empty. Inside, the band was playing some slow, sad instrumental Jack didn't recognize. A few couples were hug-dancing, swaying across the dance floor in tiny steps.

At the bar, Jack greeted Paco, the bartender for this

shift, a rotund old Hispanic gentleman who didn't have much to do this evening besides polish the glassware.

"*Buenas noches, Jack, como está?*" Paco said.

"Can't exactly say how things are going," Jack replied. "Where's Sarita?" His voice sounded stiff to him. He hoped Paco didn't catch the tones of worry and anger.

Paco shrugged. "Sarita is gone. She didn't even say adios."

"Tell me about it, Paco."

"Nothing to tell. I called her mother and she said Sarita went to Mexico with an old friend."

"She say who the friend was?"

"No, Jack. She just told me an old amigo had come to get her."

It hit Jack hard. Paco saw it.

"Can I buy you a drink, Jack?"

Jack shook his head. "Thanks, Paco. I gotta be going."

He got back in his cruiser and drove past every place he thought she might be. He drove past her mother's house. The MG was there. But he knew she wasn't with it. She was in Mexico with Cash like Hackett said.

It was after midnight by the time he pulled up to the Sheriff's Station. Purvis was dozing behind his desk, the shotgun loose across his lap. He awoke with a start when he heard footsteps, looked up to see Jack. Purvis scrambled to his feet.

"Trouble, sir?"

"Can't sleep," Jack said. "I thought I'd catch up on the paperwork. Sign out, I'll hold the fort."

"Yes, sir. Be heading on home." Purvis unloaded the shotgun and put it back on the rack. "Hell of a damn day, wasn't it? Never have figured out what happened to them damn phones."

Jack didn't bother to remind him that the phone company had figured it out that afternoon. Purvis made a beeline for his car before Jack could change his mind and make him stay.

Once he was alone, Jack went over to the holding cells. Atwater and Coker were lying on their bunks, wide-awake. Jack pulled the keys out of his pocket and unlocked the door to Coker's cell, then to Atwater's.

As he swung open Atwater's door Jack said, "You better call your boss, Buck. We're going to Mexico."

29

"One thing never changes," Biddle said. "The great thing about being in the army is you always go first-class."

"So what else is new?" Coker sneered.

The five remaining commandos, along with Jack Benteen, were riding a battered, blue converted school bus on an unpaved, heavily rutted back road deep within the Mexican state of Chihuahua. The bus was jammed. Rickety old school buses are the backbone of local transportation throughout Central America. On this bus, as one would expect, the local farmers were hauling their chickens, pigs, and eggs to market.

The transmission screamed as the driver sloppily downshifted on a turn. The occupants of the bus strained to hold their seats as the ungainly vehicle cornered a little faster than prudence and the creaking suspension might have dictated. But, though the tattered cotton fringe over the windshield swung sideways from the lateral G-forces, the plastic Jesus glued to the dashboard held on and the bus remained upright.

The absurdity of this team of highly trained commandos riding in a school bus carrying livestock would have been laughable, except for the mission. The space that had started closing in since the gunfight at the Rincon Norte was quickly squeezing Jack toward Cash, as Jack had always known it would.

Atwater and Coker had taken the Ranger to their base camp in the Benrey foothills.

"We've got to move fast," Jack had told Hackett.

"Tomorrow?"

"We've got to move now. I've already got too much explaining to do. Bank robbery is a federal crime; the F.B.I. is involved. They know about Buck and Coker here and they're likely to start a manhunt when everybody notices they're not in prison where they belong."

Jack's logic was unassailable. Twenty minutes later, they piled into the station wagon with McRose behind the wheel. They drove to El Paso, where they parked near the border crossing. From there, they split up into groups of two to avoid drawing attention to themselves. Hackett told Jack to accompany him, but Jack had insisted on going with Buck, for one simple reason, which he kept to himself: Jack had cut Atwater a break on two separate occasions—on the night he caught the "drunken" Atwater and McRose, and the day he let Atwater out of jail. If these men wanted him dead, Atwater would be the one who wanted it least.

They had all walked across the border into Ciudad Juarez. Each of the commandos carried a small arsenal with him, concealed in a duffel bag, a daypack, under a jacket. As usual, Mexican Customs didn't check any of them. Americans, after all, were good visitors, bringing dollars to spend in a poor country. It would be inhospitable to examine them too closely.

Once in Juarez, the pairs took cabs to the bus station, where they joined up again on the bus to San Luis.

"Heroes," Atwater said to Jack so the others could hear, "we're goddamn heroes, but heroes gotta have a cause. With things being too confusing these days, it ain't easy. So I support my country and my buddies. And I don't ask no questions."

"That's real deep, Buck," Biddle said, poison in his voice. "Real deep." He wouldn't forgive Atwater and Coker—and especially Hackett—for Fry's death.

Buck ignored the insult. "Yeah, real deep. Except that lately I'm not so sure about anything. So let's go kick some ass. Same old same."

To Jack, Atwater looked forlorn, almost childlike, like some bad boy, too far gone for redemption, who could still look back on his life and realize that something terrible had gone wrong.

The way the seating worked out, Hackett and Mc-Rose were directly behind Jack. Hackett leaned forward and tapped Jack on the shoulder. "We have about another thirty miles to our objective, I figure this is the time to get a few things straight."

"What do you have in mind?"

"You're used to working free-lance, Benteen, but on this ops you do as you're told. Like a good soldier."

It was Jack's turn to smirk. "I'll do my best."

"You got a real treat in store for you, watching this team go to work." Hackett cast a glance at McRose. "Larry's not just *any* soldier. You put Larry out when the sun goes down and you get body count. You wake up in the morning and Larry's drinking orange juice, sitting there with a pile of fresh ears," Hackett bragged. He turned to McRose. "No illusions about turning civilian, right, Larry?"

"Not as long as I keep working in third-world countries," McRose answered cryptically.

Hackett passed a bottle to Jack. "Whisky. Single malt. Distilled in a very small stream in the north of Scotland. Good stuff."

Jack didn't take the bottle.

"You don't like whisky?" Hackett asked.

"I've told you before, I'm particular who I drink with," Jack replied.

Hackett took a drink himself and leered at Jack. "I don't believe that, Benteen. In my opinion, you're just naturally hostile."

Jack didn't bother to reply. He stared at the desolate scrub-valley scenery thinking he was like a rattlesnake in a nest of vipers.

30

It was midday by the time the bus arrived in San Luis. The town loomed out of the dry hill country, baking in the sun, a dust cloud blurring the discrete outlines of objects like a canvas by Monet, the smoky fires of street vendors further clogging the air. It was a big Tuesday, Mexican Independence Day, September 16th, and San Luis was crowded with celebration.

When Jack first caught sight of the Hotel Isabella, its dark Spanish Gothic lines chilled his heart. He knew before Hackett told him that he would find Cash there. Smoke rose from two large fires on the plaza in front of the hotel and a foul smell of burning beef wafted down to the town below.

The "dirty half-dozen" split up into pairs again and casually made their way to a two-story rooming house at the end of the main street. Hackett got there first and rented a room. He insisted on one overlooking the street. It gave him a clear view of the whole town, from the lone adobe church at the far end of the street to Cash's stronghold above.

They had timed it perfectly: the town was unaccustomed to seeing gringos, other than the few that came and went for Cash's businesses, but the commandos could use the festivities for cover.

Once the team members were safely ensconced in the rooming house, they began their surveillance. Jack sat apart from the rest, waiting for his chance at Cash, and his chance to get Sarita back. He couldn't believe she had really come back to Cash of her own free will. He suspected the wily Cash had planned it, somehow manipulated Sarita and her anger at and frustration with Jack. Surely Cash knew that Sarita was the bait that would lure Jack to him.

Hackett was training a pair of binoculars out the window at the area surrounding the hotel. "Bailey must be on the premises. His chopper's here under heavy security."

The glasses were powerful and he could see every detail of what went on up above: the helicopter was parked at one end of the crowded courtyard, surrounded by a half dozen of Cash's mercenaries. Hackett swept the glasses across the courtyard and picked up Lupo and Monday on the steps to the cantina, surveying the guards and the peasants celebrating around the cookfires, some of them tending to huge slabs of beef, spitted, and left to smolder on the flames. The beef was Cash's token gift to the community for the fiesta, but nobody cared enough to cook it well. Indulging in Cash's cocaine, marijuana, and liquor was the preferred mode of celebration.

The binoculars caught Merv and an armed goon with two heavy black suitcases coming out of the Isabella's entrance and crossing the veranda. Merv went to the helicopter. The pilot of the Giselle loaded the suitcases, climbed inside, and took off, the powerful turbine-and-rotor thunder echoing off the hillsides. Merv watched the Giselle go, his thinning hair and string tie blowing back in the prop wash.

Hackett started listing off the Isabella's defensive

precautions. "Okay, Biddle, take this down: healthy complement of automatic weapons—AK-forty-sevens, Uzis—"

"Uzis?" Coker interrupted.

"What'd you expect?" McRose asked. "Bad breath and sharp sticks?"

Hackett refocused the binoculars and continued: "Machine-gun nest, twin thirty-calibers, on the ground, south side of the courtyard perimeter. Opposite corner, north side, same thing." He searched the Isabella's windows. "M-sixty in a balcony window." Further checking revealed: "Twin thirties nested either side of the roof, covering the courtyard."

Hackett stepped back from the window and closed the shutters. "Four tripod-mounted machine guns plus an M-sixty in the center, with a gunner and an ammo feeder at each one. Whoever set up the perimeter knows his business. Courtyard entrance to the hotel's their open field of crossfire. Stay out of that kill zone. We'll bypass it, flank 'em, and simultaneously hit from inside."

Jack opened the small satchel he had carried with him from Texas. Inside he had his gunbelt and his badge. Even though the badge had no authority in Mexico, he pinned it on. Part of what he was doing was personal and didn't call for a badge, but part of his own mission was to call on Cash in his official capacity as well. The badge would let Cash know that, and though it might make it more dangerous, Jack wanted to give Cash fair warning.

Hackett took a deep breath and began circling the room. He addressed his men, stern, no-nonsense. His premission briefing. "Okay, I know what you're all thinking. Fucking cowboys and Indians. Kamikaze panic-assed Mickey Mouse bullshit. You blame command. You blame me. We lost Fry, right? Didn't we?"

His gaze hardened, singled out Biddle. "Humping ComOps' white clock?"

Biddle met Hackett's stare for a moment but quickly turned away. Then Hackett turned back to the rest of his men, psyching them out, getting their adrenaline running for the big show to follow, making sure they were ready to follow his orders to the grave if necessary.

"You're afraid we're going to lose more. Right? Am I right? If I'm right, let's hear it!"

Biddle looked up. "Yeah. It sucks, sir."

Hackett faced Biddle again. "Okay. I'm telling you straight. This is a win, but it's going to be a tough one. Extra innings. Hardball all the way."

Jack pulled his gunbelt out of the satchel. He was an outsider here. He certainly didn't consider himself one of Hackett's men. He just listened and watched, seeing for himself what kind of game Hackett was playing. Jack's own plan was clear to him: get Sarita, get Cash, and get out. Whatever the army boys were planning was going to come down hard and he would have to move fast to stay out of the way.

McRose eyed Hackett. "Last time out we fucked up. We lost one of our own. We got a lot to make up for, sir."

"Let's go get 'em for Fry," Coker agreed.

"I'm with you, baby," Atwater said. "All the way. Me and Coker especially got to do a number."

Hackett nodded. "Okay. So how many are ready to do it?"

Biddle still hadn't spoken.

"What about it, Charlie?"

Biddle was reluctant, bitter. Hackett figured once Biddle was in the heat of battle he'd forget Fry and work for the objectives.

Biddle finally looked up again. "I'll be all I can be," he said with ironic finality.

"That's all I expect," Hackett replied gently. "We all miss Fry, Charlie. *I* miss Fry. Bear that in mind."

Jack cleared the action of his .45, then jammed in a full clip. He slipped a few more loaded clips into an eyeglass case that hung inside his boot. "I'm set." He faced Hackett.

"You said you wanted thirty minutes with the head honcho. You got it." Jack nodded, but Hackett continued, warning him. "Not a minute more, Benteen. Thirty minutes, then we're coming in."

"It's all I need," Jack said. "Thirty minutes." He opened the door.

"Hey, Ranger," Atwater called. "You going in alone against all them Uzis?"

Jack nodded. "Me and Cash go back a long way. We used to be friends."

Then he was gone. The door slammed behind him and the commandos heard his footsteps disappearing down the hallway outside.

"That's one crazy motherfucker." Atwater grinned. "But I like the way he does it."

"Shut up, Buck," Hackett said. "We aren't here to give testimonials to the Ranger. Listen, all of you. Now that he's gone I can speak freely. We are here to terminate our target with extreme prejudice. Remember rule number two? Excepting members of the immediate family there are no friendlies."

"Wait a minute," Coker complained, "the cowboy's a friendly. He let us out of jail."

"Yeah, why frag him too?" Atwater asked.

"I repeat," Hackett said, his voice hard, his eyes dead, *"excepting members of the immediate family there are no friendlies."* The sound of a mariachi band drifted in from the festivities outside. "If the cowboy gets back," Hackett continued, "he'll leak." He focused his cold gray eyes on Atwater, then Coker. "You want our ops compromised?"

"No, sir," Coker said.

"Can't say I do," came Atwater's reply. "But it sure seems a shame, don't it?"

"Major?" Biddle spoke. "Are you sure you're not going to hang out to dry on this?"

"I've got my orders, Charlie. I'm carrying them out." Hackett's eyes got harder, his voice more commanding as he pushed his men the way he needed them to go. Get the questions out now, he thought, so I can nip each one in the bud. He was patient about it. He could afford to be.

"Very unusual, sir," McRose offered.

"What is?"

"Ordering termination of an American civilian peace officer clearly loyal to the country and in the process of trying to bring a criminal to justice."

Coker, Atwater, and Biddle exchanged glances, wowed by McRose's breach of military etiquette.

Hackett stayed riveted on McRose. "It is *very* unusual, Sergeant. And you will do as you are commanded."

McRose thought about it for a moment. It didn't sound morally right but not much of this ops had. Right now, there wasn't much choice. So he replied, "Yes, sir."

But his heart wasn't in it.

31

Jack squeezed through the thronging streets toward the road that climbed to the Hotel Isabella. He had thought that facing the moment of truth would be hard, but with each step he felt lighter. The ordeal was almost over. Soon Jack would be able to close the Cash Bailey file, one way or the other.

A battered jeep careened past him on the narrow road, forcing him into the brush and kicking up the fine red silt into a thick dust cloud as it went by. The jeep was loaded with drunken goons armed with automatic rifles. It was another warning that Cash wasn't to be fooled with carelessly. Like a hornet, Cash would sting viciously if angered.

On the plaza in front of the hotel, a group of Mexican Indians played eerie melancholy music on wooden pan pipes. A string of firecrackers went off. A series of rapid-fire explosions echoed below in the village. Smoke poured across the small plateau. The blackened beef carcasses hung over their fires. The drunken revelers maundered about. One man stumbled into a cookfire, then rolled himself out again as those around him laughed. More of Cash's guards were interspersed among the crowd.

People stared at the tall gringo wearing his badge and his gun, an apparition from another time. But Jack reached the veranda to the hotel unmolested. He stopped near a young hard-looking man with long hair and a broken front tooth who was staring at him.

"Go on inside, get Cash Bailey."

Jack pointed at the door. The man didn't understand the English, but he scurried inside. Jack turned and walked back to the small fountain that graced the plaza. From the center of the small pool rose a weathered marble statue of the Virgin Mary, facing the entrance to the hotel. Jack put his back to the fountain. Like Mary, he turned to the hotel. Near him, a young mother nursed her baby. The woman was no more than sixteen. Beside her, another child played at her bare feet.

Lupo and Monday stepped out of the hotel cantina's main entrance onto the veranda, led by the young man Jack sent inside. They spotted Jack and moved down the main stairway toward him. Monday loosened his big .44-caliber Smith & Wesson revolver in its holster and Lupo held a shotgun slung over his shoulder. The stock had been sawed down to a pistol grip so Lupo could quickly whip the gun into position.

Jack stood his ground. "Tell your boss Jack Benteen is here and wants to talk to him."

Lupo held out his hand. "Your pistol first, hombre."

Jack shook his head almost imperceptibly. "I told you before, nobody gets my gun without somebody getting hurt."

Monday smiled and looked at Lupo, as if to say, "Okay. I guess we have to hurt him." The two men instinctively stepped back to give each other more room to move. Around the trio, people scrambled to get out of the potential line of fire. The Indians stopped blowing their pipes. Suddenly there was dead silence except for the crackling of the cookfires.

But Lupo finally shook his head at Monday. "Go tell Cash. See what he says."

Disappointed, Monday moved off toward the cantina, pushing his revolver back snugly into its holster.

The commandos watched from the windows of the rooming house, Hackett using the binoculars, the rest just looking.

"What's with the cowboy?" McRose asked nervously. "That's as far as he goes?"

They could see Jack and Lupo. Both of them were now in the clear; everyone else in the courtyard had backed out of the way.

"Sonofabitch will get himself stitched in the crossfire if that's where he's going to make his stand," Hackett said.

Then Cash came out of the doorway on the veranda, wearing his white linen suit and white Stetson, brandishing a half-empty bottle of tequila.

Hackett passed the binoculars to McRose. "That's Bailey, the head honcho. Grab a look, everybody. He's our prime target."

Cash took a swig from the bottle and looked at Jack. "Well, there he is." His suit was filthy. He looked like he hadn't slept in a week. He thrust his chin in Jack's direction and spoke to Lupo and Monday. "You watch out now. He's a snake, that old boy. Roll up your sleeves, get the tip of his tongue, and pull it till he pops. *Then* we'll know what we got!" He strolled out to the edge of the veranda and stopped at the top of the stairs.

Jack approached the bottom of the steps, wondering whether Cash being wired out of his gourd would help or hinder him.

The two friends gone bad faced each other, two warriors ritually facing off to battle for their lives.

Cash beamed, a crazy glint to his eyes. "How you doing, Jack? I expected you'd show up sooner or later. Did you come for me? Or Sarita?"

"I came to take you *both* home, Cash. I think that'd be the best all around."

Cash squinted at Jack, trying to focus through his drunkenness. He was angry that Jack had been so predictable and followed Sarita down to San Luis. It would have been *better* all around if the Holy Ranger had stayed in Texas where he belonged. But it was too late now; the cards were dealt and all that was left was to play the hand.

"Well now, Jack," Cash said, "you can *have* Sarita. It seems like me and her aren't doing real well together. But when it comes to inviting me back across the river . . ." He laughed.

"I'm not inviting you, Cash. You don't have any choice."

"Jesus Christ, I always knew you had balls, but I didn't think you were crazy!" Cash gestured at the men around him. There were perhaps twenty desperadoes, all heavily armed killers.

"I don't give a damn about your private army." Jack ignored the threat. "This is just between you and me, Cash. I'm calling you out. It's personal. Just me and you."

"Not leaving me any alternative but to settle our differences. That right, amigo? No room to maneuver." Stupid, Cash thought, what Jack's doing isn't right for either of us, but it's his game.

"I want to see Sarita, Cash. Make sure she's okay. Then we'll settle up."

Cash drank again. "Why sure, that's only fair. What the hell, you think I want you worried about her when you should be concentrating on killing me?" He smiled broadly. "I think we'd better have your gun first, or I don't guess you get to see the love of your life. I wouldn't want you hooking up with her with a gun in your hand. Hell, you'd start acting real heroic and blaze away at all these terrible boys I got working for me. You'd turn it into the Alamo, Jack. Old Cash wouldn't want that." He paused, then said pointedly, "Old Cash wants you for himself."

But Jack remained adamant. "It's a bad habit, giving up your gun."

Cash shrugged. "Okay, forget Sarita. I'll go and get my popper and we'll settle up right here and now."

Sarita was the bottom line and Cash knew it. Jack slowly took his .45 out of its holster and tossed it to Cash. Cash hefted it, felt its warmth, admired the grips, then slipped it into a jacket pocket.

"You'll get it back in time for our little finish-up. You know me. I always keep my promises."

Jack allowed himself a smile. "Aw hell, I know that, Cash. The problem is trying to get one out of you."

Cash came down the stairs to Jack and put an arm around his shoulders. "Jack, boy, you have no idea how good it is to see you."

Jack let Cash lead him up to the hotel, smelling the booze on his breath, feeling the crazy vibes from the man who had once been his best friend.

"People here," Cash said, ambling across the veranda with Jack, "I am telling you, they can't follow Cash in the verbal sphere. At all. When I'm flying, son, it's *solo*. You know that feeling, when you're talking along, then you pause for one minute, look around real careful, and you know in your heart it's all just wasted? All your private jokes and subtle conversations have been just sailing right on past."

Listening to him, Jack had a sense of what life had really been like for Cash: lonely, misunderstood. He smiled gently and said, "You know me, Cash. I like to keep the conversation real simple."

"Hell you do, Jack, hell you do," Cash roared with sudden mirth. "I miss you, old buddy. It's too bad you turned out to be such a shitheel and wouldn't accept my business proposition. We'd have done great by each other." They reached the double oak doors that were the entrance to the hotel. "Come on in and we'll rustle up old Sarita," Cash said, a twinge of sadness in his voice. "Then we'll have us our little fun. I promise."

Hackett and his men watched Jack and Cash go in through the hotel cantina doorway.

Hackett turned from the window, binoculars in hand. "Okay. The cowboy's got Bailey diverted. Now let's move."

"Wait a minute," Biddle said. "You told the cowboy he'd have thirty minutes before we—"

"That's now inoperative. We have our mission," Hackett replied tersely. "Let's move it, *now*. Unless you want to take over command, Charlie?"

Biddle turned his eyes away from Hackett's challenge.

"Let's roll," Hackett told the men.

The commandos readied for action, each running through the bag he had brought, pulling out weapons, assembling, loading. McRose pulled a dirty bandanna from his daypack. Inside was a fat bundle of shotgun shells wrapped together with rosary beads. McRose untied the beads and dumped the shells into his pockets, then rammed ten of them into the magazine that ran the length of the barrel of his sawed-off 12-gauge riot gun.

Biddle packed away a Steyr Aug, broken down into pieces. The Steyr was a "bullpup" type gun, so called because the magazine is located behind the trigger instead of ahead of it, which results in a shorter stock and a shorter overall length, which suited Biddle's compact frame fairly well. But smaller size was only a side benefit: the Aug, all plastic except for the ventilated barrel, carried the knock-down power of a small cannon and had a deadly accurate scope without crosshairs, just a small black circle that didn't block the "pilot's" view of exactly where the bullet would land. The gun stashed neatly in a satchel where Biddle could carry it unnoticed.

Hackett strapped a .357 revolver under his jacket and slipped a K-Bar knife into an upside-down sheath at the small of his back. Coker and Atwater each took a small MAC-10 Ingram and a few clips of ammunition. In addition, Atwater hauled along a number of assorted blasting caps, fuses, and timers that always stayed in his weapons pack for emergencies.

"The timing's crucial," Hackett told them. "We've got to mesh it up. Everything goes down to the second. At exactly fifteen hundred and forty hours we infiltrate the hotel. I'll be in point position."

It was fifteen-twenty now. They had twenty minutes to cross the town and climb the hill.

"Once inside," Hackett continued, "Atwater will take out the M-sixty overlooking the balcony, then hit the machine-gun nest on the roof—north quadrant. Biddle will take out the twin thirties on the south quadrant. Coker stays back near the courtyard."

Coker nodded, psyching himself up.

"Until you hear Atwater and Biddle open fire. Then you take out the machine gun at the south base of the perimeter, then move across to the north. McRose will be point man in the corridors. Mop 'em up, Larry. Make sure it's clear for the rest of us. If anybody doesn't make it, take the job over yourself."

The men listened attentively, waiting for his summary.

"Up until the opening blast I want a silent operation. That will give me time to pull together all the national security documents I can get my hands on before all hell breaks loose."

"What about fall-back?" McRose asked, wondering how they were supposed to cover their asses if anything went wrong.

"There is no fall-back position," Hackett said with shocking finality. "There is no compromise with victory. We hit and we hit *fast*. It'll be over by sixteen-hundred hours."

"But what about the documents?" McRose insisted. "How do we back you up?"

"That's my responsibility, Sergeant, and *mine alone*."

"Yes, sir," McRose echoed dumbly. "Your responsibility."

But he didn't accept Hackett's authority anymore. All of the commandos were getting the feeling that something was wrong. The mission was an ugly one—that sometimes happened. But they always knew the parameters within which they were operating. Hackett had kept them in the dark all along, and now that they were marching into the very heart of darkness they were still blind.

One by one, the commandos made their way out onto the street. Hackett had given them serapes and straw hats as simple cover to get them to the hotel. Each man edged into the crowd. Around them, firecrackers and festivities provided a perfect diversion.

In the minds of Biddle, Atwater, Coker, and McRose echoed only one thought, the major's final words: "Everybody remember: two prime targets," Hackett had said. "Whoever spots Bailey and the cowboy: shoot to kill."

32

Cash led Jack through the bustling cantina to the base of an inner stairway that led to the upper floors. They were tailed by Monday and Lupo, who watched Jack intensely, waiting for him to make any move that Cash didn't approve of. Jack scoped out his surroundings. It was, it seemed to him, a sad place. Cash's workers were not wealthy like Cash was. They didn't even dream of the kind of money the operation really controlled. Mostly they were poor men who had taken advantage of the employment opportunity Cash's business offered. Other than Cash's army, most of the patrons of the cantina weren't armed, nor were they especially dangerous. This was an impoverished town to which Cash had brought a kind of Faustian prosperity. Cash couldn't even enjoy his wealth. He looked mortally tired, half crazed by his life, by his isolation.

But things were the way they were. Cash and Jack were enemies, they had no choice anymore. Each one was set to destroy the other, or so it seemed. For now, Jack only wanted to see Sarita. There would be no other satisfaction in the finale, he realized.

"Go on up," Cash said. "Check out Sarita. I'll be

waiting over there." He indicated a raised area with a large table in front of the mariachi band. "Don't keep me waiting too long, Jack. I get lonely real fast down here."

"Where's her room?" Jack asked.

"Take him up to Rosa," Cash told Lupo. "She'll take care of him."

In Spanish, Lupo told Cash, "I haven't seen Rosa in a while. Maybe she's not upstairs?"

"How in the hell would I know where she is?" Cash spoke in English, suddenly flaming with anger. "You think I got nothing better to occupy my mind than keeping track of Jezebels?"

Lupo didn't understand. "Jeza-who?"

"Whores! Whores, *pendejo!*" Cash grabbed Jack's arm, looked into his eyes with a desperation Jack didn't understand. "You see, amigo, you see? This is what I'm telling you. I'm a prospector panning for gold in a latrine."

Cash's self-pity was disturbing, and though Jack felt sorry for the man, he shrugged off Cash's hand. "Don't give me this crap. Where is she, Cash?"

Then Cash's mood swung again. He was suddenly a sorry drunk, apologizing sloppily, fawning. "She's okay, Jack. She kept telling me she needed time. I finally got disgusted and gave her a private room. She can have all the time she wants in there." Then, temper flaring again, he turned to Lupo. "You heard the hombre! He wants his woman! Go find Rosa or I'll hang your balls on your sombrero!"

"Hokay, hokay," Lupo muttered, cowed by Cash's wrath. He slung his battered shotgun over his shoulder again and started up the stairs and called to Jack, *"Venga,* hombre. I find you Rosa."

Cash watched his old buddy climb the stairs behind Lupo, passing through the glow of the stairway window. The light streamed in around Jack like a halo.

Goddamn, Cash thought, he looks like an angel in the stained glass of a church window. Old Saint Jack, coming to take me home. Then Jack was out of the light again and Cash stared out into the infinite sky beyond with a peaceful smile on his face, while Saint Jack climbed toward the heavens himself, looking for Sarita.

Lupo marched down the hall, Jack close behind. Monday brought up the rear, his massive bulk seeming to fill the corridor. On one side of the corridor was an open railing from which Jack could see out over the cantina floor below. Raucous laughter, yelling, cursing, music from the band mixed with the cries of ecstasy from behind the closed doors on the other side.

Lupo pushed past the whores and the johns coming and going through the busy hall, shouting, "Rosa! *Madre de putas!* Rosa!"

A door suddenly banged open beside them, revealing Rosa, a pretty, overly made-up whore of forty, clutching a chihuahua to the red lacy bodice frills near her ample breasts.

"*Que?*" Rosa inquired, looking at Jack with a smile. She asked Lupo, "*Amigo del patron?* Is he a friend of the boss?"

"*Sí*—no." Lupo wasn't sure how to answer. In Spanish he said: "Cash says you know where to find Sarita."

Jack was boiling. His Spanish wasn't good enough to follow Lupo and Rosa's lickety-split patois.

"Sarita? *O esa!*—oh her!" Rosa exclaimed. "I thought she worked here—*yo creí que trabajaba aquí.* I put her in a room like the rest of the whores—*las putas.*"

Jack understood the word *putas* and Rosa savored his reaction. She slyly grinned at Lupo.

"You want to have some fun?" Rosa asked, still speaking only Spanish. "Tell this gringo how many men she has had here." Rosa let out a peal of laughter. "Go ahead—*andale!* Tell him. I want to see his face!"

Lupo laughed as well. Rosa was always good for a practical joke and this one would be a chance to get even with the gringo without making Cash too mad. Monday smiled, uncomprehending as Lupo and Rosa doubled over with mirth.

Lupo turned to Jack. "She make big mistake, amigo. Big mistake!" he said in his broken English.

"What mistake?" Jack suddenly felt his heart tighten in his chest.

"Rosa"—Lupo wiped tears of laughter from his eyes—"has allowed some *muchachos* to be fucking your girl. Three *muchachos* who like girls what sing, you know?"

"Where? Which room?" Jack demanded.

Rosa laughed harder. She got the reaction she wanted from Jack and it made her day.

Lupo shrugged, apologetic but still grinning. "She don't know which room, gringo. She's a stupid whore."

Jack set off down the hall and started ripping open doors, followed by Lupo, Monday, and Rosa's continued peals.

"Big mistake, gringo," Lupo called after him. "But maybe they didn't fuck her too much."

"Yeah, only a little," Monday said. "Maybe she likes it, man. Ever think of that?"

Rosa came down the hall after them, yelling at Jack in Spanish.

Lupo asked, "What's the big deal, man? You gringos come down here all the time and fuck our girls. Why can't we fuck your girls a little bit?"

But Jack ignored the taunts as he pushed the whores out of his way, crashing open door after door. He burst into one room to find one of Cash's armed goons on top of a woman whose long, dark hair could have been Sarita's. He kicked the man's gun out of reach and pulled him away. But instead of Sarita, he found the hard, used face of a Mexican whore.

Rosa opened a door across the corridor.

"Hey, gringo! Quick!" Lupo called. *"Muchachos* all over on this one here!"

Monday peered into the room. "One *muchacho* . . . two *muchacho* . . . three *muchacho!* This must be it, man!"

Jack wheeled with murder in his heart and raced in the direction of the room, but suddenly a door opened nearby and he stopped dead.

Sarita was standing by herself in an open doorway, relief flooding her face. "Jack!"

He ran to her, held her in his arms. They slid into the room and closed the door behind them. There was no one else inside.

"You okay?" Jack asked softly.

She nodded, her eyes wet but not quite crying. "Now. I'm okay now." She clung to him. "Jack, I'm so sorry. Everything got so messed up, when all the time I've loved only you!" She hugged him tighter. "You won't push me away anymore?"

Jack shook his head, holding her tight. "I only pushed you away because of Cash. I knew we were headed for a showdown and I didn't want you in the middle."

"We'll make it together, Jack?"

"I think so," he whispered. "I think we've got a chance."

Lupo knocked on the door and shouted, "Hey, gringo, time to go. You got what you wanted, now I bring you back to Cash."

33

Biddle strolled in through the cantina entrance during a lull in the music. He had shed his disguise, was now wearing his trademark oxford shirt and slacks and was carrying a satchel. He looked grim. The mission sucked, but he had to go through with it. A soldier took the bad along with the good. Werewolf Operatives were no different.

Curiously, nobody in the cantina paid much attention to the diminutive black man. The band started another number, "Relámpago," a bouncy trumpet piece that seemed inappropriate to Biddle. If only they knew . . .

He walked up to the bar and squeezed in between the thugs and the rest of the drunks. The bartender, a short, balding man in a white apron, raised an eyebrow at him.

"Cerveza, por favor," Biddle said.

The bartender opened a cold Corona and set it down on the bar. Biddle paid with a U.S. dollar and, with a gesture, told the bartender to keep the change.

A couple of whores made a beeline for the new customer, one of them racing to squeeze next to Biddle before the other could move in. She scowled off her co-worker, then smiled at Biddle.

Biddle returned the smile. "What's your little name?"

"Fifty bucks," she replied, putting an arm over his shoulder.

Biddle grabbed her ass. "Let me call you Thirty."

She smiled again. "Hokay. Let's go, gringo. *Vamonos.*"

She pulled him toward the stairway that Saint Jack had ascended.

"Gotta be a room with a view," Biddle said.

The whore hustled him up the stairs and to her room, happy for the work. As she shut the door behind her Jack and Sarita came out of the room where Sarita had been staying. Lupo and Monday escorted them downstairs to Cash's table.

Inside the room, the whore started stripping off her simple dress but, to her surprise, Biddle just walked past her and went to the window that overlooked the courtyard. Below him, he watched the other commandos moving among the revelers. The room was perfect. It had a clear view of the gun nest on the far wing.

"Okay, Thirty," Biddle said, turning back to the whore. "Into bed."

Just wearing panties, she said, "First the money," and rubbed her thumb against her fingers for illustration.

"Here," Biddle said. He pulled out his wallet and handed her a sheaf of small bills. "Don't stop to count."

She took the money. The panties came off and she sat down on the bed, lay back seductively. "Are you in some kind of hurry?"

"Come on." Biddle was brusque. "Under the sheets. I don't need any conversation."

The whore pulled a sheet over her.

"Now on your side, baby," Biddle continued. "Look at the wall."

"The wall? For why I got to look at the wall?" She didn't like the turn this trick was taking.

"'Cause it turns me on," Biddle told her.

"Hey, I don't think I wanna fuck with you," she said. She started to get out of the bed, but Biddle shoved her back down.

"You do like I say." Biddle's voice was poison now. "You turn your head and look at me and it'll be the last thing you ever see. Dig?"

She shrank away from him. He put his satchel on the bed and pulled out the sections of the Aug, then started clipping them together.

The whore's eyes went wide, then, terrified, she slowly faced the wall, trembling.

"Don't kill me, gringo," she pleaded. "I won't look, don't kill me." She crossed herself and began whispering her prayers in Spanish.

With expert speed, Biddle finished assembling the rifle and attached the scope.

Atwater went past some Cash-owned federales in knee-high leather boots who were fraternizing with some of the whores huddling in the shade of an archway that opened to the hillside behind the hotel. Nobody cast him a second glance as he went through the passage and slipped into a rear doorway. He found himself in a dilapidated narrow wooden stairwell that led upward. He started climbing the steps, but heard voices and bootsteps, so quickly backtracked. At the bottom to one side was the door he came in from. Next to it was another door.

Atwater turned the knob. It was another stairway leading down into darkness. This stairway was of old stone flags, dusty but well trodden. He closed the door behind him as a couple of armed goons came into view, then went down the stairs in the darkness, feeling his way. When he got to the bottom, he lit up a pack of matches.

He was in an old storage cellar. It was filled with wooden crates that he easily recognized. The crates held a cache of arms, mostly U.S., some Soviet, some Israeli. M-16s, AK-47s, Uzis, machine guns, pistols, grenades, boxes and boxes of ammunition. There was enough weaponry and munitions to supply a much larger army than Cash's.

Atwater was amazed. Hackett hadn't told them much about the true nature of their target. All he had been able to glean was that the head honcho controlled a drug empire. Here, though, was more solid proof that the man might, indeed, pose a threat to national security. But, he reflected, there was no way to launch an attack on the United States from tiny San Luis, unless deeper in this cellar was a missile silo. And so he stumbled on the truth: trading in arms facilitated the drug business and vice versa. This, he reasoned, was the storage depot for black-market weapons on their way to destabilizing Central America or elsewhere. In return, America could stay high. A reasonable trade, Atwater thought.

Atwater started going through the boxes. There were lots of them, all filled to brimming with lethal hardware. Atwater estimated there was more than a million dollars' worth here. He kept looking, then finally found what he had hoped for: kegs of black powder, then fifty kilos of plastique. Maybe twenty times what he needed to turn the hotel into a pile of broken rock.

"Eureka!" Now, for Atwater, this underground hole had turned into some kind of creepy heaven. The fuses and blasting caps would come in handy. He quickly spread the explosives around the basement and tapped a blasting cap into each charge. He worked quickly, knowing he didn't have much time, determined to leave his signature on the commandos' handiwork in San Luis.

"Yeah, baby, now we're talking!" he exclaimed to himself as he worked. The explosives were going to his head, the way good whiskey would go to another man's. Atwater was in his element when working with volatile substances. He found a timer and set it to fuse the blasting caps. He didn't know how much time he had, but estimated that thirty more minutes would be enough to do what they had to do. If Hackett's plan was carried out with any degree of success, it would be over in plenty of time for the commandos to get clear before the hotel went sky-high.

That done, he headed back up the stairs, whistling happily as he went. He had left a loose cannon behind him, to smash the gunwales out when the ship started tossing in the storm. With any luck, he thought, maybe the major wouldn't get out soon enough.

Ignorant of the commandos' infiltration of his stronghold, Cash sat in the cantina watching a girl dance for him on a nearby tabletop to the accompaniment of the house band. Around him, his coarse henchmen shouted bravos to the girl, leering, lusting after her. But Cash was only bored. Bored by the girl. Bored by the feast spread out before him, the fine wines, the sumptuous plates of fruits and meats and salads. Cash was like the Roman emperor Caligula, who indulged his vast appetites for pleasure and for power, but who ultimately satiated himself.

When he spotted Monday and Lupo leading Jack and Sarita across the floor to him, he waved the girl and crowding goons away. His old friends were seated at the table, Sarita huddled between Jack and Cash, making a point of staying closer to Jack. She was scared. Even Jack's presence didn't lessen her apprehension about what was to come.

"How'd the big reunion go?" Cash was expansive, ignoring or ignorant of their resentment. "Much hugging and kissing and tears of joy?"

"Yeah, something like that," Jack said. "Now I want my gun, Cash."

Cash made a face. "First, we gotta have us a last drink together. And *then* the big final-finito." He looked at Sarita. "Gonna disappoint you, baby. You've been saving everything for my old friend Jack. Gonna make you real unhappy when you watch me shoot him down." His face darkened as he yelled to a waiter, suddenly piqued by the lack of service. "Hey, Miguel! Beer for my amigo! Champagne for me and my *querida!* Pronto!"

"I don't want nothing, Cash," Sarita said. "I just want you to say Jack and I can leave."

"Aw, hell." Cash looked pained. "I taught you better manners than that, honey. You're my guest and don't you forget it." He was quite at home using the word *guest* as a threat. "She'll train up real good," he assured Jack. "Half an hour and it all comes back, good as new." He lowered his voice. "I didn't hurt her. Believe me, partner."

Then Cash exploded at the help again. "Champagne, goddamn it! *Miguel!*" Then just as suddenly he was smiling patronizingly at Sarita. "Now ain't this nice? Ain't this just lovely, darling? Tell Jack the truth, did I hurt you? Or did anyone? You tell him if we did."

Sarita shook her head.

"Well, of course I didn't." Cash assumed the manner of a gruff uncle. "Why I've known old Sarita for years. Used to neck with her, pick her up in my Chevy, and tear off some ass."

He pulled a wicked-looking dagger from his jacket,

teasingly played the tip against a long curl of Sarita's hair, turning the knife to wind the hair around it. Jack made a move toward him, but Lupo's shotgun was suddenly cocked and shoved in his face, Lupo's eyes afire. He was looking for a good excuse to pull the trigger. Jack backed off.

"Yeah, didn't we, honey?" Cash asked dreamily. "Used to tear off some ass. Damn near got married, remember? Went looking for spoons. Knives and forks and spoons and crap."

"Let's get to it, Cash," Jack demanded. "Let's deal."

Cash's reverie turned dark as he stood and looked at Jack. "Then after *I* left, *you* came along and climbed in her drawers. Then I don't know who-all she was with when she went off on her singing tours. Probably fiddlers and such. Dopers. Jew drummers. Niggers with trumpets."

Jack boiled, longing for his gun, longing for Cash's blood. "I'm telling you," he fumed, "let's get to it, Cash! Now!"

But Cash was still taking his time. "When there's an occasion to celebrate, like you two being back together, you gotta rise up to it," he rambled. He fumbled in his pockets and brought out a long glass vial full of cocaine. He filled the cap and snorted, then refilled for his other nostril, gasping, his eyes watering as the heavy dose entered his bloodstream.

His attention off of Jack and Sarita for a moment, Cash spotted a large tan-suited Mexican man, whose thick bald head stuck out above the dark heads of the other men. It was Cueball, the man who had "snaked" Garcia.

"Hey, Jesus!" Cash bellowed and waved. "Come on over!"

The man moved toward him, spoke to Cash in Spanish. "Sure, boss. How's everything with you?"

Cash thrust out his jaw, nodded his head tentatively. "Everything's fine. Just fine. Excepting one thing, Jesus. And this'll fix it." He pulled out his pistol and gave the man one blast in the forehead from only a foot away. Jesus was knocked back violently, the top of his head ripped open. He hit the floor, dead. The red-tiled floor got redder. The band stopped playing. Cash's snub-nosed .44 magnum was still smoking at his side. The cantina was silent.

Cash turned back to Jack and shook his head. "And I *liked* him. I honest to Christ really liked old Jesus, until yesterday when his account showed up short. It ain't so much the money. It's the bad example, and the fact that I *trusted* the man." He turned to Monday. "Haul him out of here. Ain't nice for the ladies to see a dead coyote." Then he faced Jack again. "It's real good country down here. A man can get away with anything as long as he just keeps paying his friends. What they need down here is a good old-fashioned revolution, you know that?"

Monday grabbed the dead man by one leg and dragged him across the floor toward the rear exit, leaving a bloody trail in his wake.

Cash turned toward his musicians. "Get some music going!" He gestured with the pistol. "What the hell is going on here? Get some music going or I'll shoot the damn band. I want it sweet, goddamn it! We got us a loving couple here!"

The band struck up "Relámpago" and Cash put away his gun. He set up some glasses and poured the champagne a wary Miguel had brought over.

"We gotta drink to your happy life together," he told Jack and Sarita. He raised a glass. "For as long as it lasts." He drank alone. "You just sit on back, Jack. I need a little more conversation before you get your gun and we settle up."

Cash, too, was a loose cannon. His fiery temper and his madness played a counterpoint to Atwater's hidden threat ticking away below them.

Hackett and McRose came in by the same stairway Buck had used. They shed their disguises and went up to an upper second floor. Coker was in the courtyard out in front, standing in position to take the first gun nest. Biddle had his assigned roof gun emplacement in his sights, ready for Buck's signal.

As the two commandos made their way along the corridor they turned a corner to find themselves face-to-face with two armed goons patrolling the halls. Before the goons could react, Hackett's K-Bar knife was buried in one of them. McRose's shotgun was out, but Hackett pushed it aside, drew a silenced pistol, and shot the other man in the back as he ran.

"Get the bodies out of sight," Hackett ordered. "Then get to Bailey. I've got to move in on the docs we're after. You're on your own from here."

McRose opened a nearby door. Catapulting in, he surprised another of Cash's henchmen, stripped to the waist, shaving at a mirror. Whirling with his straight razor, the man slashed at McRose.

McRose easily ducked under the wide arc of the razor, pushed the razor hand away, and twisted the man's wrist, forcing him to drop the blade. He kept moving, pulling the man with him, scooping up the razor as it fell. He turned and opened the man's throat, severing the carotid artery. The man died quickly as the blood flow intended for his brain ran elsewhere. McRose stepped over the quickly spreading pool of scarlet and began to drag the bodies in from the hall.

When he left McRose, Hackett moved quickly down the hallways, searching for Cash's offices. He kicked open doors as he went. The rooms up here were mostly empty—no whores, but nothing Hackett wanted either. He kept looking. Time was growing short, in more ways than he realized.

34

"Now ain't this nice," Cash said, like an overbearing matron at a Houston charity tea. "Ain't this just lovely? Two amigos drinking like old times. Let me tell you it stirs something way way down. Almost too deep to verbalize." Cash polished off some more of the champagne. Jack and Sarita's glasses were untouched. "What I keep thinking is how come we can't be friends no more, Jack boy? I'm serious. I am."

It was obvious that Cash's question came from his warped heart. But Jack and Cash both knew it was way too late now. They had to play out the string.

Jack looked into his beer as he spoke. "You and me grew up together, Cash. Best friends. Then I left. Went out to Dallas, Houston, Chicago, wherever. Couldn't make any of it work, 'cause I was just running away from who I was. When my dad died, I came home to bury him and to face up to things. Face up to my dad, my granddad, the way I was raised. When I put the badge on, things felt right. Third-generation Ranger, doing something I believed in, something most people believed in. No more kid stuff. And I looked around for my old friend Cash. Wanted him to be part of things. But he was gone. And later I found out he was gone bad. Gone real bad."

"Goddamn, Jack," Cash said with a big grin. "You got it all wrong. *You* went bad on *me.* Lost your sense of humor. Went and got yourself outfitted government-issue."

Jack ignored him, still staring into his beer, talking in a monotone, getting his bitterness over their situation out of him, so he would be free to act when the time came.

"You almost made it, Cash. Five years down here. Deep cover for the D.E.A.—"

"Ain't it rich?" Cash laughed. "Old Cash working for the law. Paid off real good, though."

"You couldn't stick to the straight and narrow!" Jack accused him.

Cash frowned, his face darkening. "I turned when I saw the light!" he rhapsodized. "It came shining down on me, Jack, illuminating what road I had to take. It made me see I could get everything I wanted. Get it all!"

"Didn't shine up the right and wrong of it, though?" Jack asked quietly.

"Ain't no right and wrong," Cash insisted. "There's only *choices*. And everybody's got to make their own. That's God-given. And who the hell're you or anybody to take that away? I'm a poor boy that rose up. I'm not going to let anybody take away what I got."

"Like you said, Cash, we've all got choices," Jack acknowledged with a nod of resignation. Then, to his alarm, he saw Atwater crossing the cantina to the bar.

Jack got up.

"Where are you going?" Cash demanded.

"To get me a tequila."

"Sit on down. I got people to get you a drink, Jack."

But Jack moved off toward the bar, saying, "I'll get it myself, Cash. I like getting things for myself."

Cash let him go. He wanted a last chance at Sarita alone. He turned to her. "You know, baby," he began, "I go to lunch with the governor of this here state, and I go to Mexico City for them big charity balls. Christ A'mighty, ain't no one like old Cash for feeding porch monkeys and peons and saving whales and such. But I got no one to talk to. No one from home. Nobody who understands me at all."

Sarita listened, trembling inside. Cash was pensive now, but he was unpredictable. He would pour out his soft side, share his hurts, his broken dreams, reveal how lonely he was, then suddenly turn, like he did to poor Jesus, and reveal his scarred, ugly, evil side.

"I got a surprise for you, Sarita," he said, standing up. "I got the band to learn your number-one song. That song you always said was your favorite, the one your mama taught you."

"Cash," Sarita protested as he took her hands and drew her to her feet, "Jesus Christ." She began crying.

At Cash's signal, the band began playing a plaintive border song, "Pero Ay Qué Triste." Cash steered Sarita onto the dance floor in front of the band and held her close.

"Sing it, honey," he whispered in her ear. "Come on. Soft on my shoulder. Just one more old time. Sing for me real sweet. It just might put old Cash in a better mood. Might not want to kill Jack anymore."

Sarita began to sing softly, tears streaming down her face, hoping that her song could extinguish the flames of madness burning in Cash's heart.

Across the cantina, Jack squeezed in next to Atwater at the bar. He signaled the bartender for a tequila, then spoke to Buck without looking at him, in case Cash was watching and might suspect complicity.

"Buck!" Jack hissed. "The major said he'd give me thirty minutes with Cash."

"He changed it, man," Atwater replied. "I'm doing a little recon here."

"What change?" Jack demanded. "Tell me, god-damn it."

"Everything got moved up fifteen minutes. Don't stay out in the open, it's all coming down."

Jack glanced at Atwater, who was staring at their reflection in the bar mirror.

"We're supposed to shoot you on sight and that don't sit too well with me. I thank you for getting me out of your jail and treating me decent. Go for yourself, Ranger."

Buck started to leave, but had one more remark for Jack. "Fire in the hole, Ranger. Maybe twenty minutes left." Then Atwater disappeared into the crowd. Moments later, Jack saw him go up the stairs to the second floor.

Fire in the hole. Jack knew the term. It was used by blasters who were setting dynamite. They called out "fire in the hole!" to warn others that they were about to set off a charge. Jack socked back his shot of tequila and urgently returned to Cash and Sarita. He saw them swaying together on the dance floor.

Sarita kept crying as she sang, Cash holding her tight.

"I'm giving you a reprieve, honey," Cash said to her. "It's *me* you want to be with, I know that. I was the first. I'll always be the first."

"No, Cash," she said softly, but he wouldn't believe her.

"You hush now and listen to me," he said. "All that went wrong with you and me the last few days—you not wanting to go to bed with me because you felt you owed Jack I don't know what—that's all in the past. I'm going to forget it like it never was. What we'll do, we'll go to Cancun, get us a bungalow, swim in that emerald sea and find our way back to where we once were."

Sarita broke away from him, horrified, her revulsion overcoming her fear of the man.

"You're crazy, Cash," she cried out. "You've gone crazy!"

She ran to Jack, who had started moving toward them on the floor. He held her and stared at Cash, standing alone in the middle of the room.

Cash was furious, sullen. He had failed. The string was almost played out and now it was time to reel in the line. Slowly he took out Jack's gun and tossed it to him.

"Here you go, amigo," Cash said. Jack caught the gun and slipped it into his empty holster. "Showdown," Cash said with finality. "Whoever's left standing gets Sarita."

"Let's deal, Cash," Jack said. "I don't want to have to kill you."

"Out in the sun, Jack." Cash ignored the request for negotiation. "I need some sun."

He walked out to the courtyard, his entourage of goons and mercenaries pressing Jack and Sarita along behind him.

Merv was in his office, sorting stacks of receipts. A money-counting machine was clacking away in the corner. Merv rested his elbows on his desk for a moment, checking the output on his computer screen. Things were running along okay. Another hour and he would be done with the accounts for the day. He rubbed his eyes. They suffered horribly from the day-long work of staring at tiny figures representing very large numbers.

Merv moved some papers around, then suddenly stopped. There was blood smeared on them. He checked his hands, wondering if he had a paper cut.

Then another drop of blood appeared, followed shortly by another. Merv looked up. The ceiling was bleeding. A ribbon of blood was snaking out of a crack, running to the end of the crack and forming drops.

Merv dashed into the hall, screaming, "Blood! It's running blood!"

Around the corner, Hackett heard the scream. He quickly ran to the intersection of the halls and ran into Merv, who was panicked. Hackett quickly holstered his gun and grabbed him.

"My fucking ceiling's bleeding!" Merv shouted.

Merv wheeled around to face Hackett and his jaw dropped open with surprise.

"Major . . ."

"I've been looking for you, Merv," Hackett said.

"What are you doing here?" Merv wanted to know.

"Big raid," Hackett said. "The D.E.A.'s made a deal with the federales. No more chickenshit local-level drug enforcement—"

"Christ!" Merv cut him off. "I can't believe it. But after that damn bank robbery—"

"They're targeting the records," Hackett said. "Got to stash them away. Where do you keep them?"

"In my office," Merv replied. "Wait a minute, I don't get it. Is this tied in to the robbery?"

"Yeah." Hackett nodded. "Now let's go. No time to talk."

"Shit." Merv started off at a trot back to his office, Hackett following close behind. "Everything's gone crazy around here. Especially Cash. He's real crazy since he heard about the bank."

They went into Merv's office. The blood from McRose's kill upstairs was still dripping. It had formed a pool on the papers on Merv's desk.

"It's still bleeding," Merv said. "Can you believe it? I got a bleeding ceiling! Somebody up there must be hurt pretty bad."

"Get the records!" Hackett ordered.

Merv went to the large iron safe and quickly spun out

the combination as Hackett stood by impatiently. All the money Major Hackett had illegally acquired was worthless if the government wouldn't let him live to spend it.

"This is it, ain't it?" Cash crowed to Jack. "The big final-final. I'm gonna give you a real good chance, Jack. Just 'cause we used to be amigos."

They were out in the sunshine on the hotel's veranda surrounded by Cash's men, who were eager for the show.

"Back to back. Count off ten paces. Then we both start blazing away. Blast each other to the Land of Glory and may the better man win. And keep Sarita."

"You do what you gotta do, Cash," Jack replied stiffly.

"That's the spirit, Jack." Cash grinned crazily. "I like your attitude."

Sarita suddenly rushed at Cash, cursing him in Spanish. She tried to pound at him, but he easily caught her wrists and held her off. He enjoyed feeling her writhe under his grip.

Monday lumbered up and grabbed her. He held her so she couldn't twist away, despite her valiant struggle.

"It's all right, honey." Cash smiled. "You've come this far with two old buddies, you might as well see them finish it up. We're just two bull elks locking horns over the best cow in the herd."

"No, Cash! Please!" Sarita pleaded.

"Show us some tit if you want to be useful," Cash suggested. "Give us some motivation." He thrust the bottle he had carried outside to Lupo. "Here, hold the tequila."

Cash walked up to Jack and turned back to back with him. Both men took out their pistols, held them pointing up, like an old-time New Orleans duel.

"One . . ." Cash counted and stepped. "Two."

Sarita burst into sobs. "No! Please! Cash!"

"Aw, shit," Cash said. He broke off the count and crossed to Sarita. "Honey, if you are gonna cry, it just fucks it all up! It lowers the whole tone. I mean this ain't just dogshit we're doing here. These are the men you love putting it on the line!"

He reached out and tore her skirt at the waist.

"A little more leg! That's a good girl." He walked back to Jack, smiling. "No change in old Sarita. Tear off a piece there, you always get meat."

Sarita went berserk and started raving again in Spanish. "You sonofabitch, Cash! Give me a gun and I'll shoot you myself!"

"Stand in line, baby," Cash said. He turned to Jack smiling. "Now we are *all* cooking. Yes, sir, we got the proper attitude now."

Merv swung open the big safe door and took out a small ledger. The rest of the safe was filled with bundles of money.

"Is that everything?" Hackett asked. "All my business dealings with Cash, all his dealings?"

"This is it," Merv confirmed.

Hackett reached for the ledger, but Merv drew back.

"Let's have it," Hackett ordered.

"I can't do that," Merv said. "It's the only copy. All the early records were stolen from Cash's safe-deposit box at the bank. This is the only record left and it belongs to Cash."

"I'm a partner, for Christ's sake!" Hackett sounded disappointed in Merv. "I put my ass on the line to supply munitions to Cash. I want to keep him out of trouble as much as me! Now hand it over!"

Hackett moved toward Merv and Merv backed away.

"I can't let you have it, Paul. Not without Cash's say-so. He'd be really pissed. He'd kill me."

Hackett's hand went behind his back as he kept

advancing on Merv. The hand slipped under the jacket and pulled down the K-Bar, but he kept it hidden behind him.

"Really?" Hackett asked to distract Merv. He stepped in quickly and brought the knife up under Merv's rib cage, thrusting it into the heart from below.

Merv felt the hard steel slide in, got a quick taste of blood in his mouth. He felt Hackett twist the blade and the blood start to pour out of his chest.

"Why, Paul?" Merv was surprised, betrayed, seeking a final grain of understanding about why he had to die.

Hackett pulled the blade out of Merv, showing no emotion at all. He stabbed the K-Bar into the desktop and picked up the ledger. Hackett owed Merv nothing . . . an explanation least of all.

"You didn't have to . . . do that, Paul. I never crossed you. Not once." Merv slipped to the floor and died.

Hackett heard a movement in the doorway and spun around.

McRose was standing there, his shotgun trained on Hackett. "He called you Paul," McRose said accusingly. And now you're going to die for it, he thought.

35

Jack and Cash were back to back again, standing in the center of the veranda. Around them, Cash's enforcers watched in silence. Monday held Sarita tightly and she stared at the proceedings wide-eyed.

"Fire on ten," Cash said. "Everybody ready?"

His men shouted back, gleeful. No matter what the outcome, they couldn't lose.

"You do the counting, Lupo. Anytime."

Cash straightened up behind Jack. He could feel the adrenaline rushing through him.

"I'm ready," Jack said.

Lupo stood tall and proudly began to count. He thought this would be more fun than a cockfight.

"Uno!"

The women who were outside quickly herded their children away from the veranda.

The duelists took their first steps.

"Dos!"

The more prudent onlookers began streaming down the hill, away from the arena of combat.

Tres!"

Some of Cash's more squeamish whores shielded their eyes.

"Cuatro!"

A tied-up donkey in the courtyard looked at the to-do on the veranda with an expression that seemed to say, "And people call *me* stupid?"

Almost everyone left but Sarita and Jack was enjoying the show. Monday rubbed his crotch against Sarita as he held her. But she was numb and didn't even try to protest.

"You two knew each other," McRose said, his finger tightening on the trigger.

Hackett smiled ingenuously. "No way, Larry. He mixed me up with somebody else." But as soon as the words were out of his mouth he knew it was the wrong thing to say.

McRose shook his head and kept the gun leveled at Hackett.

Hackett eyed his knife, which was frustratingly out of reach. Setting it down had been a big mistake.

"Let's have a look at the ledger," McRose said.

"Put the gun down, Larry, or I'll have you court-martialed!" Hackett ordered.

"Hand it over or I'll frag you," McRose replied calmly, thinking he should frag him anyway.

"Wait," Hackett said, resigned. He changed his tack. "Hear me out. The safe's full of money. I'll cut you in for half. More than half. We can get away clean."

McRose just stared at him as the pieces fell together in his mind. He and the other operatives had been taking orders from a renegade.

"I said more than half!" Hackett mouthed. "I'll give you half the ten million! It hasn't been picked up! It's waiting there for me!"

McRose nodded. Now he understood. Hackett had been giving them the shaft, KY Jelly not included.

"That's what made the mission smell," he said. "You sonofabitch. Why? Why'd you do it?"

The answer to that question was buried deep in Hackett. Just as he had been compelled to burn his bridges with every other phase of his life to join the Dead List, he had decided to effectively disappear from the face of the earth as far as the military was concerned as well. He would be born again, remade into a man with no past, no allegiances, and lots of money to spend. He had risked a lot to get here. Hackett hoped that if he could show McRose what kindred spirits they were, he would once again beat the odds and survive.

"I've served our country for twenty years," Hackett said angrily. "I've done every dirty job anyone ever asked. I've been places and done things I just don't think people should ever have to do. And for what? Enemies get rewarded. Friends are betrayed, causes sold out—shelved till the next fiscal year. There aren't any heroes, Larry. You and me are nothing but numbers on some bureaucrat's desk."

"The government didn't have anything to do with this, did they?" McRose asked. "You cut the orders yourself. And you wanted all of us to die so you could walk away with ten million dollars."

"You stupid asshole, when are you going to wake up and take a look around you?" Hackett retorted. "They don't care. A couple more missions, you'll be just like me, Sergeant. And then what are you going to do?"

For the first time ever, Hackett looked vulnerable. He whispered, pleadingly, "It's a lot of money, Larry."

"Sure is," McRose agreed. "But it isn't worth selling out men who would die for you."

"So what are you going to do?" Hackett asked. "It's your choice. You could retire rich, disappear without a trace."

"First thing we're going to do," McRose told him, "is let the cowboy have his thirty minutes. We're soldiers in the United States Army. We gave our word. He's got five more minutes."

"Then what?" Hackett wanted to know.

"I'll do what I have to."

The door leading to the second-story balcony swung open. One of Cash's guards leaped through, a rifle held at the hip, trained on McRose.

Before the man could fire, McRose swung his shotgun and pulled the trigger, taking a bite from the goon's shoulder.

The man staggered backward, but was still standing, so McRose fired again, catching him square in the chest.

Hackett wheeled and dived into a French window to one side, crashed through into the next room.

As Lupo called *"diez!"* the goon's body crashed through the balcony railing. The body fell backward onto the veranda, landing right between Jack and Cash.

Hackett burst out into the hallway and started running. Two more armed guards headed for him. He pulled out his pistol and fired twice. Both men went down.

McRose had quickly followed Hackett through the glass doors. Hackett was already gone. McRose cursed him and headed out into the hallway, saw Hackett disappear around the corner, and heard another gunshot as Hackett ran across another member of Cash's goon squad.

When the goon landed between them, Jack and Cash whirled. Cash looked up at Merv's office, then down at the dead man. When he looked up at Jack, his face was contorted with rage.

"You think you tricked me, don't you, Jack? Didn't come down here alone!" He suddenly raised his gun and fired.

But Jack was out of the line of fire, diving over the edge of the veranda, firing at Cash as he jumped.

At the sound of gunfire, Atwater stepped into the room with the M-60. He started firing, quickly killing the gunner and loader and the two guards with them. The gunner fell over the gun and it swung up and around, trigger on, splintering the room into kindling wood. Atwater stayed low, moved around it, and pulled the man off.

Atwater swung the M-60 and fired on the roof nest he was assigned to hit. He quickly clipped the gunner and the loader. Then he turned the gun down to the courtyard and opened fire to cover Coker's run to the other nest.

Coker crossed the courtyard at a run, dodging back and forth, opening fire on Cash's guards with his Ingram as he headed for the other machine-gun nest. Around him men were dying, some shooting back, some running.

The whole courtyard was being peppered with bullets. Tables were shot in half. The sides of beef were knocked off their spits into the fires.

Atwater cursed as the M-60 jammed. Rather than fool with it, he vaulted out the window and ran across the balcony toward where the twin .30s waited on the roof above.

Sarita was still on her feet on the veranda, totally exposed, holding both hands to her ears, trying to shut out the roars of the guns around her. Jack ran up the steps and lunged to shield her. Cash jumped toward Sarita at the same time. Both men missed her and slid behind cover as the last gunners on the roof opened up with their twin .30s.

Everybody was firing at everybody else at this point. There was no clear point of attack. Hackett's plan had worked: attack from all points caused bedlam. There were, in fact, no friendlies.

Jack and Cash cursed at each other, traded shots as

they scrambled for separate cover, both trying to get to Sarita.

Biddle fired a quick burst from the window of the whore's room. He had a clean line of fire to the twin .30s. The gun went silent as the Aug took the gunner's head off. The loader moved in and Biddle took him out as well.

Suddenly the whore's room was torn apart by bullets as the other gun nest on the ground spotted Biddle. The bullets shattered the window, but Biddle had already ducked to the floor. He crawled over to the side as the whore on the bed screamed in terror. She got up and desperately ran for the door, still tangled in the sheets.

She almost reached it before the trail of .30-caliber bullets plowed into her. The impact threw her against the wall and held her there for a moment as the bullets tore into her. Then she slid down, propped up in a grotesque sitting position against the wall, the sheet half covering her, a bloody shroud.

Satisfied that Biddle was out of commission, the gunner turned the snout of his machine gun toward Coker, who was almost upon him. Coker fired and ducked, using the gunner's own sandbags as cover.

It gave Biddle time to jump out the window onto the ledge. He fired at the gunner who was aiming at Coker. A quick trigger pull and the gunner was out of the running. Coker shot the loader in the head as he tried to take control of the gun.

He wheeled and spewed the remaining bullets in his Ingram to hold off the goons charging him. He tossed the empty Ingram at them and got behind the machine gun. He pressed the dual triggers and let it rip in a sweeping arc across the face of the hotel. Windows exploded. Chunks of stucco flew off into the courtyard below.

On the veranda, Sarita was lying between two dead

goons. Monday had taken a couple of hits in the shoulder and had let go of her. He was in the open screaming crazily, wildly firing his revolver. Miraculously, Monday wasn't yet riddled with bullets.

Cash had taken cover behind one of the large wooden columns while Jack stayed low behind the stone wall surrounding the veranda, each man trying to level down on the other.

Upstairs, Biddle galloped down the hallway, screaming a war cry like a banshee as he blasted away at the goons who were abandoning their whores and bolting out of the rooms.

Rosa burst out of her doorway, clutching her chihuahua. She screamed at the pile of corpses littering the hall. Hysterically, she kept screaming as she rushed down the hall. She stumbled over a body and fell on her little dog. She got up. The dog was dead, squashed like a bug.

She tossed it away and started running again. Two panicked goons came around a corner firing. Rose just happened to be in the way and died screaming obscenities at them.

Biddle came up behind the two goons. They turned and they died as the Aug spoke. He was on auto-pilot now.

A door opened behind Biddle as he was reloading. A whore ran at him with a butcher's knife held high. He calmly snapped in a fresh clip and stitched her across the middle.

Simultaneously, another goon stepped from behind a door and started firing, shredding another whore who stepped between him and Biddle. Biddle took a bullet in the leg and he started to fall. He managed to turn and fire, knocking his attacker back into the room he had stepped out of.

Biddle tried to get up, but his leg buckled underneath him and he sat down hard. He cursed and started crawling, dragging the bad leg behind him. He heard footsteps behind him and rolled over to fire. This time, though, it was McRose. Biddle held his fire just in time.

"We've been fucked over by the major!" McRose said as he examined Biddle's leg.

"What the shit are you talking about?" Biddle grimaced as McRose's fingers probed his wounds.

"The national security line was bullshit!" McRose summed it up. "Records implicated him! He was working with Bailey, wanted to clean up and cover his ass. The bank robbery was for real. The money's waiting for him where we left it in El Paso."

"Fry was wasted for nothing," Biddle said, boiling with rage.

"That's what I mean!" McRose confirmed. "He wants all of us to buy it! *We're* the ones who get terminated with extreme prejudice!"

Suddenly Biddle was crying. His leg was throbbing, the pain getting worse. "How the hell can we get out of here?" he asked.

"We blast our way! We've got no choice!" McRose helped Biddle to his feet. "But we hunt the major! If you see him, kill him like an animal!" Maybe they would get out alive, but either way, Hackett would pay.

As they started down the hallway a number of men came up the stairs toward them. Side by side, the two commandos opened fire and advanced, McRose pumping out lead from his shotgun as Biddle's Aug chattered away. Biddle tried to ignore the pain in his leg, walked haltingly as best he could. McRose stuck by him as they made their way to the stairs.

Atwater peeked over the roof parapet beside the machine gun. He hoisted himself over the leaking sandbags and into the nest, pushing away the bodies of the dead gunners. Down in the courtyard, he could see Coker blasting away from his own position. He took a cigar butt from his pocket and lit it, then turned on the machine gun, pumping the Giselle full of lead, grounding it permanently.

Down in the courtyard, Coker was suddenly knocked backward by a hit in the chest. He struggled back to the gun and decapitated his attacker with a hail of lead. Then the gun was empty. He picked up an AK-47 lying in the nest. He climbed over the sandbags and marched forward, firing as he went. The pain in his chest was searing, stunning. He wasn't aware of the three men who jumped over the courtyard wall behind him until he heard their guns. They kept firing as he fell screaming, grabbing a clothesline for support and taking it down with him. They emptied their automatic weapons into his dying body. Coker was almost grateful.

As McRose and Biddle made it to the bottom of the stairs that Saint Jack had once climbed, Hackett furtively ran across the other side of the cantina toward the door to the veranda.

McRose fired. Hackett took a hit in the leg but kept moving. McRose moved after Hackett, Biddle hobbling right behind him, determined to kill the major if it was the last thing they ever did.

Up on the roof, Atwater started taking a lot of flak. Bullets whistled in from behind him. He turned to see men on the hillside above the hotel. He started to turn the gun when the men on the hill beat him to the punch, firing continuously with their Uzis and AKs and M-16s, jerking him back and forth. Buck went down, immobile but not yet dead. He held on to a glimmer of consciousness and waited for the Big Bang, thinking of the surprise he had left cooking in the basement. Not a bad way to go, he thought with a smile. He tried to move but couldn't, so he puffed on the cigar as his right lung gurgled with blood and he prepared himself to die.

Jack had kept firing to cover Sarita. Suddenly he realized Cash was gone. There was no sign of him anywhere. He ran across the veranda to Sarita, pulled her to her feet, and dragged her after him, running toward an old military jeep parked near a side stairway. He started the jeep and jammed it into gear as bullets hailed around them. The wheels kicked up a covering cloud of dust as he tore across the plaza toward the road into the village. Moving through a murderous stream of fire, they made it through the stone gate leading down. They careened down the steep hill, Sarita holding on with all her strength to keep from being pitched from the vehicle. They were out of the line of fire until the men on the hill behind picked them up and laid down a trail of gunfire behind them.

Hackett burst through the doorway to the veranda, firing as he limped onward, fighting through an endless stream of gunmen. He struggled to the steps leading to the courtyard. Behind him, McRose and Biddle stepped through the door and opened fire, hitting him more than a dozen times. Hackett plunged forward and rolled to the bottom of the steps. He could no longer stand. He dragged himself across the courtyard toward the fountain.

Biddle and McRose moved across the veranda to the place where they had shot Hackett and saw him creeping toward the fountain. Hackett crawled into the dirty water and pulled himself up, gripping the statue of the Virgin as his support. He turned to fire again but McRose and Biddle didn't give him the chance. They emptied their weapons into him. Hackett's blood splattered the statue and stained the pool as he sank under the water, bullets still splashing around him.

Suddenly Biddle felt himself grabbed by the neck. He struggled and tried to cry out but emitted only a hoarse gasp. Monday had come up alongside him, lifted him by the neck, and closed Biddle's windpipe with his huge hands. McRose quickly slipped another shell into his shotgun and salvoed Monday, knocking him down.

Behind him six desperadoes pointed their guns and fired, taking down McRose and Biddle together. The last thing McRose saw was the statue of Mary wearing Hackett's blood. Mission accomplished, he thought.

After the desperadoes finished off McRose and Biddle, they stopped firing. The courtyard was quiet. No gunfire. No fiesta. No bands. Just silence and sprawled corpses lying in the sun. A mangy dog trotted by and urinated on a dead man, then moved on. The survivors had mostly fled to the shelter of their homes in the village below.

Up in his machine-gun nest/deathbed, Atwater figured it was almost time for his last word. He was right.

Deep below in the cellar, the timer he had left switched on. The blasting caps triggered Atwater's carefully placed charges and the basement turned into a roaring inferno. Atwater heard the rumble beneath him and died with a smile on his face. He had just pushed the reset button for San Luis.

36

Jack swung the jeep in a one-eighty turn and brought it to a halt as the Isabella blew skyward. He and Sarita watched as the hotel seemed to rise up a few feet in the air in one giant piece, then its lines slowly softened as the roar of the explosion grew and the building started to disintegrate. Suddenly the thing was flying apart, a billion shards of stone and wood and glass and mortar. The walls tumbled. The roof expanded upward and outward in a black howling smoky flaming cloud, its tiles slicing through the air like shrapnel.

It was an awesome sight. In seconds, the sprawling hotel was a pile of rubble, some of it on the ground, some of it still airborne as the echo of the blast rocked back and forth between the hills. Fire in the hole, Jack mused; Atwater had found a simple solution to a complex problem.

Sarita cried out and buried her face against Jack. He comforted her with one arm and the words he thought she wanted to hear. "I figure Cash is dead. The army boys must have got him—or the blast did," he said. "Best thing for us is to haul ass out of here."

267

But as he turned to drive off there was Cash at the other end of the street, alone, gun in hand.

The fragments of the hotel started to fall around them in a black, eerie rain.

Jack slipped a fresh clip into his gun and got out of the jeep. He and Cash advanced toward each other slowly. Sarita, quietly crying, moved out of the line of fire. Jack and Cash held their ground thirty paces apart.

"You ready?" Jack asked.

"You're fucking right I'm ready!" Cash bellowed. "Jesus H. Christ A'mighty, you think I got all day to fuck around here? It's after four!" He seemed oblivious to the destruction of the Hotel Isabella.

The two men stared each other down, each waiting for the other to make the first move.

"We got to do things right, Jack. Fair's fair. Why don't you have our old girlfriend there count to three. Then you and me'll start having our fun."

"Sarita," Jack called over his shoulder, keeping his eyes on Cash. "Count!"

But she just wept until Jack repeated his command harshly.

"You're *both* crazy," she cried. She couldn't sanction the contest.

Cash was disgusted. "Well then, amigo, let's you and me do it. If we get to it, we can have anything we want, including pussy and beer. Right, Jack?"

Cash's .44 magnum lunged upward and fired, but Jack was quicker. His bullet struck Cash high in the chest, not a mortal wound.

Cash staggered back, his face contorted with pain and disbelief, red blood further staining the dirty white suit.

"Give it up, Cash!" Jack called. "I'm telling you to give it up!" He held his fire, looking for a sign of surrender.

"I can't! Don't you understand I can't?" Cash cried out.

"I'll take you home, Cash, just give it up."

Cash smiled in spite of the pain. Old Saint Jack was still talking about taking him home. And he would, too. But not the home Jack had in mind.

"I told you before, I'm in too deep, amigo!" He raised his gun and fired twice, but his aim was worthless.

Jack returned fire, emptying the gun, six more rounds, into Cash, as Cash's bullets went astray. Cash dropped his gun and fell to his knees. He clutched at his chest as if he could hold in the spurting blood.

"Goddamn, Jack," he gasped, "I think you killed me." He moved his hands from his chest and his blood rushed out, taking his life along with it. Cash had gotten what he hoped for: he never wanted to win the duel, he just somehow wanted everything to be *final*.

Jack was silent. Sarita sobbed softly. Jack put another clip in his gun and went to Sarita, hugged her to him. "I never wanted you to be part of all this," he told her. "That's why I drove you away. Now I'm driving you back—to be Mrs. Benteen, if you'll have me."

Still crying, Sarita nodded and held him tighter.

They had started walking to the jeep when Lupo and a dozen other heavily armed goons walked around the corner, their guns leveled and ready.

Jack froze with his gun pointed at Lupo. "Tell him he's got a choice," he said to Sarita. "We can stop right now, or keep on going. Tell him," Jack urged her, as she remained speechless.

She spoke to Lupo in Spanish, but he replied to Jack in his broken English.

"You want to trade, hombre?"

"What's the offer?"

"You and her go home. We don't kill you," Lupo

told him. "Someday you do me a favor. When we need somebody to get let out of jail or to look other way when somebody goes through the fence . . ."

"No deal," Jack replied. "The badge isn't for sale."

"Not *one* favor?" Lupo pressed. "Big mistake, let me tell you. Now you're going to die."

"I did you a favor." Jack gestured at Cash's body. "Now *you* get to wear the white suit."

Lupo considered it for a moment, then slowly lowered his gun, showing his gold tooth in a smile. "Hokay. *Muy bien*. Cash was *loco* for sure." He spun his finger at his temple to illustrate. "It's true. You did us a favor. No more working for gringos with big friends. From now on, we're in the dope business for ourselves."

Jack and Sarita backed toward the jeep before Lupo could change his mind.

"You do me one favor, right, señor? It's a good deal," Lupo called.

"I'll think about it," Jack said as he helped Sarita into the right seat and crossed around to the driver's seat himself.

Lupo nodded. "I trust you. *Vaya con Dios, amigo*. We'll see you again sometime."

Hoping Lupo was wrong, Jack started the jeep and rolled away slowly, leaving San Luis behind. The villagers would be talking about today for generations to come. The wounds would be a long time healing. Jack's final image of San Luis was of Lupo in the rearview mirror, wearing Cash's hat, pulling Cash's boots off, then his jewelry. Lupo would soon become every bit the despot Cash had been.

For a half hour they motored in silence, moving slowly along the curving unpaved mountain roads that wound through the scrub oak and mesquite. Finally Sarita started to sing softly. It was the song Cash had asked her to sing.

Sarita's voice was high and thin; she was still crying. "It was Cash's last request," she told Jack.

Jack took her hand as he drove. "I like that song," he said. "I always did."

The sadness was behind them now in the smoking ruins of San Luis. They drove through the lengthening shadows, north toward the border.